How to Fake Your Death

Death

(& Other Illusions of Exile)

Tennison Long

Also by the author:

Glorious Verve
When We Ran The Master Plan
Of Tribe & Empire
On Becoming Yesterday's Actors
tex●tu●al
The Devolution

Long Hand Publications
www.tennisonlong.com

For Anthony Bourdain...

Three things cannot be long hidden: the sun, the moon, and the truth...Confucius

Everyone must come out of his exile in his own way...Martin Buber

Life is a relentless expulsion from where we come from and an ongoing deportation to alien realms. We are in exile and our greatest dream is to return to the lost land. It is the greatest dream because no matter how long our exile is going to last, the dream will remain. It is the greatest dream because when we finally care only for this dream, then our exile will be over...Franco Santoro

BEGINNING OF DOCUMENT

<u>CONFIDENTIAL</u> [Unclassified upon removal of enclosures]
National Security Agency
2 January 1981
Washington D. C.
Subject: **Alt Vault Dossier #1**
Document Type: Memorandum

1. There was an air of disbelief with the entire meeting. Those present reported a surreal element, even what some described as "utterly incomprehensible." A round table meet up of the very much alive Elvis Pressley, Jim Morrison, and John Lennon. Slight modifications to their aesthetics left them with their looks, that yes this could be who you think it is but not likely as they are very publicly dead, and because these men looked older than their final photos. Except for Lennon, who had been "assassinated" by a deranged fan just one year ago. Elvis maintained his good looks, had lost approximately 70 pounds and allowed his hair to go grey. While Jim Morrison had put on weight and was clean shaven

which made him unrecognizable from his later-years bearded look. All three international superstars had been brought in by a secret government group, recruited to make rights from their wrongs and pay back the government that helped them disappear from their own celebrity. All three known for their penchants for younger girls, their mission was to locate active pedophiles within the ranks of Hollywood, rock 'n' roll, big business and Washington. They knew who were the dirtiest. They knew what certain men liked. And they had the cover of anonymity as their own existence had been wiped with high profile deaths and subsequent highly publicized fandom mourning and unbelievable posthumous success.

2. They were up for the challenge, and they wanted justice for all the injustice they had seen in their fast-paced lives. There was intrigue in the unveiling of high crimes explored at the intersection of where their prior life ceased and the real freedom began. Like when you know less than when you started, your own movements through the thought process and the commitment of the crime. Conflicts quieted at the heart of drama while escape was provided by whimsical follies. These were men who had been abused, and in return abused substances, their families, their lovers and children. Once disenfranchised they were then buried in money and fame. Catharsis came through personal expression. They

wanted to be human again and create new masterpieces.

3. "We are artists so we look inside ourselves to understand that human potential even if unpleasant or surreal, it's there for the taking, the madness, the evil and the light," Jim Morrison pontificated.

4. "Once you can imagine doing a thing, you are now capable of doing it, and as this feeling envelops your whole being you must be cognizant of that potential for unleashed new emotions," said John Lennon.

5. "I hate crime, especially those committed on children. I don't like to see it or hear about it. But I like the challenge of gaining the knowledge to discover who did it, and having a say in what is going to happen next," from Elvis.

WARNING: Authorized Persons Only [Civil and/or Criminal Penalties Apply to Unauthorized Access]
Report Class: ~~Secret~~
Country: USA

ELVIS PRESLEY (January 8, 1935 –), AKA Elvis, is an American singer and actor. Regarded as perhaps the most significant cultural icon of the 20th century, he is commonly referred to as "The King" or "King of Rock and Roll."

On a Memphis evening in August of 1977, Presley was to take a flight to begin a Midwest tour. But that afternoon he was discovered unresponsive on his bathroom floor. Firsthand accounts recount that it was as if he had frozen up while seated on the toilet then fell forward. His bodyguards attempted to revive him at the scene, and during the time he was being transported to Baptist Memorial Hospital he would transpire. Upon arrival at the hospital, 3:30pm local time, he was pronounced dead. When news of his passing broke there was instant international mourning and intrigue. Rumors were that he had overdosed, and that is what Elvis wanted his fans to think. He could go out sympathetically. After all, he had descended into the label of Fat Elvis and looked and felt decades older than his recorded death age of 42. The plan was simpler than most would assume. There were a mere three people who were paid off for signatures and witness accounts. Within 20 minutes of arrival at the hospital Elvis had left the building. He was on a Learjet 23 to the Caribbean within 45 minutes of being discovered in his bathroom. He was one hour into his flight before the news of his "untimely and unfortunate" passing broke.

WARNING: Authorized Persons Only [Civil and/or Criminal Penalties Apply to Unauthorized Access]
Report Class: Secret
Country: USA

JAMES DOUGLAS MORRISON (December 8, 1943 –), AKA Jim Morrison or "The Lizard King," is an American songwriter, poet and singer, who was lead vocalist of the rock band The Doors. Considered one of rock's most iconic front men, Morrison endured a reputation for erratic behavior, poetic lyrics, a growling voice, and a movie star rawness that all the more contributed to the mythos of his untimely death at the age of 27 in a Paris apartment. Well known for his alcoholism, The Lizard King often performed drunk, with many notoriously wild performances marred by inebriation that involved his own on-stage nudity that sometimes ended with back stage arrests. Final official details of his life included a solitary bath, in his girlfriend Pamela Courson's apartment located at 17 rue Beautreillis, Paris. The staged scene consisted of melted candles surrounding a Hausmannian tub, with emptied bottles of his favorite libation, American whiskey. The body used was that of a homeless Algerian man who resembled Jim. By the time authorities were called to the scene, Jim was en route by train to Gibraltar, in southern Spain, where he would then take the 17-mile crossing of the Mediterranean by ferry to Morocco. He spent his first few years exiled in Marrakech where, under the guise of an American professor on sabbatical, he befriended an unknowing Mick Jagger and various Euro celebrities through his shamanistic charm and poetic style of speech. His French autopsy resulted in "unknown cause of death." His tomb at Pere Lachaise is a perennial top ten Parisian tourist destination.

JOHN LENNON (October 9, 1940 –), is an English songwriter, singer, and peace activist best known as founder and co-lead vocalist of the Beatles. His partnership with Paul McCartney resulted in some of the most famous songs ever written. Along with his second wife, Yoko Ono, he formed the Plastic Ono Band in 1969. The Beatles broke up the following year. In 1975 he quit the music business to raise his son Sean. Under the archway of his Manhattan apartment building--The Dakota--he was shot by self-proclaimed "superfan" Mark David Chapman. The five shots that were fired from the .38 special revolver at his torso were blanks. Lennon collapsed and Chapman sat next to him reading a copy of JD Salinger's Catcher in the Rye. The police that arrived, hired by Lennon two weeks prior, were crisis actors. The two males dressed as NYPD put him into the back of their cruiser. They drove to Teterboro and Lennon boarded a Cessna that flew north. The body that was cremated three days later at the Ferncliff cemetery was that of a 45-year-old indigent stolen from Potter's Field.

END OF DOCUMENT

Forbidden Knowledge

Life comes down to forbidden knowledge, all of those morsels and tidbits that were kept from us for our own protection, sanity, impoverishment, or weakness, yet having the adverse effect of depriving us of liberty, as if we are controlled by being told what to know, whether that be something top secret or the heartbeat inducing embrace of a new lover. Fundamental is the ability to dream while knowing that what we choose is not constructed for us, it's cherry picked by someone else, to end in a nightmare of their choosing. We can be hijacked into the fake infinite loop like being flipped into a new television channel or subjugated by a mouse click, to then question the nature of illusion or break free from the remaining controls of personal history, and the perceptions that our past can no longer dictate our future.

It is in these opening pages that I must express the importance of the false versions of history that litter the fabric of our lives. Oh yes, I am going there. Not so much about mind control but about seedling into your brain's circuitry the self-doubt that comes about with questioning the narrative. What narrative, you ask. All of the sum of everything that has been told to us, for say, the last 200,000 years. No wayback machine is needed to investigate the past or to attempt to make rights from our wrongs. No, that is much too daunting of a task. All that matters now is the present. Misinformation, smokescreens, mythology, fairy tales, all fed to us in order to shine the light toward the directions we must head. To question this is to be labeled a conspiracy theorist, not so much demonized but quite possibly laughed at and belittled for having such independent thoughts. Don't mind them, they are the small-minded. Much of what you will learn in this book will counter the narrative, and your viewpoints going forward will be forever altered. It isn't so much the high drama of cloak-wearing Euro elites drinking from chalices of blood as it is a few clicks on the keyboard here or there, tweaks to the coding, and soft manipulations to the positions of power. Oh, and avoid getting killed off in the process.

Those who control history control what people know of history. Make sense? It's about confusing the population in order to, say, suppress their knowledge of, say, who they are, or where it is they came from, both geographically and from the lineage or stock of person. With the advent of religion and science they could take it to the next level from the ancients, a re-programming of the mind that would parlay ignorance into servitude. Yes I know I am getting dark here, please stay with me. It is with this concept that we must go forth challenging the official story of what we know while seeking out the fundamental knowledge that has been suppressed and written out of our history, the stories and layers of information never told, and a further unfolding of the untold. Some mysteries of the past will bring to light logical explanations and, as the onion is peeled, there will be an ever-increasing clarity as conspiracy turns to testament. Herein begins the reading, enjoy.

When Her Royal Highness The Princess of Wales Diana Secretly Met With John Fitzgerald Kennedy Jr.

Anonymous ID; TB+ANS Sun 05 Nov 20:53:48 <u>No. 148105</u> ViewReport
Her Royal Highness (HRH)
Prince of Camelot
Relevance?
Secret meeting?
What is the operation's name?
Who is John Travolta?
~~Active~~
False flag
Queen Mother
Exit stage/right
Hiding in plain sight
XOXO

Summertime, NYC, 1995 - British royalty and American Camelot, their meeting at the Carlyle hotel went undetected. They were both married and high profile targets of paparazzi focus. The cover story for their teams was that this meeting was in order to discuss Princess Di appearing on the cover of John Kennedy Jr's new political magazine George. Detailed accounts of this "logistical nightmare" have been recounted by John John's executive assistant RoseMarie Terenzio. "Their biggest concern was a leak to the paparazzi and the subsequent pictures splashed across international tabloids," which would fuel speculation to what these two potential paramours had done alone together in a room. The final maneuver planned was to have them walk together into the lobby of the hotel. That way if there was a media blowup the meeting would be claimed to be just that. Any talk of nefarious cheating or a sexual liaison squashed with the fact that neither of them entered through the side door. Only two staffers from each team knew of the meeting that day, which lasted over an hour and a half. The two were alone in the presidential suite the entire time. After extended small talk about their mutual friend Mother Theresa, they made love twice, and John John would later confide with a friend that he was surprised by how tall Diana was and how much her legs turned him on. Their chemistry was undeniable and both were suddenly enraptured out of their own simultaneous dull existences. John had experienced a fling with Daryl Hannah since his marriage, something of a farewell fuck, and Di had continued to sleep with her personal trainer at the time. But what existed between these two was special, the stuff of fairy tales and what married couples ideally should feel. Yet passion delayed is passion denied. Or vice versa. There was the heightened thrill, especially for Diana, of being caught, something that she would be fine with, almost an attempt at reckless abandon to blow up her own world. But not for John who was scared to lose half of his dwindling fortune. In what had become a routine, his wife, Carolyn, would threaten to take half ownership of his magazine if he ever cheated on her. These threats were often delivered under a cloud of cocaine-fueled drunkenness. So his libidinous waning was offset by the thought of having to co-edit his political rag with her and this idea made him sick.

There was just too much in the way of any planned avenue for Diana and John to make it work as a couple living in London and New York. Even the potential for their new coupling to break the tabloids as the new definition of an uber power couple, one with equal parts of charm and love from the public. And there was still time for Diana to have another child, the grandson or granddaughter of JFK who would also be the sibling to the future King of England.

Hours after the meeting, still reeling in the post-coital bliss, John penned Diana a love letter, of sorts. He had it sent by bike messenger to her security detail while Diana remained in NYC for a gala event:

Dearest Di, I do not know how this started and certainly do not know how it will end, but somewhere along the line I fell for you. Your crystal eyes are hypnotizing and your smile is captivating, your legs are exquisite and your accent so charming.

Even in these immediate waning hours of our time together I desperately long to wrap my arms around you. The sadness you feel, that you so honestly shared with me, is almost too much to bear. I wish I could carry the burden of your pain. In my loneliness I only imagine what it would be like to be together but all is forbidden for now. This fruit of temptation never looked more delicious. I don't know how to let go so I will plan for a fantasy where we can be together because without you I want the world to stop. When you said you loved me my heart skipped a beat but I didn't want you to know. In my transparency there is part of me that doesn't want you to know how I really feel, maybe it's just the little boy who cannot relinquish the love for fear of being hurt again. When we cure ourselves of these complicated and messy lives maybe we can reunite. For now, time will have to pass with our conversations in secret and knowing that you are always just outside of the room for me. XOXO, John

A copy of the note was xeroxed and faxed to the Private Secretary's Office of the Queen at Buckingham Palace per her majesty's instructions. Her intelligence team went to work deciphering the letter for any hidden meaning or other messages undetected from a "superficial read."

Tampongate & The Loneliness of Being Royal

MSM narrative

His Royal Highness

"Horse Face"

Feminine "hygiene"

Loud & Clear

Sunday Bloody Sunday

Mr Wonderful

Enter: Dodie Fayed

~~Chariots of Fire~~

Define Arab?

Backgrounds

Countermoves

To label Diana as depressed or an active bulimic would be unfair without adjusting for the influence from the man in her life, Prince Charles. He and his family as a whole never treated her well. There was an ostracizing vibe to how they handled her, almost as if she was toxic waste. The reasonings ran deep but are too complex to unpack here and now. A much despised aspect within the royal family was her popularity with the common people, a certain every woman capacity at charm, with a demure smile that would later establish her as the "People's Princess." She brought the spotlight to a decades-long lull of dullness in the royal family. But even amid all of this sunlight there was still the cloudy darkness of the loosely guarded secret that Charles was a perverted sexual deviant. And that he was still in love with his lifelong girlfriend Camilla Parker-Bowles, a woman one year his senior. The fairy tell story of Diana Frances Spencer marrying Prince Charles in the biggest global event of 1981 was fraught with her own internal insecurities as well as an obsession with Charles' own lingering love for Camilla.

Much of the early years of her marriage would foreshadow the remaining days of her public life, providing fodder for misguided gossip and fake news. A lesson could be learned that every little girl's dreams of being a princess doesn't always end happily ever after. After just a few dates Charles and Diana were engaged. Tabloids began to make note of Diana's "pudgy" appearance so she began a strict diet that spiraled into an eating disorder. Food was still important in helping to fill a missing void so she began throwing up what she ate. Diana knew that Charles was still seeing Camilla. Diana confessed to being "out of her depth," going back to her thoughts walking down the aisle of Saint Paul's Cathedral. She knew there would be an onslaught of problems with her marriage. She knew she couldn't sustain having another woman in her marriage. She knew her marriage would never be a happy one. Jump forward twelve years, to 1993, and the public release of what came to be known as the "Charles & Camilla Tapes." Transcripts and recordings that would shock the British public to the core. The tabloids had obtained secretly recorded phone conversations between the two and the resulting revelation confirmed what most had assumed for years, that Charles was indeed a massive pervert.

Prince Charles: "Oh, God, I'll just live inside your trousers or something. It would be much easier!"
Camilla: "What are you going to turn into, a pair of knickers? (both laughing). Oh, you're going to come back as a pair of knickers."
Prince Charles: "Or, God forbid, a Tampax. Just my luck!" (laughs)
Camilla: "You are a complete idiot! (laughs) Oh, what a wonderful idea."
Prince Charles: "My luck to be chucked down a lavatory and go on and on forever swirling round on the top, never going down."

The fallout from the tapes, later to be known as Camillagate, or Tampongate, brought favor and sympathy to Diana and her image of an outsider princess. Charles' family members, at least publicly, were shocked and disgusted by "such depravity." This was the open window that Diana needed to get out of the marriage. Within one month she was separated from Charles, publicly declaring that the tampon references made her physically "sick."

The repercussion from the scandal was big but some thought it was not big enough. Many questioned if Charles' reputation could ever be repaired, also if he was fit to one day ascend to the throne as King of England. All these years later Charles is married to Camilla and he is in fine standing with the British public, partially through his own hints at abdicating the throne directly to his oldest son William upon the death of his mother.

Yet Diana had her own amorous indiscretions to answer for. It was well known that following her 1981 wedding to Charles she had settled into an unhappy marriage. So who could blame her for seeking comfort in other men? As early as 1985 Diana fell in love with her bodyguard Barry Mannakee, who was killed in a motorcycle accident within two years of them meeting. But perhaps the biggest fish in her stable of men was James Hewitt, the biological father of Prince Harry. A polo player and cavalry officer, Diana met him at a party in 1986. He charmingly offered her to help with her fear of horses. Their riding lessons took on new meaning with afternoon delights. The affair lasted five years and, other than producing her second child, it left Diana heartbroken. Hewitt, over the years, has personally disputed being Harry's father, even though they look very much identical. He claims Harry was already a year old when he met Diana. This claim can be debunked by their own publicly declared timelines and royal secret service logs.

Diana would have her own telephone sex scandal with her lover James Gilbey, a car dealer and heir to the Gilbey gin fortune. He had affectionately nicknamed her Squidgy, and in what was to be later known as Squidgygate, the tapes that surfaced in 1992 (recorded in 1989), included conversations where Gilbey called Diana Squidgy 53 times. Their affair quietly ended and he never spoke of it to the media.

Art dealer Oliver Hoare, although her senior by 16 years, was Diana's sexual kryptonite. She was instantly attracted to him and within days of their first meeting they were arranging for "nooner" hook ups. She confided in an interview shortly before her death that he was the "first man to arouse me physically." When he cut off the relationship in order to marry the tycoon Diane de Waldner de Freundstein Diana became irate and was left desperate. This desperation was revealed when she bombarded his house phone with hundreds of calls pleading for him to call off the marriage.

It was in 1995 at a gym that she met English rugby player Will Carling, whom she asked for private training sessions. Their affair led to the collapse of his marriage to a well known television host. Scorned, his wife blasted Diana in the media by saying she was nothing more than a home wrecker repeating destructive behavior that had been instigated on her previously. It was a psychological analysis that gave the public a sliver of sympathy for what Diana had dealt with for years with Camilla.

Later in 1995 Diana began dating Pakistani-British heart surgeon Hasnat Khan, who she affectionately nicknamed Mr Wonderful. She had hoped to marry him and even traveled to Pakistan to meet his family. He insisted if they were to marry that they would have to move to Pakistan, far away from the press, so they could maintain some semblance of a normal life. She didn't want to leave her young sons, as well she wanted someone with more time available to spend with her. Someone like Dodi Fayed.

Scenes from an Unhappy Marriage & Subsequent Plane Crash

Anonymous ID; TB+ANS Tue 07 Feb 01:23:28 <u>No.</u> <u>148106</u> ViewReport
Who owns Camelot?
Sexiest Man ~~Alive~~
20 N Moore Street NYC
What is relevance?
Cocaine Carolyn
Jackie O legacy at stake?
George Magazine spy operation for Mossad
Calvin Klein model ~~recruitment~~
Fidel Castro activated
Essex County airport compromised
Cape Cod Hyannis Port clear
USS Briscoe
POTUS Clinton "compromised"
Church of St Thomas <u>More</u> eulogy
Part of legend
"Imminent" but delayed return to spotlight

He shared with those closest to him that all he wanted at this point in his life was to have children but that whenever he brought it up with his wife Carolyn she would change the subject and even refuse to have sex with him. Furthermore, he shared, it wasn't just about sex or kids, it had become impossible to talk about anything with his wife. They had become total strangers. Talk of divorce was on the horizon, in fact, it was the only possible transgression from this point forward. The marriage in fact had soured shortly after their grand wedding on an island off the coast of Georgia. Collectively they maintained their unhappiness as a well-guarded secret. Even the fact that they lived apart, he at the Stanhope Hotel, and her at their Tribeca loft. Born from their marriage was a new Kennedy myth, that a man who could have the woman of his choosing chose an undistinguished bride, neither famous nor rich.

The wet dream fervor of the Cinderella story casting of Prince Charming finding love in a commoner turned out to be a private hell that evolved into domestic violence, fueled by drugs and alcohol. The initial thrill of fast-becoming a fashion icon, Carolyn succumbed to a narcissistic disposition she never knew she possessed. On par with John's own dusting of megalomania, with his paparazzi teasings of riding his bike shirtless through Manhattan or laying out in Central Park for the touristic throngs, in the mega-stardom was an emptiness very few could relate to, similar to what he would describe as the feeling of "being ignored." They tried marriage counseling, of course without anybody knowing, even within their closest circles so as to avoid any leaks to the press. But these sessions failed as the counselor would ask about Carolyn's drug use and she would dramatically storm out. Word is they attempted counseling just twice. She also despised John's loft where they lived. It was the quintessential NYC bachelor pad and according to her had "the coldest feel." Located at 20 North Moore Street the penthouse loft was 2,600 square feet, consisting of just 2 bedrooms and was decorated with sentimental furniture from Jackie O, exercise equipment, and a curious amount of empty photo frames.

Her behavior was beginning to exhibit signs of clinical depression and the facade she so masterfully had built around her emotion was beginning to crack under the pressure of being married to America's most famous man. She couldn't handle going out on the town, socializing, meeting up for lengthy dinners, all the things that were part of John's life. She was also sensitive to male desertion as her parents had divorced when she was young and even as an adult the relationship with her father was estranged. John's focus was on his new magazine which involved working late, combined with his penchant for evening workouts, both of which led her to accuse him of affairs. John was not about her lifestyle.

One evening he returned home to discover her passed out on the floor after a cocaine binge with her inner circle of gay fashionista friends. Some of these people had keys to their loft. He insisted on referring to them all as "cokeheads" and not by their names. Acquaintances began to spread the word that Carolyn was into more than cocaine, that her likings had evolved to other street drugs. On a rare occasion that John spent the day at home, sick with the flu, she spent the day making trips to the bathroom. Perhaps it was a deflection tactic but she began calling John a fag and ramped up her own trashy talk and attempts at being irreverent. The relationship eventually turned for the violent resulting in his trip to the ER for a severed wrist nerve which he explained off as a workout injury. Even a black eye he suffered during an extended weekend at Mar-a-Lago was played off as a fall. But it was in fact the rageful response to the presence of John's old flame Daryl Hannah who was staying at the Florida resort as a guest of Donald Trump. Because of so much manipulation John knew he couldn't leave Carolyn and that she would never let him go.

He had come around to an awareness of "borderline personality disorder," something that perfectly described Carolyn's behavior. An emotional dysregulation affliction, BPD symptoms included emotional instability, worthlessness, impulsivity, insecurities, and impaired social relationships. The kicker was that most of this behind-the-scenes behavior was played out through projection at others, basically blaming one's own traits on family and friends, through a gaslighting effect. And with her deep concern of rejection, John felt that Carolyn had been damaged by

26

her father and these issues were now transposed into his marriage. Her insecurities that John would one day leave her could very well involve a scorched earth finale. This is what kept John awake at night.

The insecurities ran deep and continued to fuel the manipulation. Cocaine and other drugs made her paranoid. She tried to poison the closest relationships in John's life, with his sister and business partners. Privately reinforcing to him that people only liked him because of his name. The magazine, George, was already a slight failure and the frayed relationship with his executive team only made the untimely demise of the magazine more of a possibility. John's biggest dream at this point was to have a son, in fact he already had picked a name, Flynn, as a nod to the family's Irish heritage. Carolyn's new reason for no children was the fact she couldn't imagine raising them in the fishbowl of their lives. John confided to his sister that he always wanted a strong-willed woman like their mother and that he overlooked that with Carolyn, choosing her because of her sense of style that was very much a marked attribute of his mother. There was a chic and ethereal quality to her that was reminiscent of Jackie O and this mysterious air of unavailability was somewhat comforting to John because it made him feel protected.

John's inner circle began to see the wearing effects of his disastrous marriage, leaving him physically drained and uncharacteristically grouchy. He explained it off as his Grave's disease flaring up. But there was something else, something more was disturbing him. He did not share it with friends, but he discovered that Carolyn was cheating on him with her ex-boyfriend, a Calvin Klein underwear model. He learned that their sexual liaisons took place during their entire marriage. The fateful night that John confronted her about the affair she grabbed an oversized metal candlestick, with a burning candle, and threw it into the floor-to-ceiling window of their loft, shattering the glass out onto the sidewalk three floors below. She confessed in her fit of rage that she loved her ex-boyfriend more than John and admitted that their marriage was a mistake. In true borderline fashion she insulted John with the mention that her ex was a better lover with a "more delicious cock." In a last ditch effort to save the marriage John took her on a Caribbean trip and pleaded during the five day stay that she take her antidepressants. The trip ended in failure with the couple sleeping in separate rooms and Carolyn continuing with her illicit drug use. In the downtime John continued his work as publisher and editor-in-chief of his magazine, realizing that he felt most fulfilled with this title and role. He was excited for his forthcoming interview with Fidel Castro. Advertising revenues were improving as the magazine was slowly becoming the hottest political magazine on the market. But any divorce by the couple could jeopardize its future.

Before her death, John's mother had questioned his entering of the cutthroat magazine business, after all John had zero experience in journalism or media, and very publicly had failed the New York state bar exam twice. He wanted to prove to her, even in death, that he could make the magazine as big as anything and would continue on inspired by her. Besides, he got off on high risk activities, and the adrenaline he got from being in his office making numerous decisions per day was just as thrilling as sailing around Nantucket or rollerblading through Central Park. It had been a well-guarded secret, something that only a few people knew or suspected, and was primarily put to bed with the death of Jackie O, that John had dyslexia and attention-deficit disorder. He grew up taking Ritalin to raise his body's dopamine levels but as an adult he did not believe in these drugs and began to search out activities that could substitute for that "missing rush." He signed up for flying lessons and after 300 hours became licensed and bought a single engine plane from a New Jersey businessman. The Piper Saratoga plane, for which he paid $300,000 USD, was parked at Essex County airport.

On July 16, 1999, with John at the controls of the plane, and Carolyn and her sister as the only passengers, they took off with their ultimate destination being the Cape Cod Hyannis Port Kennedy family compound, for the marriage of his cousin Rory Kennedy. The flight started off normally, in generally good weather, but conditions rapidly worsened with a bank of haze arriving from the Atlantic to the east. John climbed to an altitude of 3,000 feet to get above this unexpectant weather pattern, but in the process lost visuals of the coastline below. Nine minutes into the flight Carolyn and her sister Lauren were passed out from the

Midazolam sedative he put into their pre-flight mimosas. The small parachute stowed under his seat slipped onto his back and front buckled while he opened the side door. He disengaged the autopilot and pointed the plane into a nosedive position while jumping out. He pulled the rip chord immediately and within the planned twenty second descent splashed down in the cold Atlantic water. Within two minutes he was rescued by Zodiac boat and disappeared. It was several hours before family members reported to the Coast Guard the possibility that the plane was missing. It would be two days before pieces of wreckage made the shoreline. On day three Navy divers found the wreckage on the ocean floor, 116 feet below. With two female bodies recovered, the naval commander sent back a solo diver to get the "body of JFK Jr" which was retrieved in the dark of night and all three bodies were cremated the next morning in a small crematorium on Martha's Vineyard. The ashes were brought back out to sea on day four and ceremonially spread off the Navy destroyer, the USS Briscoe. A private mass for JFK Jr took place on day five at Manhattan's Church of St Thomas More. Day eight NTSB declared there were no mechanical malfunctions and the accident was deemed pilot error, adding that the "pilot was inexperienced and became disoriented and lost control." Senator Ted Kennedy, John's uncle, eulogized: "From the first day of his life, John seemed to belong not only to our family, but to the American family. He had a legacy, and he learned to treasure it. He was part of a legend, and he learned to live with it."

Conspiracy Thinking, How Could You?

Anonymous ID; TB+ANS Wed 09 Mar 8:12:23 <u>No.</u>
<u>148109</u> ViewReport
Worldview MSM compromised
System worship programming
09.11.01
Self-imprisonment
Coward's Fantasy
Robotic radicals activated
Chatter siding w/ right wing
Brought by light
Identification-history-background

The mainstream media as the most powerful entity on earth often disregards its inherent obligation from being bestowed upon so much power. Oh, you don't say? They can make the guilty appear innocent through controlling the masses either through narrative creation or the outright suppression of truth. Sometimes there are engineered events that involve crisis actors and the bringing together of like-minded nefarious groups from academia, politics, corporations, think tanks, big media, the ultra-wealthy, or anyone in power who shares a mutual servitude to the system. This world-view programming is crucial to any tyrannical control of information and is dispensed by news fixers, those clever higher ups in the system, to disseminate a message that will be collectively spoon fed to the public. Oh, this can't' be, the people wouldn't fall for this? Yes, because the majority of the audience are system worshippers, those who never question the structure and because of their own weak mentality they become the glue that holds it all together. Look around at what happens when the narrative is challenged? When skeptical citizens had the audacity to question the events of September 11, 2001. Those critical thoughts were not allowed to be contemplated within the shared dialogue, rather this countering discourse was relegated to the fringe sidelines with the other loons. Because you are a loon now. You see how that works? You may even be labeled a moron who waxes poetic for an epidemic of gibberish. When you tell people what they already know, or suspect, they will thank you for it, while if you tell them something they do not want to hear, or something truly exotic, they will hate you for it. How can you blame them? When you are exiled into some self-imprisonment do you really want your jailer rattling the cage? Furthermore when the system is coming at you with all guns ablaze you tend to be overwhelmed which leads to this omnipotent force giving you full license to succumb to inaction. This is called the Coward's Fantasy. And by limiting the spectrum of acceptable opinion the people assume the role of obedient and passive onlookers to their own demise, and as system servers robot radicals or right wingers will fall for the same indoctrination. I know this is heavy chatter but I needed to get it out of the way earlier rather than later because no words will suffice when the forthcoming revelations are finally brought to light.

Elvis is Alive!

Anonymous ID; TB+ANS Thu 08 Apr 11:02:13 <u>No. 148205</u> ViewReport
Elvis Sighting Society false flag operation
Stage name
Rock 'n' roller
FBI Vaults
Graceland
King of Pop
Define: ~~child~~ bride
Funeral procession
~~Fat~~ Elvis
Kodak relevance
Muhammed Ali
Burger King importance
Elvis Week
"lot lizards"
G-Men
Ground "zero"

When Elvis passed away due to heart failure he left millions of worldwide fans stunned. It was too much for some to bear so alternative speculation grew within smaller groups of skeptics that the king of rock 'n' roll perhaps did not die. Statements from doctors and reports from coroners didn't matter to those who believed Elvis faked it all and went into hiding. Why? In order to avoid the fame he came to despise. When the sightings ensued the Elvis Sighting Society was formed to track locations and dates. Theories were floated that Elvis went into hiding to escape the mafia, into his own form of witness protection because the FBI refused to help him out, after the FBI had recruited him to assist in infiltrating a criminal outfit called The Fraternity, consisting of an elaborate network of racketeers. Elvis reluctantly signed on, but did it out of his love for law enforcement. In an undercover operation that involved him buying a "hot" airplane it was revealed that Elvis was an informant, a mole, and was now at risk. Vast databases of documents proving this theory exist in the FBI vaults, but let's not get into it here. Some believers insist on looking no further than his tombstone and the misspelling of his name as some proof of the cover-up. His middle name was spelled incorrectly Aaron instead of the correct Aron, with the theory that it would be taboo if he was still alive to correctly spell out his name on a tombstone. Skeptics that obsess on debunking theories like this claim that Elvis had changed the spelling himself years back. But alas there was no proof to this claim, and the tombstone theory lives on as further proof to Elvis being alive.

Many years after his "death" there were slip ups involving his wife Priscilla and daughter Lisa Marie when they would be interviewed about him. They tended to speak of him as if he was alive, and that there was still communication with him. It was easy to label these women as nutty and confused, having lived such a life of opulence generated by Elvis's posthumous cash cow operations, endless royalties and the absurd revenues from Graceland. Priscilla was experimental with plastic surgery and as a child bride, first dating Elvis when she was 14 years old, she had no penchant for ever dating again. Many had their opinions of Lisa Marie's questionable sanity validated when she married, if even only briefly, the King of Pop, Michael Jackson.

The first legitimate sighting of Elvis post-mortem was of him purchasing a one-way ticket from Memphis to Bueno Aires, using the name Jon Burrows. This was the pseudonym he used when he checked into hotels. Questions about his funeral persisted. Actual footage of the ceremony show the pallbearers having difficulty with the copper coffin, as it weighed well over 1,000 pounds. The theory behind this was that indeed it was Elvis in the casket, but alive, and there had been a cooling system built within the coffin. Those who approached the open casket noticed that the "dead" body appeared to be sweating. Remember, Elvis was a good actor so keeping a straight dead man's face through all of this was not too much of a stretch. Additional theories were that the cadaver was actually made of wax and the sweat was in fact the wax melting. Under either of these scenarios

Elvis was not dead. Reports showed that at the time of his death, Elvis weighed in at more than 250 lbs with what were described as "the arteries of an 80-year old." Official cause of death was "hypertensive heart failure with advanced atherosclerotic heart disease." In other words, a massive heart attack. It was not a big surprise within his inner circle when toxicology reports revealed a dozen different drugs in his system. Under Tennessee law, the details of the toxicology report, and the polypharmacy effect, those who wrote prescriptions, and doctors who signed off, will be made public in the year 2027, 50 years after his "death."

The next significant sighting was by a fan at Graceland. While taking photos of the pool house he captured the silhouette shadow of a man sitting in the doorway. Upon further examination he resembled Elvis. Experts at Kodak were contacted and verified that the photo had not been doctored. The photo, now infamously known as "The Poolhouse Photo," was analyzed and discussed at length on Larry King Live. Nothing came of it, but it did seed hope for the believers, and more non-evidence for the skeptics. A 1984 magazine photo of Muhammad Ali had a man in the background who appeared to be Elvis. He was off to the side, laughing. It was quickly played down by the magazine, leading to the issue being sold out. When asked who it was, Ali, who could not lie due to his devout Islamic faith, said "That's my friend Elvis." The late 1980s were full of what had become daily Elvis sightings. Overweight men in jumpsuits ordering to-go food at Burger King, Elvis's favorite restaurant, were the number one type of sighting. A close second place were sightings of him pumping gas and loading up on junk food in convenience stores.

But the real coup de grace of all Elvis sightings was in 2016. Surveillance video of a Graceland groundskeeper, in a video that came to be known as "Groundskeeper Presley," an older man, gray-haired in a baseball cap, wearing an "Elvis Week" t-shirt, signals to the camera a peace sign as he passes it by. Some believers have claimed it was not a peace sign but a numerological symbol denoting the number two. In these sightings Elvis lives on immortal for his fans, and he remains everywhere for their worship.

Yet, the reality is this, Elvis loved the freedom of the road so he became a long-haul trucker. He is still at it today in his early 80s. And he moonlights as a child predator hunter. He picks up CB radio conversations, with their subculture codings and secret nuanced ways of conveying coordinates of young girls, even boys, the motels where they are at, or the truck stops where they are pimped out as lot lizards. Sometimes it's a private residence, no pimps involved, where the parents are out of town and some young girl, "bless her heart," may be seeking some missing validation in her life and just reaching out on the interwebs and makes contact with the wrong dude, "some bad hombre," a guy hauling carpet across country who makes a side trip into small town America, with a sex toy and some wine coolers, to meet a 14-year-old. Sometimes these can be elaborate sting operations, but most often they are not. Just a lonely girl getting set up for a drunken rape. It tends to always be a bad time.

Elvis had retired from actually visiting the crime scenes, now he called them in, even sent emails to the FBI, continuing his lifelong relationship with the G-Men. While he had uncovered something bigger and more nefarious, he has kept it to himself so far, for his own safety mostly, as he didn't have full trust in the FBI anymore. He believed many agents had been compromised and were being used by high-level politicians.

He had uncovered a vast network, starting with the sleaziest of low lives, pimps who procured and traded one or two girls at a time, upward to the high grade connoisseurs of wealthy businessmen who bought girls in bulk, and then used them in blackmail operations. Much of Washington DC were consumers. If it wasn't an actual politician it was their adult child implicated. Or business partner, which was bad enough. The money would all link back to the same source, the Sinaloa cartel. The narco operation was heavily leveraged in this endeavor and pressed hard on the political elite, Hollywood, and the sports world. It explained the push for open borders. "Nothing is as it appears," when I spoke with him on the phone. "It's a messed up world Tony, I don't even recognize it sometimes." I felt like a giddy school girl when we set up to meet at a truck stop outside of Albuquerque, what Elvis called "ground zero of the pedo game."

The Hypothetical #Clintonbodycount

Anonymous ID; TB+ANS Fri 15 Dec 02:13:49 <u>No. 148305</u> ViewReport
HRC residence NYC
Podesta emails
Middle "East"
Lolita Express transport?
Currency stabilization counter move
Kenyan Resort
Huma Abedin (HA) = Mrs Carlos Danger
Orgy Island
"Personal music room"
Malaysian IT
Air Traffic ~~Control~~
Palm Beach Crawler
"I wish I'd never met him"
FDNY ambulance

In a move to set her up for a run at the White House in the far-off distant year of 2008, Hillary Rodham Clinton established her home residence in New

York State. This would allow her to run for the vacated senate seat by Senator Patrick Moynihan. But there were many other candidates who were better-suited for the job and much more popular, after all she wasn't a real New Yorker on any level and her connection to an exorbitant amount of suicides plagued her. One name alone could back burner any interest in her, and the necessary donations to her campaign coffers, even to her newly formed Clinton Foundation, and that was John Fitzgerald Kenney, Jr. As the consummate New Yorker, the name recognition, not only within political circles but as well pop culture, the reigning People Magazine "Sexiest Man Alive," John John had been a resident of New York City since the age of three. Hillary was nothing more than a Southerner, carpetbagger, and thinly-veiled corrupted quasi politician, carrying the baggage of her own past not to mention her husband and his wayward sexual ways. This is when Hillary ramped up her own killing spree, the early days of the infamous Clinton Body Count, what the media would speculate was coincidence but free thinkers were inclined to label as her kiss of death. Many lists have the total deaths at around 35 people (and counting). Mostly suicides but there have been botched robberies that ended with a shooting, or car or plane accidents, even heart attacks. Of course there is no direct evidence to any of the deaths, but the logic goes back to this question, how many people do you personally know that have died in the prime years of their lives? Maybe one or two? Most notable from the Clinton circle was the deputy White House counsel Vince Foster who had worked with Hillary in Little Rock years before joining the Clinton administration. Under the cloud of having failed the president in the vetting process of his Attorney General pick, Mr. Foster went to a quiet spot on the banks of the Potomac and shot himself, twice in the head. Years on was another high profile death, this time Seth Rich, a Democratic National Committee staffer who was shot and killed during a robbery. Mr. Rich had months prior to his untimely death released DNC emails to WikiLeaks, including many that were damaging to Hillary.

The WikiLeaks/Clinton drop involved 20,000 pages of emails hacked from a basement server in Hillary's house. They involved mostly political gossip and Clinton world squabbling, the obvious blending of public and private funds, and rampant quid pro quos. Yet eerily not included were the Podesta emails. Why are they so important you ask? On the surface, and this is bad, the Podesta emails detail the gifting of large amounts of money from foreign actors. Like million dollar birthday payments to Bill or Hillary from Middle East countries. Nothing to see here folks. Alas the more ominous emails, the ones detailing the trafficking of children, of orders placed for specific types of kids and orders fulfilled, when those come to light there will be hell to pay. In Hillary's own words, "If I am ever indicted I will take half of Washington with me." Or this gem, "We are all going to hang from nooses." Either way it sounds bad.

Enter Jeffrey Epstein. With direct ties to Hillary, he was a donor but also played host to her and Bill at his private island, and sprawling New Mexico ranch. As well he had lent them his private plane, a Boeing 727 affectionately known as the Lolita Express, on many occasions. Their relationship went all the way back to 1995 when Epstein had visited the Clinton White House, even staying the night in the Lincoln Bedroom. That meeting was documented as a discussion about "currency stabilization." After Bill left office their friendship deepened, while Bill launched philanthropic initiatives he also got the bug of hanging out with celebrities and rich people. He had that cache and swagger of being an ex-president. But what he really liked about Epstein was the private plane and access to women, especially young girls. Their first trip together was to Africa, under the cover of combating HIV/AIDS. What really went down, rumored by secret service agents, were small scale orgies on the plane and at the Kenyan resort, Elsa' Kopje Lodge, an eco-friendly boutique hotel nestled on Mughwango Hill overlooking the Meru plains. The rustic cottages adjacent to the country's national rhino sanctuary provided a sense of privacy for the illicit sex with minors, comforting Bill with peace of mind while Mossad agents monitored live feeds and recorded any action they deemed incriminating.

If the girls involved were underage there was no way to know as they were runaways or undocumented slave types who were recruited from city slums for their beauty. Epstein's teams of recruiters knew what western elites liked most, youth. In Africa this is combined with the jungle fever, that forbidden fruit of a nubile specimen, something harkening back to the slave owner DNA. And of course, like any high-level Mossad agent, Epstein had it all under surveillance. Their second trip together was to Europe, this time without Bill's secret service detail. This was followed with a trip to Epstein's famed Little St. James Island, in the US Virgin Islands, a trip that included Hillary. She was okay with Bill's extramarital peccadillos as long as her chief of staff Huma Abedin was around. So Huma went too, and her and Hillary shared their own villa. Any speculation of that relationship relied on the lipstick lesbian attractiveness of Huma, with the much older dykish Hillary playing a top type.

It was apparent that Huma's husband, Anthony Weiner, was straight even though he set off gaydars with his flamboyance and heightened sex drive. What had been reported, through channels of close friends of the couple, was that their sex life ended after the conception of their son. What Huma explained off as Anthony's stress from work, and not wanting to damage the in utero baby, was nothing more than his new interest in texting and virtual relationships with younger women. Huma had had sexual relations with Hillary over the years, especially when Hillary was Secretary of State and Huma was her aide who was always by her side, sharing large suites during their foreign stays. Security details had walked in once, in Cairo, on Huma going down on

Hillary while she was on her blackberry. Hence Anthony had no issues when Huma was needed by Hillary, or had to travel for several days, he enjoyed the time alone. More to come on that.

Epstein's island was a place that nearby islanders had referred to as Orgy Island, Island of Sin, or Pedophile Island, even though Epstein himself tried to get the nickname Little St. Jeff's to catch on to no avail. Purchased in 1998 for just under $8 million, the 72-acre island was Epstein's main residence. Upon his ownership much of the interior was redone in order to better hide the elaborate surveillance system a team of Malaysian IT contractors installed. Under contract by the Israeli government they never knew who the owner of the house was, nor were they allowed into the two offices that Epstein maintained. This was where the security boxes were located, and their installation was handled directly by Mossad agents. After the island was raided by FBI agents and these offices were examined the agents noted the exquisite photography of nude women, young ones, mostly topless in tropical settings, likely taken on the island. It was all part of the ruse that Epstein himself was a raging pedo who couldn't control his obsession with young women. Conspiracy theorists like to point to the mysterious blue striped temple with a gold dome, what workers and staff have explained off as his personal music room, where Epstein liked to be alone and play piano. Yet the acoustic walls allowed the mind to wander to more nefarious purposes, possibly that of a torture room. Word had spread on the internet that the temple concealed a hidden underground location which included a 3-level elevator. Noted by investigators was that the temple's front door, an oversized reclaimed wood door, had its reinforcing lock bar on the exterior rather than the interior. To further the intrigue statements by Israeli contractors claimed that the building is a personal gym.

But I digress, girls as young as 12 were brought to the island by boat. Once on the island, after a preliminary offshore grooming ritual, the girls were coerced into their initial sexual encounters. Typically hand jobs after a full body massage. It wasn't what they had imagined. The grooming consisted of telling them they would work as hostesses, offering drinks and cigars to the owner of the island and his guests. No funny business. Many of these girls were virgins and had never left their small villages in Eastern Europe and South America. Within the initial days of arrival, and conversations with other more seasoned girls, it was clear they were under a hostage type of situation. One girl tried to swim away from the island. To keep her from drowning or being eaten by sharks the security team formed a search party and rescued her. They were indeed kept children, stripped of their passports and renamed as a way to further distance themselves from who they were. But this was also juxtaposed with a life of topless ATV riding, sunbathing, drinking and smoking, with personal chefs for morning omelets, afternoon naps and yoga classes. For some it was an envious life and they accepted whatever downside consequences were required of them when new guests arrived.

Many of the flights into the island had layovers in Marrakech or Mexico City. Places where authorities would overlook passports for a few hundred dollars in tips. During the time at the airports customs would clear the travelers' documents while the girls were allowed to shop duty free, bringing back onto the plane bags of designer perfumes and jewelry. Dressed in oversized college sweatshirts they were able to pass off as wealthy of-age girls traveling with family. Air traffic controllers from St Thomas, and Palm Beach, witnessed sometimes a dozen underage girls getting off and on the plane, assuming that the authorities were doing something if in fact any of these activities were nefarious in nature.

A documented statement by Virginia Roberts, once one of these island girls, claims to have witnessed Bill Clinton with two underage girls in the infamous 12-person Jacuzzi. She even asked Epstein if that was the former president, and he replied "Yes, he is gonna owe me a few favors." Bill Clinton has repeatedly denied any and all allegations of visiting the island. His office has issued three statements countering the flight logs to the island that recorded 27 visits by the former president. The last documented guest to the island was former Israeli Prime Minister Ehud Barak. When Epstein died Barak released the following statement, "I wish I'd never met him."

Epstein was very much a sycophant, or power elite "crawler." A charismatic player within the crust of high society who flatters his way into contributing a vital role in world affairs, in his case through blackmail. This required an acquiescence to hero worshipper, conceding his own free thought and narcissism to a false perception of greatness in others. At times he was used for the same thing with his mark attempting to ascend the hierarchy through his own societal climbing. It was all about what those above you demand of those below. An example would be the Royal Family with the rituals of bowing and kneeling, and the symbology of injustice and manufactured control to project an ethereal grasp on the power they so feebly held onto. Or the ambition in titles and refusal to ever be criticized for obscene wealth. Epstein brought various tricks of this trade to the island, implementing his own chamber room within a domed temple that involved pagan type rituals that would hasten the indoctrination of the more desirable island girls while promoting him, in their eyes, to a godlike figure. Not so much a cult leader figure type but one of super human. When the temple was examined by authorities they discovered a trap door to a tunnel that led to a subterranean garage containing a fully stocked and functional New York City ambulance, prompting many to assume the room was used for torture, the ultimate tool for indoctrination.

Diana Dies in Paris Car Crash

Anonymous ID; TB+ANS Sat 12 Jul 03:33:58 <u>No.</u> <u>148235</u> ViewReport
Conspiracy Theory
Define
Queen "at wheel"
Who is ~~real~~ enemy?
Trevor Rees-Jones
Missing 2 hour window
Ritz Paris
Mercedes outrun by moped?
Henri Paul crisis actor ~~filmography~~
"Gross under accounting"
Dodi Fayed
EMT CPR
Michael Jay
Pitie-Salpetriere
Repossi Jewelers
Prozac & Tiapridal
Royal Air Force Northolt base
"Gross negligence"
"A new dawn has broken"
Cool Britannia
Westminster Abbey
Future King?
MI6
Dodi child?
green light

In the early hours of August 31, 1997, Diana, Princess of Wales, was pronounced dead in a French hospital after a violent car crash in the Parisian Alma Tunnel. Her driver died at the scene, as well as her Egyptian boyfriend, Dodi Fayed. The only survivor was her bodyguard, Trevor Rees-Jones, who suffered serious injuries while seated in the front passenger seat of the Mercedes.

An abbreviated chronology of her activities leading up to the crash:

August 30, 16:42 hours (Central European Standard Time): Diana and her boyfriend arrive at the famed Ritz Paris. They enter through the back door and go directly to the Imperial Suite. The hotel was owned by her boyfriend's father, Londoner and Egyptian businessman Mohammed Fayed.

17:15 hours: The couple take showers, likely after making love.

17:45 hours: Dodi leaves the hotel for a short walk to Repossi Jewelers where he buys two rings that were later found in the hotel room.

19:00 hours: The couple exit the Ritz via the rear entrance and are driven to Dodi's residence, a small but chic apartment, adjacent to the Arc de Triomphe.

*There is a 2 hour gap of time that has not been accurately reconstructed by any journalist, investigator or authority. What took place in the apartment that night is likely to never be known.

21:50 hours: The couple enter the Ritz through the main entrance, going directly to the hotel's restaurant, L'Espadon, where Diana orders Dover sole, a mushroom and asparagus omelet and vegetable tempura. There has been some speculation that Diana was eating for two, pregnant with her Egyptian boyfriend's first child. Dodi became suspicious that the waiters were in fact paparazzi and that some of the other patrons in the restaurant were undercover reporters. He ordered that their meals be delivered to their room.

August 31, 00:20 hours: In order to evade photographers, the couple, along with Diana's royal detail bodyguard, leave the hotel through its rear entrance. Ritz security employee Henri Paul is waiting for them with his black Mercedes S280. Paul had been drinking that night, what was reported to have been a single Scotch, and a single beer. This later was proven to be a "gross under accounting." His blood alcohol level was determined to be three times the French legal limit. A third autopsy, through testing his spinal cord, determined he was also under the influence of Prozac and Tiapridal.

00:23 hours: Paul's speeding Mercedes, in an attempt to outrun a trail of following photographers, mostly on motorcycles, is unable to navigate the bend of the Pont de l'Alma tunnel and collides head on with a concrete pillar. In a move that ran contrary to Royal security details, Diana's bodyguard, mere moments before the impact, buckled his own seat belt. Di's boyfriend Dodi Fayed died at the scene, as well as the driver. Immediately following the accident, Dr. Frederic Maillez, driving in his own car, came upon the scene and with limited medical supplies tended to Diana until the ambulances arrived. First responders used a chainsaw to extract Diana from the car.

01:20 hours: After stabilizing Diana at the scene of the accident, the ambulance transported her to the hospital. She reportedly suffered cardiac arrest along the way and EMTs performed CPR.

01:42 hours: British Ambassador to France, Michael Jay, learns of the accident and contacts Queen Elizabeth's private secretary.

02:02 hours: Diana arrives by ambulance to Pitie-Salpetriere Hospital. Within fifteen minutes she undergoes surgery.

04:00 hours: Diana, Princess of Wales, is pronounced dead.

03:32 hours: Diana--the people's princess, queen of hearts--still alive, is transported by medi-vac helicopter to an undisclosed location in the Swiss Alps.

04:55 hours: Hospital anesthesiologist Dr. Bruno Riou tells the crowding media, "Diana's body arrived in a condition of serious hemorrhage and shock. An urgent surgery showed a severe wound to the left pulmonary vein. Despite the closure of this wound and the two-hour external and internal cardiac massage, no official respiratory circulation could be established..."

18:15 hours: Accompanied by her sisters, Lady Sarah McCorquodale and Lady Jane Fellowes, along with Prince Charles, Di's body is transported from the hospital to Charles de Gaulle airport (CDG) for the short trip to the Royal Air Force Northolt base in South Ruislip, a London suburb. A ceremonial guard awaits and carries her royal standard-draped coffin to an awaiting hearse.

The media shitstorm that followed was unprecedented. Blame was primarily placed on the paparazzi who followed Diana's car. Investigations revealed that her driver lost control of the vehicle at a high speed and that he was intoxicated and under the influence of antidepressant and antipsychotic drugs. Furthermore it was revealed that nobody was wearing seatbelts, except for Di's personal bodyguard. A British inquest, nearly a decade later, placed all blame on the driver, with a verdict of "unlawful killing" through "gross negligence." The Queen, who many believed was behind the assassination of a pregnant Lady Di, remained stoic and this led to a permanent wane in her popularity. The People's Princess, or how she so coyly referred to herself, the Queen of Hearts, was laid to rest with a funeral which was globally viewed by 2.5 billion people, including herself.

There are times in history when you can feel a nation changing its course, and the summer of 1997 was very much that for the British Empire. Tony Blair's Labour Party won in a landslide, and his acceptance address to the nation included this gem, "A new dawn has broken, has it not?" Cool Britannia was resurrected from 60s culture as England's own new label, a counter punch to American Grunge, because now it was all about the cool kids. Rooted in the transient fashion of the London house music scene, mega bands such as Oasis and Blur along with fashion designers encapsulated the uplifting mood from the mid 1990s to Y2K. There was a renewal in British pride, in the Union Jack, and a stunning growth spurt to the economy.

What nobody knew then was that London was in its last days of glory. Britain, the envy of Europe, was grasping onto an identity that would no longer return. It was perhaps the beginning of the end of Continental Europe, and this spectre in the rearview mirror was the birth of the Brexit movement. Then Diana died. Blair told the cameras, the morning that England woke to the shattering news, that "Diana was the people's princess." Over one million bouquets were left on the doorstep of her Kensington Palace home. Her funeral at Westminster Abbey was held a full month later, on

September 6, with three million people out on the streets of London. It was certainly a landmark in modern history, but now so many years on, there isn't much talk of Diana, a shocking notion after such a lionization of the mother of the future King. The once-most photographed woman in the world has a neglected grave at Althorp, with the overgrown vegetation a metaphor of the slide from her own heyday and that watchful tabloid eye. This has historians murmuring the monarchy is on its last legs, but with the marriage of William and Kate there has been a stabilizing of the ship. Royal watchers and those obsessed with the Queen say there is nothing to be concerned about, as long as there are small children there will always be hope. And when beautiful young women die the collective tears will provide for a quixotic intoxication, blending the outpouring of sentimentalism with solemn promises of hope for the dwindling empire.

Much of the evidence to date shows that the British intelligence agency, MI6, on orders from senior members of the royal family, carried out the assassination of Diana. Documents, interviews and witness evidence were successfully suppressed at the time, but have since come to light revealing the perplexing, yet plausible, notion that the Queen had her former daughter-in-law killed. An inquest into Diana's murder produced cross-examinations that revealed there were two failed assassination attempts on other world leaders in the six months before Diana's untimely demise. Could these have been practice runs? When

French intelligence reported to MI6 that Diana was likely pregnant with Dodi Fayed's child, and well into her second trimester, this is when the Queen gave the green light to the operation.

Operation Camouflage, a History

Anonymous ID; TB+ANS Mon 15 Aug 03:53:48 <u>No. 148705</u> ViewReport
Parliament
French ~~Resistance~~
Imperial War Museum
Operation Camouflage
22 surgeries 43 scars
Elite
Underground
Body dysmorphia?
"Special" access
Post-op "freed hostage"

In 1945, British Army Colonel James Hitchison, a high profile member of Parliament, requested a disguise before parachuting into Nazi-occupied France to aid the French Resistance. So he went under the knife. A face surgery was performed, nothing like it was ever done in the past.

Under the auspices of Britain's Special Operations Executive, a secret organization was established to dispatch clandestine operatives to global hot spots to encourage resistance and set off sabotage within enemy territory. In order to cull these covert actors the government enlisted psychologists and psychiatrists to assess and select the best possible. Sometimes the best person for the job was a royal or someone from Parliament. Maybe even a well-known celebrity of sorts. This is when it would be required to change the appearance of someone's face. The first surgeries were ordered to disguise two secret agents before trips into Denmark and France. More detailed storytelling of the surgeries can be found within the Imperial War Museum, and the files of the National Archives in the town of Kew, just outside of London. More is still coming to light with the ongoing declassification of wartime files, now 70 and 80 years on.

"Operation Camouflage" was tasked with ensuring that agents headed into enemy territory would blend in when they arrived. Of course this meant more than just the appearance of their face, but also authentic clothing, paperwork, and identification. It could even mean dentistry, making one's bridgework look more convincingly Continental, leading to better teeth for those afflicted with the British curse of crooked teeth and distracting, even off-putting, grills. Those with gold teeth had porcelain caps made, and like a fresh coat of paint on your house there is nothing more drastic or

rewarding than an aligned set of chompers. Way ahead
of their time, the early days of the vanity surgeon trend,
these doctors invented permanent makeup to address
large ears, broken noses, burn marks and scars. The
London Clinic, where much of this went down, was a
private institution secretly funded by the government,
located in Maryleborne. Experimental procedures were
green lit in order to advance the surgeries, to best see
what could be done and what could not, all while under
the urgency of Nazi advancement. Veterinarians who
specialized in clipping dog ears were brought in to clip
the tops of the ears of men. Barbaric measures were
used to shave down noses and chins, anything to reduce
the prominence of such important contributing features
of one's face. Tattoo removal was difficult, for smaller
tattoos the skin was actually removed and sewn back
together. For larger ones there was additional tattooing
done to blend the designs into something larger. One
MI6 agent was ordered to become so unrecognizable
that his own wife would not be able to recognize him.
In what played out over several days with many rotating
shift doctors, even an attending American
anesthesiologist, this secret agent went under the knife,
receiving 22 surgeries with 43 resulting scars. It was a 10
day recovery process. After his time in combat he
retired to a secret life in the countryside. It wasn't until
his own death in 1986 that his obituary, pre-written and
sent to the paper by him, entailed his true identity. He
was the first of his kind that did not take the secret to his
grave.

Operation Camouflage continues today, run as an elite underground service, providing the best and most discreet cosmetic surgery for those entering into Interpol witness protection or wealthy elites with a dusting of body dysmorphia.

Meeting Elvis at a Truck Stop, Nothing to See Here

Anonymous ID; TB+ANS Thu 12 Jan 03:43:28 <u>No. 148165</u> ViewReport
Micky D's neon
"Bob"
24-Hour Flyer
Yes men
Big caravan
~~American~~ epidemic
Louisiana connection?
Sinaloa Cartel = Washington DC
"Older" girls
Ether rags
Charm school
CB talk
gone "senile"
Town called Stanley NM
Chain of events
kinky shit?

child servants

"Motherfuckers would die"

Ah, the smell of an American truck stop in the morning. That blended floral romance between diesel fuel and asphalt, the grit in the grime of many miles driven but even more to go, and that longing to get home, at least for some. For others the vagabond highway is already home. The American West charm in the signage design, the welcoming big arches of Micky D's or the neon in your desolation, and that greasy truck stop hamburger or hot dog that beckons after awaiting your fat ass in a hot glass box for several days before your arrival. Not the best food but not the worst out there. We all know it's too much soda that gets you on the road life. But I digress. I am here to meet Elvis, who since the early eighties has gone by Bob. Saddled up in the diner of a 24-Hour Flyer, we both order the Slammer: 2 eggs, 2 strips of bacon, and 2 hotcakes. And steaming coffee jacked with obscene amounts of caffeine as it's the drug of choice for the road, a close second to methamphetamines, so I've been told.

"When I first went off the grid, before settling into this undercover life, just after I faked it all, there were the first couple of years that I didn't know if I could make it. You see, I had to unwind from it. De-program would be the best word. Everything had been so tightly wound up for me, and my only escape had been internal with all the drugs. Then I suddenly found I'm free to roam and express myself, and I didn't have anyone

59

around me. No yes men, no team, no manager, no lawyers, no accountants, no groupies and no fans. Just me by my lonesome. I will tell you Tony, that humans are good at adapting. I lost forty pounds in a couple of months. How? Just getting off all the dope. It took me about a week of not being able to shit, the constipation was so bad I thought all the backup would kill me. This was concerning because I was in real hiding at the time. I could not just walk into a doctor's office, I was Elvis fucking Presley and there was no hiding it. After a few days of taking all the shit-inducing over the counter stuff I could find, I finally blew a head gasket. I shit damn near for two days straight. And it felt good, a full colon cleanse. I hadn't felt this incredible in years. So I stayed clean. With all the weight off, and the gray coming in on my dyed black hair, it was much easier to get back into the public. Sure, there were times when people would stare at me in a supermarket or the occasional, 'You look like Elvis, you ever hear that?' type of thing."

"How did you end up here, on the road?," I ask.

"I always wanted a job with the least amount of responsibility and the freedom of the road. That's why I loved to tour, get in that big caravan and drive town to town. It was the shows that got exhausting. I was watching TV one night and there was this commercial for trucking school and I thought that's it. I had access to a few trust accounts so after I got the license I bought my first rig."

Our waitress came by to top off our coffees, I doused mine with creamer canisters turning it that perfect shade of latte brown.

"How did you get into the pedophile hunter game, I mean, we must be jumping forward a decade or so in the story at this point?"

"It started around the mid 80s, that heyday time when kids were being abducted in rest stops along the interstates. I was seeing the missing posters at every rest stop and truck stop. And every one of them was a different kid. All of these sweet beautiful children that should have been at school or home with their families now missing. It was an American epidemic but I never heard anyone talk about it in the media. Even truckers didn't talk about it. So, like anything, if there isn't attention on it then it doesn't exist."

"Did you have any friends on the road?"

"Yes, this is what happened. My friend and co-driver Steve, it's a long story, but he would ride with me and we took turns driving and sleeping. One day he blurted out that he had an inkling that his cousin down in Louisiana was connected with the disappearances. I said, what the fuck you talking about now? This kid was a shit talker, and I liked that about him, and he had no idea who Elvis was so I didn't have to act too much around him. Turns out his cousin was a drug distributor for the Sinaloa cartel out of Mexico. Steve said he found out that it wasn't just drugs they handled, that you could also get kids from them."

"And then what?"

"We paid him a visit, brought him some booze, got the truth serum working and he explained to us how the network conducted its business. A coded fax letter would be sent from Washington DC with an "order" to the cartel. It would be decoded and the order would be placed. Let's say it was for an attractive brunette girl with long hair. A "request" would then be pushed out to the "network," usually messed up truckers, low-life pimps, and pedophiles that would drive the interstates. Then the search would begin. Malls, parks near schools, motel parking lots, rest stops and truck stops. Some of the older girls, and when I say older I mean like fourteen, would willingly get into cars and trucks. They were ready for the runaway life. Younger kids had to be forcibly abducted with fast getaways. Like at rest stops. Usually snatched from a stall then carried around the back of the building, so nobody in the parking lot could see you, and into the cab of a truck and back on the interstate. Ether rags would knock them out cold."

"Wow, just wow."

"And then the kid is taken to one of several hubs in the southwest, dropped off and the abductor is given a code he then uses to get paid. Usually it was a few thousand dollars that would be deposited into his account from a front company, something trucking related so it looked like a big haul."

"Where would these kids then go?"

"Within the network were 'charm schools' that would sort out the level of quality of the product. The hottest, I can't believe that's the term for a child, were groomed, trained in things like massage, some sex stuff and these were the girls offered to the elites. Either Washington DC people or the billionaire class. The lesser quality product was sent abroad, sometimes to Mexico for the cartels to use as bartering chips and gifts between cartels. Or even off to the Middle East or some parts of Asia, like the young boys. At this point these kids were now officially lost, never to be reunited with their families again."

"When you say Washington DC, do you know anything more?"

"Yes, hell yeah, big names, senators, congressmen, lobbyists for the top corporations, using children as pawns in their power grabs and for sex parties. All that shit that people talk about in the conspiracy circles are usually facts."

"Tell me about how much you have infiltrated it."

"I got myself a decoder sheet for all the CB talk. That way when some trucker comes on and rambles something incoherent, you don't think he might be stroking out or gone senile, rather you can actually break it down and decipher the order from Mexico."

"What about the highway patrols and state police?"

"They are in on it, just like they are in on the drug trafficking, they know what cars are loaded up and which ones to not pull over, and if they do by accident pull over the wrong car, they know quickly to let it go. Same with the coded transmissions, I think they just turn a deaf ear to it."

"These charm schools, have you ever been to one?"

"Yes, right here in New Mexico, just down Albuquerque way, outside of a town called Stanley. Big operation. The intake point is the Motel 6. The kid stays in your vehicle while you check in at the front desk. You then wait in the room with the kid, it could be up to an entire day. You get a knock at the door and are told that your money has been deposited, and there is a cash tip on your windshield. You are then instructed to leave the room and the child stays behind. I have never done this but this is officially how it plays out."

"What then?"

"From what I understand a team of sophisticated European women come for the children, the kids are warmed up to the exotic accents, the motherly touch they miss, a trigger to somehow remind them of their own mothers, anything to make them feel safe. Then they are spoiled with the good life, with their own spacious room, meals of fast food, video games and television. This goes on for a few weeks while new identification documents are made for them. Usually American passports."

My breakfast has gone cold, as I barely touched it. I am tempted to offer it to Elvis but I don't want him to lose his train of thought.

"What is the next chain of events?"

"They are sent on to their new assignments, wherever that may be. Their birth identity has been scrubbed, and it's usually been about six months since they disappeared or vanished so there is no more media coverage about them. Their own mental makeup is wiped, that usually goes first. They forget who they are, and the groomers take on the role of authority for them and they listen to what they tell them. Sometimes it isn't just sex, it could be some other kinky shit. Massages, toe sucking, reading stories, serving cocktails, lighting cigars. You have to understand these sick fucker elites, for them it's like the most exquisite pinnacle of toys. People who have always gotten their way, who have everything they can imagine, adding to their collection a sex slave, or child servant means everything."

"What do you think would happen if the average American knew about this?"

"They would bring back the guillotine and, excuse my language, motherfuckers would die."

El Chapo's Blood Alliance

Anonymous ID; TB+ANS Thu 11 Oct 21:43:28 No. 148225 ViewReport
El Chapo
"Narcotraficante"
~~global~~ sex trade
owns Mexico
Medellin Cartel in its prime?
beheading = modus operandi
"vats of alkali" = no trace
DEA
off the books $$
Coffers of Democratic Party
Gov of California
LA Congressman
Clinton Foundation?

The Sinaloa Cartel is also known as the Pacific Cartel, the Blood Alliance, The Syndicate, or the Guzman-Loera Organization. It is considered the most powerful drug trafficking operation in the world. But it's also known for money laundering and other organized crime. Their pioneering founder, Pedro Aviles Perez, was the first drug smuggler in the 1960s to use small aircraft to move product. He was considered the OG, that first generation of romanticized operative who built the foundation for the modern day narco networks. These were noblemen who refused to incorporate sex trafficking into their operations. But that changed with Joaquin Guzman, the second generation leader of Sinaloa, also known as El Chapo, the self-proclaimed "narcotraficante" who swallowed up other cartels, namely the Tijuana Cartel, into his operation. Tijuana was a global sex trade hot spot. And with that, the trafficking wing was born.

Sinaloa Cartel owns Mexico, operating in 21 of the 31 states, and is the primary distributor of cocaine, fentanyl, methamphetamines, and marijuana into the US. Some estimates have their fingerprint on over 90 percent of all product into the States. Their distribution hubs line the north-south highways from San Diego to Seattle, they own the entire drug operations of Chicago, and are slowly overtaking the northeast drug operations from the Gambinos. They have surpassed the Medellin Cartel in its prime. They kill anyone in their way: small town mayors, cops who won't go on their payroll, or anyone they think is an informant. Beheading is the modus operandi, as gruesome and inefficient as it is, it does send a strong message. Then through the power of social media, they film the bodies being dissolved in vats of alkali and post these videos to their social networks. They built the Taj Mahal of tunnels, connecting a warehouse in Tijuana with one in Otay, California. They partially own the DEA which allows them to continue to grow unthwarted. And most importantly they own the politicians of Washington DC.

Even without lobbyists they have managed to fill the coffers of Democratic candidates with more off-the-books money than imaginable. Much of it directly into the pockets of candidates and elected officials. When El Chapo was arrested he declared that he would be released within days. This did not happen but when he was on trial in a Manhattan courtroom, he testified that he gave approximately $500 million to the then-speaker of the house, to be distributed how she felt, which included "donations" to her nephew, then-Governor of California, and to the congressman for Los Angeles, and a large amount to the Clinton Foundation. The implied favor from the payout was to maintain an open border between Mexico and the States.

It turned out that El Chapo would be framed, set up, whatever you want to call it, ending up in ADX, or the US Penitentiary Administrative Maximum Facility, in Florence, Colorado. With the bigger hope that he doesn't talk further, or somehow with the fantasy of an eventual return to the cartel, it's implied that his silence now will pay dividends in the future. As with any dirty operation the cartel higher ups are known for throwing each other under the proverbial drug trade bus. During his opening statement in a Brooklyn Federal Court El Chapo laid bare that his longtime partner, Ismael Zambada Garcia, was the real mastermind of the Sinaloa operation. El Chapo claimed to be merely a scapegoat. It was a clever play because now it seemed there was a shadow operation within and perhaps El Chapo was nothing more than the public face, and impending fall guy. His own attorney said, "The world is focusing on this mythical El Chapo creature while nobody knows who Mayo Zambada even is." Named in numerous indictments over the years, Zambada has never been arrested and remains at large.

The bigger missed hook of the story was the downline operation of the child sex trafficking. Prosecutors were focused on large shipments of cocaine seized in border towns as the evidence to the crimes. This is what the grand juries liked to see in order to indict. Talk of crooked DEA agents who helped facilitate the movement of young girls seemed too esoteric and fantastical for a courtroom. Big evidence of crimes was needed. Pictures of agents with the loot, tables strewn with bricks of cash and mountains of cocaine. The stuff of Hollywood. It was like the endangered girls were too much of a hot topic story to wrap heads around. It even seemed implausible that such an operation could function on such a large level.

So there was disbelief in that high order of coordination, much like there was in 9/11 conspiracy.

In order to get a conviction any good attorney will tell you to focus on the drugs. But even more importantly, those in the know knew that the child trafficking went to the top levels of Washington DC and therefore paid off insiders in grand juries wouldn't indict, or people as high up as the Attorney General's office may intervene. Or there would be a jailhouse suicide. So they play it safe. It becomes a game of wins and losses. And anytime you are up against the biggest and baddest cartel you have the threat of your own assassination. Oh yes, those desert cowboy "sicarios," the most violent killers. Bad hombres that get off on the violence. Believe it or not, some of the orders placed to these assassins come directly from the corridors of the US Capitol. There is no hesitation in them dressing up like UPS drivers and knocking on the door of a judge in the suburbs of Virginia and putting a bullet into their forehead.

So next time you are following a big case, some new trial of the century, and when it takes a turn that doesn't make sense, know there are many invisible hands at work, puppet masters, assassins and other protectors of the underworld.

A Playmate & Her Inheritance

Anonymous ID; TB+ANS Mon 14 Mar 21:33:44 <u>No. 148995</u> ViewReport
Playboy Playmate
Medical "Examiner" [examine her]
Chloral hydrate = natural causes
"dark of night"
Seminole Police Dept
1999 POY
~~Hugh Hefner~~
Supreme Court
2 men, 1 daughter
Enter JonBenet Ramsey (JBR)
"newfound purpose"
Find JBR killer(s)

Early February, 2007, 39-year old former Playboy Playmate Anna Nicole Smith died from an accidental drug overdose in a Florida casino's hotel room. The Medical Examiner deemed it a "combined drug intoxication," but labeled the reason of death as "natural causes." Seminole Tribal investigators ruled out suicide and foul play. Chloral hydrate, a sedative used to treat insomnia, was deemed a major contributing factor to her death as well as high levels of methadone. Another contributing factor for the authorities was the recent death of her son Daniel, as well as a number of legal issues brought upon her by her much older son-in-laws, J. Howard Marshall III and E. Pierce Marshall. Furthermore she tested positive for immunoglobulin drugs, human growth hormones, and antianxiety drugs. Abscesses on her buttocks were the result of injections. This was the only superficial evidence that the body was indeed not that of Ms. Smith. The cadaver that was in the possession of the Medical Examiner was that of a Colombian bikini model, who had traveled to Miami for a Brazilian Butt Lift surgery but fell ill and died just moments before surgery. Anna Nicole Smith's attorney, Howard K. Stern, arranged for the deceased body to be transported in the dark of night to the hotel room. There was a striking resemblance between the two women and without makeup there was an unmasking affect smokescreen. Both women had had years of plastic surgery and high numbers of incisions and scarring. Both had size double D breasts. Because the death occurred on tribal land the Seminole Police Department wanted the case closed fast, meaning no speculation into criminal activity nor mention of suspicious circumstances, this included any questions about the body.

Smith grew up in Texas and when she turned 18, like other girls her age, she became a topless dancer. Her all-American look combined with an exquisite pair of natural breasts led to a personal offer by Hugh Hefner himself of her own Playboy spread, resulting in her title of 1993's Playmate of the Year. This opened her world to modelling, for which she famously became a Guess jeans model. During this time she began to self-medicate with prescription drugs. While she aged out of the limelight, very much under the public eye, she went deeper into her addiction. Her public persona became that of hot mess tabloid material, with her shenanigans and escapades juicy fodder for paparazzi and a newly-popularized television format, that of reality show. She traded in the currency of her buxom cleavage and that of former B-list star now disheveled into a battered every-mom chic, as this was her appeal.

In what in retrospect likely saved her life at the time, she met and married 89-year-old oilman J. Howard Marshall II. When he died not longer after their marriage, she inherited his $500 million fortune. Immediately she was sued by her two son-in-laws over the financial windfall, and as with anything that involved her, the media hype around it was bigger than life. She eventually took the battle all the way to the Supreme Court, winning the entirety of her deceased husband's $474,000,000 USD fortune. Looking back at it, so much of her life was comprised of unnecessary drama, too much too soon, and without so much pressure she would have had a much simpler existence, something sustainable, and not of this high wire magnitude.

During the years-long battle she had a baby girl that two different men claimed as their daughter, her personal attorney Howard K. Stern and photographer Larry Birkhead. This fed deeper into the tabloid narratives and forced Anna to realize that her life as Anna Nicole Smith had become unsustainable, that she needed to go away, to reinvent herself, to take on a new name, to change her appearance, to get sober, to even fake her own death. With the freedom that would come with the anonymity she could finally look into what she considered the crime of the century. That of who really killed JonBenet Ramsey, the child beauty queen who had died the previous Christmas. This was a mystery that shook Anna to the core. A lovely child whose flame was extinguished way too soon, it was as if Anna's newfound purpose in life was to find the killer(s). With this focus she could get off the dope, and finally absorb and feel some of the personal trauma she had been pushing away for her entire life. And I will be there for her, as her friend and possible lover, someone she can lean on, even lean into. My inner pubescent boy is piqued by the intrigue of meeting this American iconoclast. Those great tits and all.

Hugh Hefner & the Playboy Effect

Anonymous ID; TB+ANS Thu 11 Apr 05:25:44 No. 148991 ViewReport
Pajamas
Young busty women

Grotto
ANS
Freedom of speech
Centerfolds
Creepy grandfather
~~Bill Cosby~~
Defiant
$100,000,000 USD

Oh to spend your life in silk pajamas surrounded by young busty women who never age. It's one of those things you need to process in your mind, at least if you are a horny man like myself, and for your own sanity to work it through that perhaps the grass is not greener on the other side, that surely there is a downside to this lifestyle. And apparently there was. Hugh liked to control the girls. In fact he got off on that more than the famed orgies in the infamous Playboy Mansion grotto. It was something that Anna Nicole Smith witnessed first hand and helped her realize she was no longer in Texas.

Hefner to his credit was a key figure in the freedom of speech and of course without him there would be no centerfold fantasies for the last half century. With that said, as his publishing power waned he ramped up his control of house guests. There was no shortage of eighteen year olds who would want to spend their days laying out, playing volleyball, getting their hair and nails done, and eating popcorn with Hef at night in his theater room. It wasn't even a requirement to have sex with him. If you caught his eye he might comment on your body and ask where you are from, but nothing more than a creepy grandfather vibe.

Yet there was something else going on. Isn't there always? Hef liked his porn, so back in the 70s he began secretly filming his "guests" having sex with playmates. Of course to be a guest at the mansion you had to be a celebrity. He would arrange for threesomes mostly. Bring in big names like OJ Simpson or Bill Cosby. It was pre-tabloids so nothing ever got out. But the footage, after Hef watched it, would be archived in a vault in the mansion basement. It was like Epstein servers meet the Weiner hard drive.

For decades there were hushed rumors and a bravado mythology of these tapes being held in a private stash by Hef, but it didn't keep the people from attending the parties, in fact some liked the potential exhibitionistic aspect of their own performance. It built up the Hefner mythos and made him more powerful than the biggest power brokers of Hollywood.

It wasn't until his death that people began speaking ill of him. Endless amounts of girls who had similar stories of abuse and being pimped out to famous people. It was like a dam had broken and the floodgates were flowing. Celebrities kept quiet. Deflection techniques were deployed. Many well-known actors claimed to have never been to the Playboy Mansion. The big question on everyone's minds was where the tapes were. Hef was old school and liked the super 8 reel so there was minimal concern that these troves of amateur porn were somehow digitized. Word from staff was the tapes were in the basement.

So when the Playboy Mansion was sold for $100,000,000 USD to a young heir to the Twinkie dynasty, eyebrows were raised. But like any good real estate flipper, the young buyer turned around and sold the basement vault room, sight unseen, to a shell company of the Israeli government for, wait for it, $100,000,000 USD. It turned out to be one of those bargains that you only hear about in real estate folklore, that no deal like this is out there anymore. Even more so for the people on tape. The troves slipped through the crack and now were on their way to the cloud. The story went unreported as those on film were either proud of their conquests, with the footage something of their own legend making (think OJ), or the subjects were married men who had wanted this part of their past sealed. The nervous pangs of imminent release would keep these people up at night, a sort of PTSD would become their new normal. After all, this is part of any good blackmail game.

Airborne Escape Artist Event

Anonymous ID; TB+ANS Fri 13 Apr 07:45:24 <u>No. 148996</u> ViewReport
Airborne "explosions"
Yitzah Rabin "assassination"
Shabak or Shin Bet?
Yigal Amir
~~testimony~~
Blanks or toy gun?
Martha's Vineyard
"calm & collected"
"could fly itself"
Falcon jets
Camp David
POTUS Clinton
"recovered all passengers"
George Magazine
Interpol
High Intensity Radical Field (HIRF)
EgyptAir Flight 990
Janet Reno, male?
Nantucket Island
Operation Trojan Horse
51-Day Siege
False Flag op?
Tim McVeigh OKC diversion?
"Inexperienced"
Extreme weather
Curse of Camelot
Presidential ~~run~~ (2000)

Much of the conspiratorial fallout from JFK Jr's plane crash involved "airborne explosions" seen and heard by witnesses on Martha's Vineyard. Many of the unexplained factors were in direct conflict with what saturated mainstream media reports. You had to look deep for it, as these were the early days of the internet, but there were theories and reasons for taking out JFK Jr. He was scheduled to meet with high-ranking Israeli officials and agents from Mossad to reveal information he had obtained regarding the recent Yitzhak Rabin assassination. Word was that it was an inside job, pulled off by the Israeli Secret Service, also known as the Shabak, or Shin Bet.

Conspiracy theories immediately followed the assassination of Rabin, both from the left and the right, with all theories quickly squelched by the Israeli media. The official story was that a Jewish student, Yigal Amir, was apprehended within seconds of the shooting in a crowded square. He would end up being found guilty but not without lingering questions. Police reports state that there was gunpowder on Rabin's body even though he was shot from a distance that would not allow gunpowder to travel onto his person. Surgery reports detail a bullet entrance wound in the chest contradicting eyewitness reports and video footage showing him being shot in the back. The testimony of three police officers was that Rabin showed no visible wounds when placed in his car. Even though it would be a five minute walk to the hospital, his motorcade took 22 minutes to arrive, even though the streets were cordoned off, and he had the most experienced Shabak driver. Shell casings from the scene did not match Amir's gun according to police ballistics tests. A witness, one who died mysteriously in the week following the assassination, told a local news outlet that someone screamed "It's nothing, they are blanks, it's a toy gun." Amir had been employed by the Shabak two year prior in Latvia. In court he said "If I were to tell you the whole truth, the entire system would collapse," adding "I know enough to destroy this country." These comments were stricken from the public record. Shimon Peres was sworn in as Prime Minister and later became President of Israel.

Kennedy had radioed into the Martha's Vineyard airport with his location, position and trajectory all indicating a smooth routine flight. The air traffic controller on duty that evening claimed there was an "in control" element and "calm and collected" state of mind in Kennedy's voice. Within seconds of this transmission were reports of what a beachgoer said was a "craft plunging toward the ocean like a rock." Yet there was no distress being shown on the radar of the plane. It would be years before alternative radar data revealed different maneuvers, and this would be enough to prove false information had been implemented to cover up the true facts of the crash. The media liked to emphasize that Kennedy was an inexperienced pilot, glossing over the fact that he had seventeen years of experience. Instead they opted to go with the narrative of "several hundred hours of flight time," the minimum required for a license. Additionally the plane, the Piper Saratoga, was equipped with the latest in hi-tech equipment that included auto-pilot and emergency tracking systems. Some pilots would claim that this particular plane "could fly itself."

Kennedy's family first called the Hyannis airport at 2:15am when he failed to arrive. This is when the official search began. Twelve hours later, the family postponed the wedding that he was supposed to attend. The Air National Guard and Air Force began a massive air search with Falcon jets, TC-130 aircraft, and smaller helicopters over a 1,000 square mile area. In a statement issued from Camp David, where President Clinton was staying that weekend, he offered, "All our prayers and thoughts are with the families of those on board."

A leaked Interpol report claimed that Carolyn Kennedy was in her third trimester of pregnancy, as well that nearby sensors picked up a massive electromagnetic pulse as the possible cause of the crash. Something that would have "instantaneously microwaved all passengers." If the pilot was not "immediately" microwaved, "his ability to see through the blast flash would have been nearly impossible." The Interpol report was just enough to set off the conspiracy theorists down new rabbit holes, and the official quality of such Interpol reports could not be discredited by the mainstream media. What wasn't known was that the report was written by Kennedy's best friend, his editor-in-chief of George magazine, and back channeled through college friends in Lyon, France, Interpol's headquarters. Could it have been a low-grade tactical nuclear explosion? Possibly a positron beam of some sort? Otis Air Force Base in Cape Cod are the northeastern eyes in the sky for the military. TWA Flight 800, three years prior, was likely taken down by a High Intensity Radiated Field (HIRF), from some kind of military craft. Of course by accident, official or not. That day there was a Navy P-3 Orion flying extremely close to Flight 800. This is the official unofficial stance. As well this is the running theory behind EgyptAir Flight 990. Of course those who would think such conspiracies are too fantastical would only need to know that the likes of a Clinton president could pull this off. As well the threat that Kennedy was set to run for office. And that John was set to expose then-Attorney General Janet Reno in a George article. He was not just going to out her as a lesbian, but also as a male-born transsexual, within a story detailing her botched efforts that led to the Waco Massacre. Additionally, any attempted run by John at public office would resurrect the buried stories of the assassinations of his father and his uncle, Bobby Kennedy.

EgyptAir Flight 990 was a routine flight from LAX to Cairo International Airport with a stop at JFK International Airport, New York City, on October 31, 1999, until the Boeing 767 mysteriously crashed 60 miles south of Nantucket Island, Massachusetts, killing all 217 crew and passengers on board. Many family members, and the majority of polled Egyptians, believe that the US government with the assistance of the CIA and Israel took down the plane with a missile. Much of the NTSB report and official record places blame on a possible suicide mission by the pilot.

Called Operation Trojan Horse, or the Waco Massacre, the 1993 raid by the bureau of Alcohol Tobacco & Firearms agents on a religious sect, searching for illegal weapons, would lead to a gun battle and a resulting 51-day siege, culminating in tanks and tear gas and an inferno that killed 76 Branch Davidians, including 21 children. The conspiracy minded blamed cover up upon cover up by the Clinton Administration, and Attorney General Janet Reno, as the gist to this most abusive use of force by the federal government. Looking deeper in retrospect one could argue it may have been a false flag operation by Reno who was attempting to distract from her own secret, that she was a male that had transitioned to female. Years later we would learn that the Waco tragedy was the spark for the planning of Timothy McVeigh in his bombing attack of a federal building in Oklahoma City that killed 168 people in the largest act of domestic terrorism to date.

Any good conspiracy theory needs a sidebar story to spin enough confusion into the minds of the believers (or non-believers), and this was the Mossad hit job theory. That JFK Jr's chauffeur to the airport that day placed a bomb into his luggage. That then-Israeli Prime Minister Ehud Barak had reasons for John not finding out the truth of Rabin's murder. The media paraded out day and night expert after expert on aviation, using loose terminology while emphasizing the "inexperience" of the pilot and the disorientation that came with such "extreme weather." Polls found that the majority of Americans blamed JFK Jr. for the bad decision to fly that day. After all, he essentially killed his own wife and sister-in-law. The puppets and talking heads were successful in their smear campaign and the story was able to subside as just another chapter of the Curse of Camelot. Within newly-formed internet chat rooms word spread within certain conspiracy forums that JFK Jr's real ambition was to run for President in the year 2000.

Mother Teresa & Diana

Anonymous ID; TB+ANS Mon 3 May 02:32:12 <u>No. 148999</u> ViewReport
Legacy of sainthood
Baby Doc
Sex trade diaspora
Vatican City
POPE
"spiritual awakening"
~~AIDS~~
HRC
Fauci
Epstein

Any honest discussion of Mother Teresa must address her romanticized world view of poverty and suffering, as it wasn't something she tried to eradicate, instead she embraced it. And her legacy of sainthood has been marred with this sort of sickly obsession with the cult of the destitute. For all of her holiness and righteous behavior she was politically naive and this led to a friendship with Haiti's dictator Jean-Claude Baby Doc Duvalier. Baby Doc was the grandmaster of child trafficking, personally responsible for the sex trade diaspora of thousands of young Haitian girls. His final acts before exile were to hand over the non-governmental organizational powers to the Clinton Foundation rather than a less corrupt United Nations. This would give way to the No Ceilings Initiative by the Clintons and a perfect cover story for more trafficking. The other aspect of Mother Teresa's naiveté was how she would send all of the donations she received to the Apostolic Palace, Vatican City, 00120, addressed to the Pope himself. We are talking millions of dollars, and she was confident that this money would be used for the best, even though quite contrarily much of the money she sent in, especially from the 1980s to the late nineties, was used to cover up Catholic Church sex crimes.

This frail elderly Albanian woman was the visage of earthly holiness but mostly she was a shill for the elites and dictators who needed cover. Princess Diana had tried to meet with Mother Teresa in 1992 to get her the message that she was being used. Diana had prepared an elaborate fable type of monologue to best explain to this innocent woman the evils in her midst. But these dark forces were successful in shutting down the meeting by getting Mother Teresa sick with food poisoning. Diana went to the convent where they were supposed to meet, in defiance of those who were able to cancel the meeting, to send a message that she would still bring her spotlight to these unfortunate souls. After her brief tour she claimed to have her own "spiritual awakening." It would be another five years before Di and Mother Theresa were to actually meet.

The meeting took place in Calcutta, at Mother Teresa's Missionary of Charity. In private Diana was able to convey that her friendship with Baby Doc was not as it seemed. That his own exile in France was a cover story, that he had been paid off by the global elites. That his ties to the Clintons were more ominous than first thought. It was too much in too short a period of time for Mother Teresa to process. They agreed to meet in the Bronx the following year, for an AIDS event, and to continue their discussions. That would be their last meeting and nothing of sex trafficking was discussed. It was the closing chapter of the AIDS epidemic and there was a jubilance in the air. All those deaths of gay men were not in vain, there had been enough advancements in prophylactic drugs and cocktailing of other inhibitors to lower the death rates to under a single percent. At this somber gala were New York Senator Hillary Clinton, National Institute of Allergy and Infectious Disease Director Anthony Fauci, and mega donor Jeffrey Epstein.

Princess Diana would be dead the following summer, and in a kindred spiritual connection Mother Teresa would pass from natural causes a mere five days later.

Emotional Atrocities & Other Bemusements

As a species we are most interested in ourselves, and, furthermore, with the strange things we do when we go about life. That and the rush and thrill from sexual attraction. It is all-telling of our most intimate selves. It explains so much of our ethos. It's even why we like gossip, that inherent need to keep up with what others are doing. Perhaps it's about tracking our peers in order to see what we should be doing ourselves. The term gossip is an old one, stemming from when royalty would meet up to talk smack of others, they would "go sip" their tea and seek out bemusement in the schadenfreude of another's demise or failure. Stillbirths and overthrows were hot topics. Talk of affairs were all but guaranteed fodder. Sex with the enlisted help was all there really was for entertainment outside of the boring and mundane day-to-day of privileged living. Gossip is a valued currency which can make one feel recognized and heard, and almost indispensable in the most crucial of moments. There is a dissecting quality, much like an autopsy of society that entails understanding class rage, passion, desire and the fake elements of misinformation. And the loss of shame, something that healthy societies develop to stay sane. Everything evolves into a runaway situation with unintended consequences leading to insane behavior that justifies again the original spark from the match. It's about enlarging the prerogatives and potential for emotional atrocities.

Shaming others is meant as a way to dictate behavior, another method for society to let the people know what is, and what is not, acceptable. When shame is used as a threat for survival within one's family or tribe there is a default reaction to simply hide away to avoid being forced out. This behavior correction within the context of a loving relationship can lead to feelings of unworthiness. At this point it's not about the original behavior but about the beliefs of ourselves and who we have become. For survival's sake we are tasked with uncovering our basic goodness and all that has been obscured by the traumatizing within our internal climates. Free of self-judgment we can correct the internal atmosphere and live a less limiting existence.

So it is in this spirit that the reacquainting of a very much alive Lady Di and John John took place in a secluded chateau in Switzerland, nothing too fancy, but humble by the ultra-rich standards of larger than large square metric living. Void of security details and encumbrances that are attached to such planning, their first moments were fraught with the subtle panic that comes from living under such microscopic watch. The pangs of a rematch to the initial butterflies was a thrill they both had longed for in the several-months-long planning for this day. It would be a dozen minutes before their first kiss then merely moments before John slipped his hand into the athleisure yoga pants of Di. From there it advanced to a full melding of bodies and souls through to a climactic orgasm by Di that signaled to John it was his turn to finish. Such libido was not found in your typical 60 and 61 year olds.

It was in the seclusion afforded by the chateau that they could plot their next moves. This required a deep dive into The Alt Vault, a long-held secret database of faked celebrity deaths, and the going-ons of their post-celebrity re-births. It was a treasure trove of high interest reads, and included close friends of theirs. People like Gianni Versace and Prince.

But to remain on task their first person of interest was Anna Nicole Smith. In the midst of her search for JonBenet Ramsey's killer(s) Anna was in Asia and needed assistance in locating Anthony Bourdain, who did not kill himself.

<u>Anthony Bourdain Did Not Kill Himself</u>

Anonymous ID; TB+ANS Thu 3 Feb 02:24:14 <u>No.</u>
<u>148005</u> ViewReport
AB or TB "death"
Countryside of France NOT NYC
~~CNN~~
Illuminati or Trilateralists = same thing?
Harvey Weinstein
National Suicide Hotline
"deepest ~~condolences~~"
Mia Farrow
Chef
Weiner laptop
Asia Argento "fuck everyone"
Italian bloodlines
#metoo
myth creation
Hollywood, never work again
Caribbean
Assassination = DNC?

How do I know this? Because I am Anthony
Bourdain, your spirited narrator of this delicious and
delectable story, and I did not kill myself. I can get to
the details later, but let's just say for now I am safe and
my "death" was necessary for the betterment of
humanity, as my tools and resources are best used
without the spotlight of fame glaring down on me. Ok,
well, I suppose I can get to the details of my untimely
demise now, rather than later, to help shine a light on

what we are up against. With the innuendo attached to a "supposed" suicide in the "countryside" manor of France, far from my NYC home and my daughter and my girlfriend Asia Argento, the co-founder of the #metoo movement, who had been raped by Harvey Weinstein in the mid 1990s, I had a fine meal in the hotel restaurant, filmed by my CNN crew of six, then retired to my room and hung myself off a doorknob with a silk pillowcase. I don't think so. And thank you to those who did not believe this utter bullshit. Sure I got a bunch of tattoos in my fifties, and yes I was a heroin addict for some time in my twenties and thirties, but this doesn't automatically mean you are primed to take your life just when you have it all figured out and money in the bank. Furthermore I wasn't involved in some coven of witches or warlocks, or even a blood delivery service for the elites of Manhattan. Even though in my early years I cooked and served some of the Illuminati and Trilateralists there was no connection in later life or the historical precedent that I am now some Satanist coming after your babies. On a less sexier note, it was Harvey Weinstein that had me "killed."

His own elite squad of retired Mossad agents gone rogue were fooled by the striking resemblance between myself and a dying Marseillaise homeless Algerian man who accepted from me a direct deposit of $100,000 USD for his family in Algiers. The cremation took place the next day, well before notifying the American embassy in Paris. Only those within my film crew knew and as they did not believe the suicide narrative they went along with it to ensure their own safety. There was a perverse magic in what I had pulled off, and like how I enjoy making perfect food I enjoyed making a perfect death. With the logistical challenge of the scene of death out of the way, and the destruction of any DNA remains, the final piece was the media's narrative which they fell into rather quickly, without a single question as to why I would kill myself, the talking heads were quick to note my years of addiction, and my later-in-life affinity for body ink. It was enough for them to close the book on me.

"He taught us about food, but more importantly about its ability to bring us together," Barack Obama

"National Suicide Hotline 1 800 273 8255 I've brushed up against this darkness and I know it's a tempting exit but REACH OUT to ANYONE. Stay on this side of it, in the light and warmth. Where you get to try again, every day," Patton Oswalt

"My deepest condolences to his families and loved ones. He sometimes spoke of his battle with depression. I am saddened to hear it took him from us while he still had so much left to share," George Takei

"Maybe we all wanted to hang out with him. He was that cool, fun, frank, insightful. He introduced us to distant lands and to people with different traditions. And without ever preaching, he reminded us that we humans are far more alike than different. Thank you Anthony Bourdain," Mia Farrow

"According to AFSP, there are nearly 45,000 suicides every year in the US. Shocking. I was saddened to hear of the deaths of Kate Spade and Anthony Bourdain. RIP. It illustrates that success is not immune to depression. We all need to be more aware of our friends who are suffering," Bryan Cranston

"Stunned and saddened by the loss of Anthony Bourdain. He brought the world into our homes and inspired so many people to explore cultures and cities through their food. Remember that help is a phone call away US:1-800-273-TALK UK: 116 123," Gordon Ramsey

Every chef wants to serve a plate that is a reflection of their craft, along with the finest seasonal ingredients, so I left some clues to try and scare the living shit out of Harvey, as well Hillary Clinton who most likely was in cahoots to some extent with the hit job. You see, they knew I was onto them, not just their elite circles of pedophiliac activities, but I had a mirror hard drive of Anthony Weiner's laptop, more on that later, and my girlfriend Asia, who was of a certain royal Italian bloodline, and her impending high profile testimony in a Manhattan courtroom would not got over well with the Club of Rome or what-have-you Euro power brokers. As arrogant and preposterous as it sounds, do not piss off daddy.

I met Asia Argento on the set of my show, Parts Unknown, specifically the Rome edition, in 2016. We went public right away, blasting out our disgusting puppy love for each other, for all the world to see through our social media channels, declaring that yes indeed 60 year olds are still sexual, and sometimes with women 20 years their junior. Alas, was there trouble in paradise? Isn't there always?

Just hours before my suicide Asia posted a photo of herself wearing a shirt with the caption, "Fuck everyone" with an asterisked note "You know who you are." When the media caught on three hours later that I had taken my life in France she removed the post, but with the technology of screenshots her post lived on and was fresh fodder for the conspiracy set. Was this a message to Bourdain or to Weinstein, or maybe to the entire #metoo movement that was becoming frayed before our eyes with an impending implosion brought on from excessive estrogen and unresolved daddy issues?

One of our most sanctimonious attributes of being American is our ability at myth creation, often at the expense of more complicated truths. We can forgive our heroes because we want them to be perfect. If they lie to us or don't live up to their hype we rewrite the narrative to correct for their failings. Much of the sustenance behind the #metoo movement involved women who had, up to that point, defined themselves by the men in their lives, and by default protected the predators in our midst by siding with the evil in order to climb the social ladder, or ranks within Hollywood. Do you ever wonder what happened to a certain actress, say someone who had been on a several year run with a rash of successful films to then never be heard from again? Oh, maybe she retired to a cabin in Idaho to raise her family, you ponder. Or maybe she denied the advances by a power player like Weinstein and as promised never worked again.

What really piqued my curiosity was why nobody questioned my suicide, even with the one remaining glimmer in one's life, their children, well I had my daughter Ariane, and she was delicately eleven years old at the time. Could she, possibly even in the slightest, have been someone that would give me sufficient hope to stick it out long enough to get well? Doesn't look like it, as the obits were written and CNN ran some depression narrative, how it afflicts chefs and others in the restaurant industry harder than most. Well, you don't say? Could it be the late nights, the struggles with the bottle and stimulants like cocaine, maybe not having families, or, when you do, not being able to see them because of your god awful hours. Could it be that our megalomania is fed with the quasi-glint of stardom within our own kitchens, with our own bedazzled patina aesthetic, whether that be bright orange crocs or sleeves of arm tattoos, maybe a well-placed bandana to lend to the credence of your former gang life thuggery, while everyone yells back at you deferential "yes CHEF" this and that. But outside that kitchen you are a mere burnout, a societal fringe player, half vampire half mortal teetering on the brink of foreclosure number two and several years in arrears on child support. That pressure is not glamorous nor sustainable.

Anthony Bourdain, whose dark memoir about life in the kitchens of New York City made him a celebrity chef while igniting a secondary career as a food journalist, was found dead on Friday in a hotel room in France. He was 61. His death is being considered a suicide. Local authorities said the death was by hanging. "At this stage we have no reason to suspect foul play," said Christian de Rocquigny du Fayel, local prosecutor. Anthony Michael Bourdain was born June 25, 1956, in New York and grew up in Leonia, New Jersey. Mr. Bourdain never stopped marveling at the unlikelihood of his later in life success. "I should've died in my 20s. I became successful in my 40s. I became a dad in my 50s. I feel like I've stolen a really nice car and I keep looking in the rearview mirror for flashing lights." Mr. Bourdain is survived by his mother; a daughter, Ariane; and a younger brother, Christopher Bourdain. His father died in 1987.

But I digress. Asia was kryptonite. A tattooed brunette, who, dare I say, was a haggard facsimile of Uma Thurman. She wore her trauma well. A day after my death she released this endearing statement, "Anthony gave all of himself in everything that he did. His brilliant, fearless spirit touched and inspired so many, and his generosity knew no bounds. He was my love, my rock, my protector. I am beyond devastated. My thoughts are with his family. I would ask that you respect their privacy and mine." When Asia and I began dating the media rumored that she was a homewrecker and responsible for ending my marriage to Ottavia, but the truth was our marriage had been pushed to the back burner for years due to my insane schedule and because our relationship--other than parenting our beautiful

96

daughter--had become an unconventional one. Before Ottavia, I was married for twenty years to my high school sweetie, yes that vile American tradition of settling so early on to the morsel of an appetizer to deny yourself any meal later in what becomes a long life of deprivation. Her name was Nancy and when that marriage was ending I was suicidal to an extent. The media dug up this gem of a quote, the only one of its kind, to exacerbate the suicidal narrative. "After my divorce to Nancy, to cope, I went to the Caribbean where I behaved in a completely irresponsible and suicidal way. I didn't value my own life and acted accordingly. I had put myself in a very dark place and behaved recklessly in the not-too-subconscious hope that something terrible would happen. I was doing everything possible--smoking pot, drink-driving--to invite that."

In their ever reckless style, the media glossed over my last public interview stating, "I am happy in ways that I have not been in memory, happy in ways I didn't think I ever would be, for sure, and I thank my girlfriend for this contentment." She did make me happy and that is why I so publicly became an outspoken advocate for her and the #metoo movement. The fact that the media did not push any idea that perhaps my suicide was a well-planned assassination, a retaliation of sorts for my prodding and explosive new stance on the harassment of women, with people like Weinstein and Bill Clinton in the crosshairs, is baffling and confirms again that the mainstream is nothing more than an arm of the DNC. All tin foil hats aside, this is the only explanation.

This from an essay I published in the magazine Medium months before my passing: "In these current circumstances, one must pick a side. I stand unhesitatingly and unwaveringly with the women. Not out of virtue, or integrity, or moral outrage--as much as I'd like to say so--but because late in life, I met one extraordinary woman with a particularly awful story to tell, who introduced me to other extraordinary women with equally awful stories. I am grateful to them for their courage, and inspired by them. That doesn't make me any more enlightened than any other man who has begun listening and paying attention. It does make me, I hope, slightly less stupid."

My own suicide happened just days after the suicide of NYC designer Kate Spade.

Kate Spade May Not Have Killed Herself

Anonymous ID; TB+ANS Sat 5 Apr 04:23:14 No. 149995 ViewReport
No Ceilings Initiative
Haiti is Hispaniola

Clinton Foundation
WOC = weapon of choice = red scarf?
Full Participation Project
"underground world"
smokescreen
junkies
pill collectors
background
~~Earthquakes~~
Procurement of "girls"
How involved?

Kate Spade may not have killed herself. I say may because of all the questions surrounding this woman's most idealized life and the connection to her returned involvement with the Clinton Foundation, through the "No Ceilings Initiative" in Haiti. What adds to the mystery is a series of photos that her husband posted of her after her death, and what are obviously staged photos of her in the moments leading up to her demise. She was found hanged off a closet door knob with a red scarf. Debunkers will debunk the idea that Kate was in fact depressed. She was no longer involved in her namesake brand after selling her remaining stake in the business to Neiman Marcus for $59 million two years prior. A housekeeper found the body of Kate while her husband, Andy, brother of famed actor/comedian David Spade, was at home as well. It was revealed that the two had essentially separated ten months prior and were living apart within the sprawling Park Avenue apartment. It was reported that he had recently asked for a divorce, and this is all the media needed to steer their narrative away from the Clinton Foundation chatter. A further distraction tactic was deployed when Andy appeared the day after the suicide for the awaiting paparazzi wearing a mouse mask.

The Clinton Foundation No Ceilings Initiative primarily hovered around the western hemisphere's most ravished and vulnerable country, Haiti. Rife with endless opportunities for child trafficking, the island of Hispaniola was just a three and a half hour flight from New York. In order to fully index the local female children, there was an official effort at collecting pictures and names to be sorted and parked on the dark web. So the Clintons launched The Full Participation Project as an initiative to "advance the full participation of girls and women into the workplace and more importantly into the conversation." The foundation went on, "Despite progress over the last several decades, girls and women remain the majority of the world's unhealthy, unfed, and unpaid." What the initiative left out was that these were the most vulnerable population to human trafficking and modern day slavery. In order to help these girls, the Clinton Foundation ordered a data-driven analysis on gender equality. This required photos of the girls, names, vaccines, addresses, birth dates. All under the ruse that the more information obtained the better the conversation could be. Kate Spade had made several trips to Haiti to gather this information. It is still not known how much she knew, or if she was aware of her nefarious involvement.

It was not long before the internet lit up with theories of a connection between Kate and myself, that we were secret crime fighters bringing the fight to the underground world of pedo rings. Some of it was so fantastical that it strategically discredited any validity to the very real problem at hand, that pedophiles were in the highest positions of power, globally, and nobody really knew the severity and those who did, people like Kate and myself, even Chris Cornell and Chester Bennington, two remarkable men, artists, and fathers, who "killed themselves" the summer prior to my own suicide, those that had the privilege of knowing, and the onus to do something would not go there, for the threat that a wrath would be unleashed on one's family so hard that everyone you knew would be deemed somewhat in danger. You must understand, this is why there is an invisible fight and that the battles are undertaken behind the smokescreen of very highly publicized deaths, in our cases suicides, because we were fucked up people, because we were once junkies, because of our pill collections and later in life tattoos.

Chris Cornell Did Not Kill Himself

Anonymous ID; TB+ANS Tue 24 Sep 01:32:32 <u>No.</u> <u>149875</u> ViewReport

Soundgarden = garden of sound
Ativan, naloxone
Comet Ping Pong Pizza
Cornell Foundation
"head wound"
~~black book~~
Coordinated or concerted?
Broken ribs = EMT aggressive response?
"Excessive amounts of blood"
Palos Verdes Estates
~~fake news~~
Linda Ramone
Courtney Love
Bohemian Grove
NWO
dark web
Wizard of Oz
Devil's rules
Biological son of Podesta
Seth Rich
"a struggle"
ATM "robbery"
Clinton Body Count
Russian Foreign Intelligence ☐ SVR
"hit squad"

Following a Detroit gig, Soundgarden lead singer Chris Cornell shocked his fans, band mates, and the greater world by taking a handful of pills and killing himself. These included the anti-anxiety drug Ativan, barbiturates, and the anti-opioid drug naloxone. In the reeling disbelief that came about in the shock of the event, there was a convenient glossing over of why such a successful rock star, with so much to live for, a beautiful wife and two doting teenage daughters, would end his life alone in a hotel room. Without any red flags or warnings, I am here to ask, what if Chris didn't kill himself? What if he was murdered, or even staged his own suicide and is now in hiding. And his "death" is somehow tied to the much down-played Pizzagate story that refuses to go away, so fantastical on the surface, that widely discredited pizza parlor front for the Washington DC elites' personal pedophile ring. Yes, that Comet Ping Pong Pizza place. Well, the truthers are never satisfied and this official account of Cornell's demise appears fictitious in nature--in the same vein that pizzagate comes off as a narrative of bad writing--but my theory is as such: Chris along with his wife Vicky founded the Cornell Foundation for neglected children, and he was about to expose the names from a "black book" that he had mysteriously obtained. And as for the suicide scene, there is choppy audio from a Detroit police scanner mentioning a "head wound."

The Cornell Foundation was formed with the mission to "protect vulnerable children around the world." The foundation "supports organizations that provide shelter and resources for homeless, abused and at-risk youth, children living in refugee camps and victims of human trafficking." Most of their work has been private and anonymous. Chris formed the foundation based on his own experience working "in the child protection space." He had confided to close friends that he was onto something big, "earth shattering" he claimed. The deeper he dug into the underbelly of the child abuse world more and more did not make sense. There was a sense that it was well coordinated and that there was a concerted effort at cover up.

Chester Bennington, co-frontman of rock/metal band Linkin Park, committed suicide mere weeks after the death of his dear friend Chris Cornell. An ex-junkie himself it was easy to cover the story that he took his life, even though he too had so much to live for, even a new album that he was "so proud of" about to drop within days. Fans were not buying the suicide and pointed to a conspiracy that involved John Podesta, former Bill Clinton chief of staff and Hillary Clinton campaign manager, who was in charge of protecting the identities of those in the "black book." Both rockers had hung themselves with exercise bands resulting in excessive amounts of blood at the scene. Both even had broken ribs.

In lieu of a personal suicide note, Bennington penned an endearing note to his friend Chris Cornell:

I dreamt about the Beatles last night. I woke up with Rocky Raccoon playing in my head and a concerned look on my wife's face. She told me my friend had just passed away. Thoughts of you flooded my mind and I wept. I'm still weeping, with sadness, as well as gratitude for having shared some very special moments with you and your beautiful family. You have inspired me in many ways you could never have known. Your talent was pure and unrivalled. Your voice was joy and pain, anger and forgiveness, love and heartache all wrapped up into one. I suppose that's what we all are. You helped me understand that. I just watched a video of you singing "A Day In The Life" by the Beatles and thought of my dream. I'd like to think you were saying goodbye in your own way. I can't imagine a world without you in it. I pray you find peace in the next life. I send my love to your wife and children, friends and family. Thank you for allowing me to be part of your life. With all my love. Your friend.

Bennington's final moments consisted of solitude in his sprawling Palos Verdes Estates home, a master planned community on the cliff line of the Pacific Ocean on the western edges of Los Angeles County. He had returned home alone from vacation with his family in Arizona. His wife and kids would stay on for several more days to allow the singer space to prepare for his band's planned summer tour departure. The day of his death he was to reunite with his bandmates for a promotional photo shoot, instead a housecleaner discovered his hanging body. Next to his body was a half empty bottle of alcohol. This was all the news needed in order to run their narrative.

I have been loathsome to the term "fake news" but that really is what the mainstream media is now producing, even events like tornadoes get a political spin. When stars commit suicide, like my own "suicide" in France, there is no questioning allowed. The propaganda machines are run by the globalists, with the media merely players for the puppet masters of the Illuminati. Nothing more than clickbait prostitutes. With that said, the powers that be take out anyone in their way. Cornell was cremated the next day even though his family had called for a second evaluation from a different medical examiner, and the nine rib fractures were deemed "normal" for anyone who undergoes CPR. Even though most medical examiners will say maximum is three, and typical is just one. The blood at the scene raised eyebrows. The story was that Cornell convulsed during the hanging and in that process banged his head. But this blood was all over the floor, instead of where it should have been, on the door.

Along with the Podesta connection there is Linda Ramone, widow of Johnny Ramone. She is a Satanist and close friend of Courtney Love, widow of Kurt Cobain of Nirvana fame, and performance artist Marina Abramovic, who is very publicly friends with Podesta. Abramovic is known for her use of large amounts of blood in her artwork. Any talk of the Illuminati is downplayed as a mythical story about freemasons who founded America and conduct satanic rituals among the elites of Hollywood, big business and politics. Their secret society conducts rituals in places like Bohemian Grove, north of San Francisco. Many ex-presidents are members. Their goal is to overtake the world. Some believe they are fallen angels tasked with bringing the

Luciferian agenda to the globe's New World Order. Talk of baby sacrifices are seeded to make the whole story seem less plausible. But they are why there are so many missing kids in America. They can be blamed for the harvesting of blood and parabiosis blood transfusions, which they bathe in and drink. Footage of these rituals are sprinkled throughout the dark web. Linda Ramone is rumored to be an original architect of the dark web, and much of the Ramones' royalties went to funding its creation.

Luciferianism is a belief system rather than a defined religion. Consisting of admiration and venerated characteristics of Lucifer himself, as described in the Hebrew Bible, it is not Satanism, as Satan was a fallen Lucifer. The original Lucifer is one of enlightenment progressiveness and independence. That is the ultimate goal of the followers, a pursuit of enlightenment, based on principles of truth and freedom of will. Worship of the inner self with a focus on potential. Traditional dogma is not encouraged, rather a belief that we do not need deities as a basis for our moralities. And, finally, the lack of fear from external punishment because we know right from wrong. Of course this level of understanding is fluid, and whether Lucifer is in fact a mere archetype he still represents ultimate knowledge as well as being humanity's savior. If you have ever seen The Wizard of Oz you may have noticed how Oz is controlled by The Wizard. That hidden hand is very much like how society operates. We may see the celebrities or the politicians but we never see the true rulers. And why I bring this whole thing up is because those people believe in this philosophy of crap. Or is it though? Have they sold their souls to the devil, that free will that God gave man, to now play by the devil's rules? It's twisted indeed, and to get behind any such movement, as secretive as it is, requires a silence campaign or better marketing treatment pitch.

There's a lot of talk about Chester being the biological son of Podesta, and if you were to look at side by side photos of the two men you would see a striking resemblance, actually a facsimile, as they could be twins, just at different ages. Podesta was at the heart of Pizzagate, when he would frequent Comet Ping Pong Pizza in Washington DC, and host "pizza parties" which in the pedophile community is code for having sex with kids. Podesta's emails were leaked to WikiLeaks by a Democratic National Committee staffer named Seth Rich and shortly thereafter he was found murdered, in a botched robbery.

Seth Rich was not randomly murdered. On a Sunday morning in July, 4:20am to be exact, in the Bloomingdale neighborhood of Washington DC, police were notified by an automatic gunfire locator to the conscious body of Rich who had been shot twice in the back. He died at the hospital shortly after arrival. Earlier that evening he had been at Lou's City Bar, a sports pub within walking distance of his apartment. His mother talked with the media the next day, sharing "There had been a struggle. His hands were bruised, his knees were bruised, his face was bruised, and yet he had two shots to his back, and they never took anything. They didn't finish robbing him, they just took his life." Police told the family they had surveillance footage with the glimpses of the legs of two individuals who were the killers but this footage was not shared with the family. The vagueness of it all was enough to set the conspiracies off, leading back to the Clinton Body Count.

As a cover story for the mainstream media, Russian foreign intelligence, known as the SVR, circulated a false bulletin, written up to appear as an authenticated intelligence report, about the murder of Rich. This was within three days of his death. His body was still warm as it was detailed that Rich, in his role as data director in the DNC, was in fact on his way to alert the FBI to Hillary Clinton's corrupt dealings while in her role as presidential candidate, and former position as Secretary of State. And foreign donations into her foundation. Her "hit squad" is who killed Rich. Doubters of this story were quick to label it as fake news. Perhaps it was the first real big fake political conspiracy story ever pushed so quickly on the internet, or was it indeed true? The smokescreen was so wide on the story that for any morsel of fact to somehow emerge was essentially impossible, and the story was to be forever treated as conspiracy.

Don't Worry About a Thing, 'Cause Every Little Thing Gonna Be Alright

Anonymous ID; TB+ANS Sat 2 Jan 11:35:42 <u>No. 148005</u> ViewReport
Razor's edge
"Poached eggs of Normandy"
Alsace Lorraine
Looming zombie apocalypse?
Local mall Santa
Colorado mansion
Thailand "vacations"
Beauty pageant queen
~~Patsy~~
sexual "assault"?

Diana found herself intrigued by what Bob Marley was doing with his life now. A soccer teacher in Ethiopia, or a busker in South Africa? Could he have stayed in touch with his children and grandchildren? After all, this was Diana's own hope, to one day reunite with Harry and William and hold her grandchildren. The mind can play magical tricks that involve riches and honor, the void of disaster and high level moves in unison. It could be as uplifting as a chemical stimulant or a downer that affects your outlook for the entire day.

Because of the irrevocable decision to fake one's death there is the ever-present incoming threat of being exposed, for an expediency of fraud to rain down onto thee, the most uncomfortable outing of you toward your loved ones and what you put them through, that Chirssakes aha moment of clarity when it was your selfish acts that put them through such anguish and pain. Only to then ask for their patience in explaining it was for their own good, and for their survival, that assassination was imminent and to cry about it now versus later was the razor's edge decision made with everyone's security in mind. Just like your adoring dining public they want their food hot and they want it quickly.

It was that kind of process I went through when I paid so generously for the Algerian man's soon-to-be deceased body. It was with that chef's urgency that I hastened my own escape plan, to safe haven in Alsace-Lorraine. To now say that Anna Nicole and I are dating would be a stretch. I mean this girl is all woman and is refreshing to say the least. Under the facade of trauma protection is that sweet Texas girl that we all felt we once knew. In the specter of a worst case scenario she would be your best choice as a ride-or-die into a south of the border sunset or some looming zombie apocalypse. And damn those tits. Billowy pillows of abandon likened to the perfected poached eggs of Normandy. But that is a description for another day and time.

For now I must explain the purpose of this impromptu meeting in an undisclosed location between myself, Anna, John John and Lady Di. Do you remember way back to Christmas day 1996 and the death of America's little beauty pageant queen and human doll JonBenet Ramsey? The story was hot and sold ads, it got eyeballs, it was the most important story on nightly television. It was fear porn on steroids. A little girl possibly abducted then murdered then placed back into her home? Or was she taken out by the local mall Santa who became fixated on her prepubescent charms and during Christmas eve killed her in the family basement? Was it her brother who snuffed her out to get the limelight back onto his back burner demoted life. Was it even more nefarious, with some sexual peccadillos between her and her father gone awry and covered up by her momager, Patsy Ramsey? Could it have been the contractor that was remodeling their Colorado mansion? Hushed rumors circulated that the contractor vacationed annually in Thailand, not for the food but for the kids.

Anna felt a kindred connection to this much-smaller version of herself. She saw in her eyes that gaze from the lights, from the downtime in the green rooms, in the makeup chairs with only your reflection as your friend, that impulse for your own reflected visage to somehow beckon or summon the necessary verve to escape from "the life." Anna wanted to save her, but on the surface of the story it seemed it was too late. But there was word, in certain intelligence circles, that JonBenet was still very much alive, and that it was her mother who staged the murder to frame the father. That narrative, as you know, never panned out. It did leave a cloud over John Ramsey's life and resulted in numerous slander and defamation lawsuits launched by the businessman in order to clear his name.

But what if it was more to protect JonBenet from the sexual assault that Patsey believed was going on between her two children? Yes, twisted and the most difficult predicament imaginable for a parent, the incestuous molestation between siblings. John John had it on good measure from Navy intel that JonBenet was living in the hornet's nest of Thailand. Why and specifically where were now up to our motley crew of middle-aged fame survivors, assembled for the mere purpose of delayed justice, and with a go-to spirit, paired with our array of connections, we would embark on a journey to Thailand and find her.

DJ Avicii Did Not Kill Himself

Anonymous ID; TB+ANS Sun 12 Apr 4:24:54 No. 148955 ViewReport
EDM?
VIP
Marbella

Naomi Campbell
"Fierce"
"Dead inside"
Moldovan
For A Better Day
~~Paul Walker~~
Oman
SOS

His real name was Tim Bergling. But the world knew Swedish EDM musician as DJ Avicii. What wasn't so well known was he was depressed and had a problem with the party lifestyle which meant for him going days without sleep doped up on stimulants. Yet this is how he became the richest electronic deejay in the history of the world so he was doing something right. His celebrity brought him into power circles of the elite with his private gigs for which he charged $1,000,000 USD. This included a 3-hour set and time with the VIP crowd for pictures and autographs. He traveled to the most jet set of global locales, places like Marbella, Spain, or St Barts, even mansions in Aspen. And in these circles his charming boy next door disarming air had everyone wanting to be his friend. This is how he met Naomi Campbell, which led to his demise.

Naomi Campbell was the biggest black supermodel of all time. Her look and attitude defined the term "fierce" and she was sexual kryptonite to the men she dated. Once you went Naomi black you never went back. She tried to get Avicii to bed her but he wasn't interested. Deep down he felt she was out of his league, and he was intimidated by her height, and known propensity for wanting big cock. It was one night in the Las Ventanas Al Paraiso resort in Los Cabos that Naomi tried to arrange for him a threesome with two young girls. She quietly sent the girls to his room and he politely answered thinking they were fans, but when he saw they were doped up and "dead inside" he knew something was up. Both girls were Moldovan and had never heard of his music. This was a red flag so he sent them on their way but gave them his cell phone in case they ever needed anything. He saw them the next day at the resort's pool, topless and in thong bikinis, inside one of three cabanas of a New York billionaire named Jeffrey Epstein.

He knew deep down these were trafficked girls and that Naomi Campbell was playing, to a certain degree, the role of pimp. His gut left him feeling there was blackmail involved. When Avicii returned to his studio in Los Angeles he put together a music video for his song "For a Better Day" that highlighted human trafficking, with footage of hooded traffickers going on a shooting spree, killing the adults in the way. When the video was released it was mocked as a fake story, with many detractors saying that in order to eradicate child trafficking it wouldn't be through a music video. And it certainly wouldn't be a video made in Hollywood. With the amount of push back he was getting, Avicii knew he was onto something much bigger. The week the video was released actor Paul Walker was killed in a violent car crash. Paul Walker was about to release to the public the corruption and child trafficking he documented while volunteering in Haiti, specifically the Clintons' No Ceilings Initiative. Avicii released this quote on his press release regarding the video: "The promise of a better life often traps families and children into being used as tools for some of the most despicable people on Earth."

This level of peak vibration led the spiritually grounded Avicii to spin out with his own abuse of drugs and alcohol. Known for bouts of depression it was easy to massage the message of his hotel room suicide in Oman. Nobody would believe his allegations after he was gone, another young star who flamed out before his time. Hotel staff were quick to have his body removed, and by the morning local authorities had cremated his remains. His family in Sweden were denied visas to enter the country and his ashes were flown home to Stockholm on the private jet that brought him to Oman. His family held a private funeral for him at the Hedvig Eleonora Church. The family was allowed a plaque in the garden of the famed church, on the plaque is his name, birth date, death date, and these three letters: SOS.

Human Evolution as a Theme

Anonymous ID; TB+ANS Mon 23 May 1:12:12 <u>No.</u>
<u>148965</u> ViewReport
Nature of Humanity
"big brains"
biodiversity
~~screen time~~
pre-deluvian
13,000 BC
Colonize earth?
seed farm?
Jeffrey Epstein
Galaxy of DNA
"as many women as possible"

I would be remiss if I did not touch upon the story
of the last 8,000,000 years and within that time frame the
possible tampering of our reproductive systems to alter
even slightly our evolution. Who would do such a thing
you may ask? Well, aliens. Stay with me here. It's
important and makes more sense than alternative
narratives.

We began to walk on two legs before we got big
brains. Like for 4,000,000 years. What took so long?
Maybe we were busy evolving in such vastly different
environments like savannahs and jungles, beaches and
forests, or could it have been the result of some foreign
experiment? Simultaneously our stomachs got smaller as
our nervous systems grew bigger, bringing about a
heightened awareness of our surroundings and the
dangers in our midst.

When we ask what is human we must differentiate between biological anthropology and the nature of humanity. Are we more than DNA? What cultural mutations have penetrated into our breeding patterns resulting in the diversity to this point? Is this biodiversity the cause for the sooner-than-later extinction of our days? Or our ancient cells coping with modern aspects, like microwaves and other transmissions? It becomes esoteric and I hate to even go there, but to get the gist of who we are and how we came to be, and most importantly the reptilian brain's responses to the evil, as well as the driving force behind that evil (sex drive), we must explore the complexities and channels not necessarily to other dimensions, but with an openness to what may have made us.

In our modern days there are more energies at play, and information being ingested, sometimes overly processed like our food, and this numbing or coma effect results in our sense for safety being withdrawn, so instead of preventing certain catastrophe we succumb to our own prevention, resulting in personal destruction. The stronger the signals the quicker the surrender. What our brains once did our computers now do. What consisted of intimacy is now done in the virtual, screen time entertainment at your beck and call.

In ancient lore is a story of a great flood, something of a cataclysmic event consisting of a tidal wave. What resulted in its wake was a golden age, involving a human battle against extraterrestrial forces, and high tech wars and battles of gods that took place in the sky. Nutty storytelling, yes, but plausible as well. Global folklore recorded a period of endless colossal earth changes through volcanoes and earthquakes, then the upheaval of people, resulting in mass diasporas to shift populations to more habitable spaces This would be just after places like Atlantis and Alexandria were sunken forever. Pre-deluvian (before the flood), as the professionals would call it. This was around 13,000 BC. You can look into it further if it is news to you now.

But I digress. My own hypothesis is that a higher form of life engaged in the chess game of planet earth, even seeding the planet with some of their own, who look like us but have that extraterrestrial DNA. We don't know their motives but we do know we are part of an experiment. Could it be a long game plan to colonize earth? Could we be nothing more than a seed farm? My point to this fantastical yet likely truer than not sci-fi riff is that Jeffrey Epstein--yes I am bringing it home-- believed that he possessed this alien DNA, that his own sperm was the seed of the galaxy, and his later in life mission was to impregnate as many women as possible.

<u>Don't Gain the World & Lose Your Soul</u>

Anonymous ID; TB+ANS Fri 10 Feb 1:24:56 <u>No.</u>
<u>148926</u> ViewReport
Nesta
36 yo
Future resorts
Hope Road, JAMAICA
CIA = skin cancer?
Madison Square Garden
The Wailers
"an omnipresent cry in our electronic world"
"emancipate yourself"
Puppet masters
Race = narrative
Multiple Personality Disorder
Five sense ~~experience~~
Candle in the darkness
Liberate them from ~~slavery~~
Cry freedom, my brother

     There was a dark cloud that surrounded the death
of reggae superstar Bob Marley. Born Robert Nesta
Marley on February 6, 1945, in Kingston, Jamaica, he
came to be one of the most endearing, influential and
beloved humans ever born. His was an ability to tap into
your emotions through music and lyrics, and with his
platform an uncanny willingness to speak about social
injustice. The prophetic messages of his music and the
spirituality of his songs appealed to many, and gave birth
to one of the biggest genres in music. But his bright star
was dimmed too soon. During the height of his fame,

leading up to his untimely death of skin cancer, his fans could not appreciate what a legend they had in their midst. It was after his death that the bigger questions were asked, like how did he die and why so young? Was there nothing that doctors could have done? At the young age of 36 succumbing to disease in a Miami hospital was not how this was supposed to end. Detailed from his medical records was that what had started as melanoma had spread to the singer's brain, lungs and other vital organs. To save his life was impossible.

Conspiracy theorists pointed out that doctors had diagnosed his skin cancer as early as 1977. That year he had toured Europe and worked through the pain of an injured toe, reportedly from playing soccer. When his manager forced him to see a doctor while in London, it was then that a biopsy determined that the malignant tissue was indeed cancerous. With this diagnosis in mind it makes sense that doctors would enforce some oncological treatment plan and Marley could still be alive today. But the conspiracy theory is that Bob's manager was in cahoots with Bob's wife Rita to get rid of him, to take full control of his wealth and massive posthumous earning potential. His vast real estate portfolio and royalties were mind blowing. The Jamaican properties all had potential as future resorts, and his royalties were 100 percent his as he retained the copyrights on all of his music over the years. Even though it was still the 1970s, music industry insiders knew his songs were eternal classics and would be played on for generations to

come. This equation made sense, math wise Bob was
worth more dead than alive.

An alternative theory is that he was assassinated by
the CIA because of his influence among black people,
something that made the agency uncomfortable. This
theory is strengthened with the failed attempt on his life
in 1976 at his home on Hope Road in Jamaica, when
armed assailants took over his compound with Bob
eventually escaping along with his injured wife. As the
CIA wasn't able to finish the job then, they took to
inducing the cancer. This theory was supported by a
former CIA operative who on his deathbed confessed to
sending to Bob, while on tour in Europe, specifically
Paris at the time, a gift of a pair of shoes, but one with
an embedded copper wire which had been contaminated
with carcinogens. When Bob tried on the shoes his big
toe on his right foot was pricked and the cancerous cells
were introduced to his body. This theory was even
supported by Bob's personal doctor, a well-known
Bahamian, who suggested that Bob had indeed been
murdered.

What fact we do know is that the cancer was
discovered in the summer of 1977, and when he was
ultimately admitted to the Miami hospital in 1981 he was
in the final stages of skin and brain cancer. Very reliable
records back this up. It was suggested that amputating
his toe would stop the spread of cancer, but his
Rastafarian beliefs did not allow for the cutting of flesh.
However, he finally did relent and parts of his big toe

were removed and replaced with grafted flesh from his thigh. He wanted to finish the final leg of his North American tour and flew to NYC for his sold-out show at Madison Square Garden. While there he fell ill on stage and cut the show short. His band The Wailers, his closest group of friends, knew this might be it for him. The next morning he went for a jog in Central Park where he suffered a stroke that caused him to faint. His bodyguards rushed him to Sloan-Kettering Cancer Center in Manhattan. Doctors discovered how badly the cancer had spread, to all parts of his body. After some abbreviated sessions of radiation therapy it was revealed to the media that "Mr. Marley wants to thank his fans, friends and family at this difficult time. He would also continue to accept your prayers while he must suspend the remainder of his tour while he recuperates at home in Jamaica. One love."

This was the cover story. Reality was a NYC vagrant with small dreads who weighed a mere 82 pounds was sent in his stead to be treated in a German hospital in Bavaria. On the flight his dreads were completely shaved off and he was somewhat recognizable as Bob. Ten days of aggressive treatments, mostly experimental bone marrow work, were not working so it was decided by Rita that Bob be flown home to Jamaica. But en route, over the Atlantic, his condition deteriorated and the flight was diverted to Miami, to the Cedars of Lebanon Hospital. He was dead on arrival and cremated the next day. His ashes were flown home to Jamaica two days after his official death date of May 11, 1981.

Jamaican Prime Minister Edward Seaga eulogized at Bob's funeral:

"His voice was an omnipresent cry in our electronic world. His sharp features, majestic looks, and prancing style a vivid etching on the landscape of our minds. Bob Marley was never seen. He was an experience which left an indelible imprint with each encounter. Such a man cannot be erased from the mind. He is part of the collective consciousness of the nation."

Posthumous talk about Marley included mind control, that he was under a CIA spell of sorts, and through his lyrics he was crying out to his fans for help. *Emancipate yourself from mental slavery. None but ourselves can free our minds.* The mind control was subtle, nothing more than a series of repeating opinions that had been implanted subconsciously. It only became important when, and if, the programmers wanted to carry out a deed, like assassination. For Marley the puppet masters wanted the ability, if the time came, to dictate to his fans a prescribed behavior.

You may be familiar with Multiple Personality Disorder, a common mental ailment of modern times, quickly dismissed as schizophrenia or the affliction of much of the homeless population. Well, it's made up.

Nothing more than a re-framing and tagging of terms to another ailment called Dissociative Identity Disorder which results from trauma, and is formed as a coping mechanism to handle the onslaught of emotional carnage. It is part of the reptilian brain that can sort out traumatic events and compartmentalize them so as not to go insane. This way you can put up an amnesiac barrier around the memory. They did this to Bob Marley, a series of unfortunate events to try and honeycomb his mind into submission, with the end goal that he could be a messenger to his masses. But it didn't work on him. He was able to defy the binds.

My last call with Bob was by satellite phone from an undisclosed location. Bob considered himself a high level target all of these years on and was still adamant about concealing his identity and whereabouts. I must add that a conversation with him elevates the consciousness level to something planetary, those refined vibrations lend to more new energy and he leaves you better off. Isn't that what we want from all of our interactions?

"I want the five senses experience, Tony. Not to get detached but plugged in, while my human feet may be grounded I am floating into the blue sky. And when I decry what can little me do with all of this, I tell myself everything or nothing. Like the glass exploding from too high of frequencies we need to be careful when achieving that desire for universal freedom. And as a candle in the darkness for these children, the onus is on us to liberate them from the slavery. We must go to the source, the indoctrination, and away from the herd mentality. Live life under infinite awareness. Cry freedom, my brother."

Again, Anthony Bourdain Did Not Kill Himself

Anonymous ID; TB+ANS Tue 3 Jun 12:22:54 <u>No. 149005</u> ViewReport
"Media-debunked"
Kayserberg, FRANCE
#metoo hypocrite ☐ CALIF?
Hollywood "players"
91 names
Cannes Film Festival = CFF
Future lost wages = $3.5 mil USD
"Vagina-like," "barely there"
intersex?
Fournier's gangrene
~~bon vivant~~
"rebirth & revival"

Celebrity chef and bestselling writer Anthony Bourdain had no narcotics in his system at the time of his death, per the official French toxicology report. Found dead by suicide in his hotel room in Kaysersberg,

France, on a summer night while on location to film his show "Parts Unknown." He was 61. His girlfriend, Italian actress Asia Argento, had recently become a leading figure of the #MeToo movement as a result of her accusing movie producer Harvey Weinstein of raping her a decade earlier at the Cannes Film Festival. Prior to Bourdain's untimely death he had spent the better part of a year speaking out against predatory men in both the restaurant and entertainment industries. As his voice became louder and his accusations bolder, Bourdain was shunned by the media and other celebrities. He publicly called out people like Hillary and Bill Clinton, as the godparents of #MeToo as well as their involvement in Pizzagate, the "media-debunked" human trafficking and child sex ring run out of Comet Ping Pong pizzeria in suburban Washington DC.

Meanwhile, Asia Argento harbored her own secret of a 2013 "alleged" sexual assault, when she, at the age of 37, statutorily raped a 17 year-old boy on the set of a movie she was filming in California, where age of consent is 18. She quietly paid her accuser several hundred thousand dollars before he went public. Did Bourdain know about this, and if so did it lead to his suicide out of some hypocritical guilt? Word of the cash payment was eventually leaked and Ms Argento was widely discredited as a #MeToo hypocrite. Was it possible that Weinstein was behind the leak, with his retired Mossad agents working behind the scenes to ruin the names of anyone else to come forward with accusations against the shamed Hollywood producer?

It would come out a few years after the fact but Weinstein also offered up a personal hit list of Hollywood players, mostly actors, 91 names to be exact, of people he wanted killed by his team of ex-Mossad agents. The problem was with such a list how frequently the hits could be pulled off without someone putting two and two together and adding up that Weinstein was behind the plot. In addition to actors there were publicists and producers, and 43 of them were men. He figured that if all on the list were incapacitated there would be nobody left to take him down. The plan was that the former Mossad agents would pose as journalists or women's rights activists in order to get close to the women, and their deaths would be reported as accidents. None of this ever played out as the handwritten list was obtained by a prominent magazine and Weinstein was then reverse blackmailed.

There was an unforeseen boomerang effect in the woke culture of victimhood, asking how could one blame Ms Argento when she was once a victim of sexual assault herself, perhaps all she was doing was acting out as a perpetrator because of her own trauma experiences? After all, it was in 1997, in a hotel room at the Cannes Film Festival, when Weinstein forced Argento to perform oral sex on him. She admitted that consensual sexual relations went on between them for another five years. In courtroom testimony, at a much later date, many of his accusers would describe his penis as "deformed," "burned," "vagina-like," and "barely there." It was difficult to grasp a visual of him receiving oral or performing sex on a woman. One accuser believed he was "intersex" when she saw his "lack of male parts when opening his hotel robe." Attorneys for the accusers filed requests with the courts for photographs of his penis to be shown to the jurors to ensure the continuity and validity of what was being described by his accusers. In a play for sympathy, Weinstein's attorneys fessed up to Weinstein being a victim of Fournier's gangrene, a bacterial infection that enters through a cut in the genitals and mainlines the bloodstream, and in his case requiring the removal of his testicles.

Argento's own alleged statutory rape allegations detailed that she plied the teen with alcohol and cigarettes, forcing him to perform oral sex on her. She put him up in expensive hotels like the Ritz, and posted on social media pictures of them laughing together in bed. It was what professionals call "predatory and conqueror" behavior. The kid eventually sued her for $3,500,000 USD in damages, specifically for intentional infliction of emotional distress, assault and battery and future lost wages.

Shortly after Bourdain's "suicide" she shared to social media: "I am proud and honored to know you. You just did the hardest thing in the world." Many felt this was coded language, that there was a more ominous message within. Because of the side narrative of Argento's own misdeeds, it allowed for a smokescreen to cover the suicide of Bourdain, and not allow for any questioning of this most selfish act. After all, why would such a global bon vivant want to kill himself? In an interview shortly before his demise, Bourdain said "I've been seeing up close the kind of vilification and humiliation and risk and pain and terror that come with speaking out about this kind of thing." He even confessed to re-examining his own macho and bad boy persona. It surprised him that it took so long but he was now staring down a new battle with his own toxic maleness, having to adhere to new rules in the game while re-examining the carnage he had left in his wake for much of his adult life. But could this masculinity also be what got him to where he was now, and wasn't it what built the great cities, wrote the best music, designed the best buildings?

Was this a man so depressed with his life that he would end it all, or was this a man who was in a later-life stage of rebirth and revival? The answers may never be known, but I will be the first to tell you.

<u>Never Tear Us Apart</u>

Anonymous ID; TB+ANS Thu 12 May 20:13:14 <u>No. 149009</u> ViewReport
Microphone
Sydney concerts

Hong Kong
"unrecognizable"
"it tasted so divine"
~~Room 524~~
Tiger Lily
Bankstown Airport
"Underworld of the Asia he loved"
Flight 370
~~Indian Ocean~~
Najib Razak
Hard drive
decoy?
Jungle Girl
~~Steve Fossett~~
Satellite imagery
"twenty years in the making"
"prominent role in 9/11"
ALIENS
"mid-air" explosions
Bermuda Triangle
MC thriller
Kinesis KL-02
"shaman high on peyote"
David Carradine = Steven Seagal?
American cinema

     Australian rock band INXS reached its heyday in
the mid to late 1980s filling the world's arenas and
stadiums. Their frontman Michael Hutchence was the
quintessential rock star who, without an amazing voice,
was able to overcome any vocal deficiencies with an

incredible and deft ability to whisper into a microphone whilst whipping his gloriously curly hair back and forth, a mane that played its own iconic role in the band. His part was so integral to the band that after his untimely death at the age of 37 in 1997 the band could not go on. They tried, through a reality TV competition show to find a replacement singer, as well as recruiting 80s solo artist Terrence Trent D'arby for a string of high profile Sydney concerts in 1999. Without Hutch there was no band. And without the band there was no Hutch.

He was now living a relatively relaxed life as a busker on the streets of his hometown, Hong Kong. Gone were the epic outfits and wavy hair, while a receding hairline and 30-pound weight gain had set in. He looked just like his father, the one that abandoned him and his mother, and while this pissed him off it made him unrecognizable as the star he once was.

The apparent suicide by auto erotic asphyxia, or what many in his inner circles claimed to be an accident, did not go down as reported. Just hours before the biggest show of their careers, a homecoming of their 20th anniversary tour's final show, Hutch took his life in room 524 of the Sydney Ritz-Carlton. All merely a ruse to stop the skid of his out of control life, if not now then never as there would surely be an eventual accident of some sorts. There was the event in Amsterdam with his girlfriend, supermodel Helene Christiensen, when he crashed his bicycle into a passing taxi and as a result permanently lost his ability to smell and taste. He confided to his close friend, rock star Bono of U2 fame, that what he was going to miss the most was the "scent of pussy and how it tasted so divine." He never was the same jovial cat after the head injury that night. Often angry and aloof, he wanted to pull his bandmates away from their global pop sound, those formulaic beats, piano, saxophone and harmonica sounds and become more aligned with the hot grunge sound coming out of Seattle. An off and on relationship with heroin was another factor into his exiled faked death post-fame life. If he didn't do something now he would never be able to see his young daughter, Tiger Lily, grow up.

So with his remaining juju he summoned his younger brother to find a look alike street junkie to be placed in his hotel room. When the switch went down, hours before the discovery of the choked-out remains, Hutch left the hotel by Vespa to the Bankstown Airport to board a private jet to Hong Kong. Years of lost time on the streets busking, gaining weight, dabbling in drugs and drinking heavily segued into a desire to flush out the pedophile underworld of the Asia he loved. His daughter was only two when he killed himself and with time he tracked his own progress, calendars, and linear thoughts with the stamp of his daughter's age at that moment in time. When she turned ten he tried to imagine the unfathomable despair that sets into the mind of a trafficked young girl. And here he was with that immoral depravity everywhere he turned.

His response to most was a low-grade vigilantism, taking johns out back and beating them silly, or robbing them of their wallets, passports, cash and jewelry to ensure they would be in heaps of trouble back home. There were instances of blackmail, when he himself needed the money, a quick pic of some overweight middle-aged British tourist getting head from a young girl. Transfers of money in $10,000 USD increments into a Bank of Hong Kong account in exchange for the flash drive. Hutch still made a point to alert the authorities after the payment.

It had been nearly two decades on when Anthony Bourdain made contact. Bourdain was nobody he had heard of, as the famed journalist chef was a later-in-life celebrity. Bourdain had never been a fan of INXS, he considered their music shit and an abomination that something so poppy could emerge into the world at the same time that garage rock was invented in NYC. But any two former junkies will always get along with their shared stories of chasing the dragon, and desire for the edgier runs at life. They were both wordsmiths and in this was a brotherhood. They both had a single daughter, Bourdain's was a teen while Hutch's was in her 20s. It was a kindred connection.

And as I switch back into the first person--Tony here--let it be known that I was more the alpha male while Michael was the gamma male. He had a charming and disarming disposition, a wicked smile and penchant for winking at all the right moments. We met at the Park

Hotel Hong Kong, in my suite, comped by a secret admirer, to discuss the mystery of missing Malaysia Airlines Flight 370, that most intriguing Boeing 777 with 239 souls aboard when it went incognito between Kuala Lumpur and Beijing. The most settled upon official word was that the plane crashed somewhere in the Indian Ocean, at least this was the narrative from Malaysia's Prime Minister Najib Razak. After months of multiple vast searches for debris of the plane nothing ever was found. Years on, one would think there would be something to wash ashore but alas zilch.

It would never be officially reported, documented, archived, registered or manifested but in all likelihood, through a series of clues, cover ups and slights of hand, the Anthony Weiner hard drive was on that plane. How do I know this for certain? I do not, but I also do not claim to know anything is for certain but if I had to guess, with what I do know, the likelihood is stronger than the alternative. And this hard drive's location may be the hottest question in certain circles of law enforcement and the powerful elite. Its acquisition will be for the betterment of society and result in demise for those involved. The laptop that sits in a police department evidence room in New York City in all likelihood is a decoy, much like the major pieces of art in the world's museums. Something we go along with knowing that for their safety we don't really need to know where the real Mona Lisa resides, but that her facsimile will do, because, like a Hallmark greeting card, it's the thought that counts.

This is all for the better as we plan our journey into the Cambodian jungle where in some likelihood the very much intact plane is parked. Rumored for years to have landed at an abandoned airstrip deep in the heart of the Ratanakiri province, where so-called Cambodian Jungle Girl emerged in 2007 (more on her later), amateur google map topologists had made rumblings about something abnormally shiny, the size of a football field, located at an abandoned airstrip last used during the Vietnam war. These were the same nerds that found the remains of American adventurer Steve Fosset in the high deserts of Nevada when a morning solo flight ended into a snowy hillside. That online search was offered up to the public via a google project assigning quadrants of satellite imagery to then be closely scanned by human eye. That search took months and in the lead up seemed like a fruitless endeavor. Until some kid found something shiny in the rocks, the debris of the Super Decathlon plane Fosset had flown out of Reno's Flying-M Ranch. It would be five more days until the Air National Guard were able to hike into the site twenty miles south of Yosemite. In the entire search process that encompassed nine days there were eight other crash sites identified, one going way back to WWII.

Back to Cambodia, there are no jungles on the planet as nasty as hers. Waterfalls, rivers, quicksand banks, thick brush, falling rocks, it was why the story of the Cambodian Jungle Girl was so alluring. The fact that a feral twenty-something woman raised alone in the jungle, or possibly abducted and held in captivity, nobody really could know as DNA tests were out of the question and there were several families claiming her as their disappeared child from two decades earlier. She didn't speak, and it wasn't just mutism, she was in fact void of language. She emerged naked, scarred and filthy from the jungle, first stealing a villager's lunch. Many of those who made first contact with her believed she was a jungle spirit. Cambodian human rights NGOs were concerned she was the victim of sexual abuse and the scarring, mostly cuts along her arms and legs, were proof of her forced imprisonment. She was able to use a spoon. Beyond that she was hopeless. Jittery with a fixed gaze stare, her best hope would be to return to the jungle, as the modern world which she could not understand was too cruel for her.

In my own selfishness I knew she would make the best guide, and I knew guides. Any city or locale I ever visited the key element was to find someone with local knowledge, that insider insight that cuts through the typical bullshit of travel. She likely could be the one for the task. In fact twenty years in the making.

The consensus among experts was that flight MH370 ran out of fuel and plunged into the sea. Either deliberately or by accident. Any contrary narrative, something more along the conspiratorial lines, was met with your typical tin foil hat debunking and discrediting campaign, that the public who buys into conspiracy theories are nutty, and in their own little minds simply trying to make sense of the world. While the rational minds among us are those who think pragmatically, with facts and science behind their theories and findings. The conspiracy set are those who are much too curious of the unknown and cannot leave anything unanswered even in the face of scarce information. The most popular theories to the fate of flight MH370 are correlated to one's belief systems and personality factors. There is the power of suggestion, this played a prominent role in 9/11 conspiracies. And just like the ease of falling for a certain unexplained, or even far-reaching theory, there is the opposite, that strong ability to believe anything and everything the media spoon feeds the public. How external sources present the narrative which is then compounded with one's ethnicity, age, religion, and, most importantly, personality.

Personality plays big in which conspiracies are believed. First off there is the notion that flight MH370 was abducted by aliens. The fact that cell phones rang long after the supposed end of the flight would prove that there was no midair explosion. The Asian Bermuda Triangle, the global opposite to the Bermuda Triangle, would explain the plane somehow vanishing then reappearing in the Atlantic where it may have crashed undetected as there were no witnesses or reasons to search there. It could have been a 9/11-style hijacking that the CIA or Interpol do not want the public to know about, as Israeli Mossad agents planned to crash the plane into a tower in Kuala Lumpur and blame it on Iran. Maybe it was a cyber hijacking, where hackers were able to reprogram the flight's computers and control its speed and direction. A less nefarious theory that the plane had cracked, and with a slow decompression in the cabin everyone eventually went unconscious. Pilot suicide has been floated, as the plane's captain had recently had his wife leave him for a younger man. But, alas, the working theory for me, the one that makes the most sense, something from the pages of a Michael Chrichton thriller, is that a team of scientists, twenty of them in fact, from the firm behind the world's smallest microcontroller, the Kinesis KL-02, with the help of drone technology, something too futuristic for here and now, took control of the plane and landed it on a remote jungle airstrip, somewhere in Cambodia.

Extraversion is the trait that brings about emotional expressiveness, like being overly talkative or a high level of sociability. Easily excitable some might say. A certain manic magic to one's heightened inclination to believe theories that are off from the mainstream narrative. Other pro social behaviors like kindness and altruism add a dimension to the required agreeableness necessary in the belief of conspiracies. High levels of thoughtfulness, commonly known as conscientiousness, align with other behaviors like being goal-directed and impulse control. Having a general sense of openness is a trait of insight and imagination that allows for the conspiratorial mind frame. And, finally, a sense of neuroticism brings about the anxiety, instability and general sadness required to suspend belief in the tangible for something more ethereal.

Not to get too deep in the weeds on time travel, but there seems to be proof around the globe of artifacts left behind by visitors from other time dimensions. Crazy, I know, but stick with me. If you really dig down into it the only real puzzle involved is the concept of time. Take that out of the equation and sequence of events becomes a garbled mess. Think about archeologists, would it not jeopardize their careers if they were to find something from the future instead of the past? Again, not to go off on a tangent here, but we do know that a certain people called the Mullions existed alone and untouched by other people 10,000 years ago along the coast of Algeria. It was an advanced culture that involved women and children utilizing tools that were otherworldly, even what seems to be prototypes of desktop computers. Many relics of this are submerged in the mud beds of the Mediterranean, likely to never be pursued. But the thing about the Mullions is that they vanished overnight. Their lingering traces were not those of bloodshed and skeletal remains, as the only things that remained were their elaborate small cities of sewer lines and fresh water delivery, and their tools. The massive earthquake in the late 800s AD, the same one that sank Alexandria, Egypt, buried all final traces of the Mullions.

Along this train of thought is the absence of proof of macroevolution in the fossil record. No evidence exists that sea worms became bigger fish then amphibians on a shoreline, to then become mammals that morphed onto two legs. Scientists admit there is too vast a difference between critical functions and body parts to transition from one environment to the other. If there was proof we would easily be able to trace it. And this beckons the question, if we came from sea worms why are there still sea worms? I know this question triggers evolutionary scientists and the anti-religion crowd, so that's why I ask it.

Before I move along back to the adventure, I must lay out the hypothetical concept that perhaps humans arrived on earth as part of a migration project from another world. Sort of colonizers who were ditched without cooperation, and these aliens were responsible for making the genetic jump, although untraceable, from sub-species to the humans we are today. The void of evidence is proof in itself, that we have been genetically altered somewhere in prehistory. Or the space dust theory, that seeding of earth with life that formed the building blocks of existence, lit up into flourishment with a subsequent reign of large-scale volcanic eruptions. This theory solves the riddle for evolutionary scientists when they ask how activation occurred for primordial conditions of first life. Regardless where you fall in regard to the argument of the beginning it is undeniable that we are made of star matter--the result of explosive transactions between energies--and the fallout of nitrogen, carbon, oxygen, only to be formed into new shapes with an undetermined destiny. But I digress.

We could take a prop plane to the site, at least in the general direction, but alas we do not accurately know where "where" is yet, and my prophetic visions, which I tend to follow like a shaman high on peyote, include the barrel role of our small plane, wings clipping the tops of the jungle trees before smoke fills the cabin and the pilot is forced to land but--like how I like my female pubic hair--there are no landing strips. Before we can arrange for travel north, we must complete the team, which would include John John and Di, myself, Hutch, Anna Nicole and Cambodian Jungle Girl. Along the way there may be a surprise appearance by David Carradine. That 1960s actor of exquisite caliber, half man half weapon, white Asian, gangster with that constipation stare. The godfather to the likes of Steven Segal, and well Steven Segal. If there was ever a more endearing contribution to the canon of American cinema I don't know what there could be.

The planning that goes into such an unknown journey, deep into the heart of darkness, is the poised vision of how it can perfectly be played out, that divine ending, in our case the capture of the killer of JonBenet or possibly the Weiner hard drive, but like the silhouetted figure of the aged-out prostitute, from a distance everything looks fine, even enticing, but as you near there is an unsettling reality that what you are confronting is not what it seemed when now in focus. It may even be worse than ever imagined, and your approach now requires a Zen-like calmness. This is the locale where I go, digging deep into my years as a chef, with a kitchen on fire and a crew filled with nothing more than cocaine and backed up tears.

Texts Radio

Anonymous ID; TB+ANS Sun 4 Jul 4:13:54 <u>No. 149010</u> ViewReport
New Age
Wolf [Matthew McConaughey]
Son's death
~~Playboy Mansion~~
vaccine
"It became a blur"
"Mind blowing in its authenticity"
sequential moment
Faked death?
"Vibrational prison cell"

"I know you are a smart man Tony, but I want to be clear, the power of attention is vital to regaining control of your experiences," said Anna Nicole Smith to me, Anthony Bourdain.

I love it when she talks to me with that New Age vibe, crystal poppin' mama, down home girly girl voice.

"If we focus on what frightens us we will connect with that energy and start fearing everything we see. It's like with what's going on with Epstein and all those girls. We must gravitate toward it but we cannot become it, we can't feed that wolf."

I love it when this attractive specimen of divine woman starts mentioning wolves and talking like Matthew McConaughey.

"You know that Cherokee Indian story, the one where the village chief tells the children that there is a terrible ongoing fight inside us all, and that it's between two wolves. One of them represents fear, inferiority, guilt, pity, regret and sorrow. While the other represents humility and love, faith and compassion. That fight is within us all. And when the children ask the chief who wins the battle, he replies the winner is the one you feed."

My boner for this woman is ridiculous and embarrassing.

"When I took it upon myself to make my life's mission to find out who killed JonBenet I knew I had to fight the programming, my conscious recognition was fully engaged to rewrite the program and to press the delete button every chance I got."

The public never gave this iconoclast of a woman a chance at brains, it was all about the overflowing brassiere and pearly white smile. Ditzy as a persona goes further in Hollywood than intellect, and this is why Anna is where she is at now. It just wasn't for her. It was making her insane. It caused her to do drugs. It led to her son's death.

"I came out of the fog into an infinite awareness. It was like I was under some spell. It got worse the longer I was in Los Angeles. My initial visits to the Playboy Mansion is what started it all. I swear I was put under a mental spell, maybe even injected with some vaccine that kept me from overthinking, forcing me to make bad decision after bad. The last authentic experience before all of that was when I had Daniel, then it became a blur."

Another boner inducing element with women like this is her clarity and the peace that comes with their oneness with the universe, something that you know if you were let into would be mind-blowing in its authenticity.

"The most basic rule for life is to always do what you think is right, but this isn't possible when you are under the spell. The legions and legions of people working against you, for the insiders who want to abuse you and use you, this is why when a tiny particle of clarity set in for me I began the process of withdrawing from the illusory reality of each sequential moment, away from the false light and toward my faked death."

Simple truths can be so devastating.

"And when I was fully unplugged I took that ache and pain to a new battlefield, one for good, the one that led me to you. Outer peace can only come from inner peace, the first peace, that oneness with others, like what you and I have going on right now between us."

I think I just came in my pants.

"If you can help me I am all yours, I know many of the secrets and players of the Hollywood underground. We need a shift in consciousness or nothing is going to change. Otherwise the vibrational prison cell will keep adding on bars."

The Hollywood Madam & the New York Politician

Anonymous ID; TB+ANS Thu 3 Jul 4:09:43 No. 149010 ViewReport
Heidi Fleiss
Black Book, Gucci [day planner]
"treasure trove"
Eliot Spitzer
Adam Schiff
Chateau Marmont
Black girl
7.0 magnitude [earthquake]

James Biden
Water Island
~~cheerleader~~
Suicide
"iceberg of pervs"
NOW ☐ #metoo

Before there was the Anthony Weiner laptop there was the Black Book of Hollywood Madam Heidi Fleiss. In actuality the black book was a Gucci day planner with red bindings and its contents were the most coveted nineties treasure trove of who is who in the Los Angeles prostitution game. And before there was an open deep state covering up sex crimes there was the LA district attorney allowing for the rich and famous to go unprosecuted. In retrospect much of it seems to have been a trial run for what was to come with Epstein and those within his reach. Many of Epstein's victims even referred to Ghislaine Maxwell as a "Heidi Fleiss" type, in that she knew how to properly groom the girls and effectively pitch them on whatever task was at hand.

New York politicians have historically been known for their sexual deviance, look no further than New York governor Eliot Spitzer and his fetish for sex with prostitutes while wearing socks. What US Senator Chuck Schumer brought to the table was his penchant for young black girls. Emphasis on young and emphasis on black. The younger and the blacker the better. And like any supply demand exchange where there was small demand there was small supply. Heidi Fleiss' specialty was procuring the most difficult of requests. If Charlie Sheen wanted five girls dressed up as cheerleaders to come over and cheer him through to orgasm, say no more. So when Chuck Schumer was visiting Los Angeles for a Beverly Hills fundraiser for local congressman Adam Schiff, and staying at the Chateau Marmont, Fleiss drove to South Central LA and "rented" an overweight twelve year old black girl. Schumer demanded discretion so Fleiss personally brought the girl to the room that had been reserved under an alias. What went on in the room is still not known to this day, but through Fleiss we know the girl survived, she would never allow murderous snuff to happen under her watch. Adam Schiff on the other hand is rumored to have covered up a murder scene in the Chateau Marmont, resulting from a gay sex hook-up turned male prostitute overdose, but I digress.

The next recorded event of Schumer's involvement with young black girls was his interest in the Haitian relief effort after a 7.0 magnitude earthquake devastated the island. Under the guise of caring New York politician, he went to Haiti to "represent the 150,000 Haitians living in New York." His visit was nothing more than an exploitive political photo op to cover for his more nefarious intention, that of sexual relations with young girls. His decades-long friendship with Bill Clinton allowed for access to the seedier parts of the slums, places where the relief workers didn't go, and in these ghetto slums were shanty whorehouses. What happened on that visit is unknown, but there is an email sent from Schumer's government email account to Hillary Clinton thanking her and Bill for "the hospitality extended to me, and that my trip was eye-opening to say the least."

The next recorded visit to the Caribbean was when Schumer traveled with his wife to Water Island, a Virgin Islands getaway a mere 8 miles from Jeffrey Epstein's famed pedo island. Water Island had been recently acquired by James Biden, brother of US politician Joe Biden, from a lobbyist who purchased the island from the Danish government then sold it to the younger Biden brother with a mortgage the lobbyist carried himself, to then casually forgive the note. (Note: years later James Biden sold the island for an estimated $10,000,000 USD.)

During this Caribbean stay, Schumer's wife stayed at Water Island while Chuck traveled to Epstein's island to visit with the New York "philanthropist," to procure more donations for his reelection. It was during the two-day stay that a photo was taken of Schumer french kissing a very young overweight black girl on the beach. When this photo circulated the internet a couple of years later the debunking sites went into hyperdrive to label the photo as a fake. Either they said it was photoshopped or that the man in the photo was not Schumer. Most everyone who has seen the photo will attest that their own gut instinct is that it is indeed him.

Murmurs of sexual indiscretion with underage girls continued for years. But the biggest and most credible was that of an affair between Schumer and a sixteen year old friend of his own daughter, Jessica. Chuck had abruptly ended the two yearlong affair with the cheerleader. But when Anthony Weiner, his protégé, had been exposed by New York tabloids as Carlos Danger, reports began to surface of this Schumer family friend committing suicide. Schumer's daughter was distraught and posted this to her social media:

"My dad is being a hypocrite and that's why I'm speaking out. When I was in high school he dated my best friend Rebecca and even got her pregnant twice. He paid for her abortions both times and spent a ton of money on her at Steak & Shake and Victoria's Secret. She fell in love with him and he broke her heart. My mom paid for her to be quiet and go away. Three years later she committed suicide."

The alleged affair had been confirmed by the girl's mother and through medical records obtained by subpoena from Planned Parenthood. She killed herself just days before her twentieth birthday. The story was properly vetted by reporters and it hit the news wires with the Associated Press first to run the story. But within a few hours the entire piece had been scrubbed from the ether, quick enough that none of the story made it into print.

When interviewed twenty years on, Fleiss said that one of the sickest clients she ever had was a New York politician. And that if there was any investigation the authorities would find "it was just the tip of a gigantic iceberg of pervs." In the highly publicized trial of Fleiss the prosecutor was selectively able to ensure that regardless of any outcome at trial that the names in the address book would not be made public and, most importantly, there would be no subsequent prosecutions of johns. After Fleiss was convicted of pandering there was outrage by the feminist group NOW who wanted the rich and powerful customers to pay for their crimes. In some ways it was an early incarnation of the #metoo movement, but as it was pre-social media there wasn't the digital grassroots traction necessary.

The Bromance of Andrew and Jeffrey

Anonymous ID; TB+ANS Sat 4 Aug 9:11:23 <u>No. 149011</u> ViewReport
"Spare to the heir"
Randy Andy
Sarah Ferguson a semi-unattractive ginger woman
"ghetto fabulous"
Access to the Prince = $750k USD
~~Qaddafi~~
Azerbaijan
Marbella SPAIN

Sharm-el-Sheik
"full-body" massages
Epstein
Debacle, embarrassment
"flame haired woman"
tragicomedy
"public's glare"
26 lovers
Jet set
Lady pimp = Ghislaine Maxwell AKA G-Max
"Myopic" view
exit switch
Mossad?

The British public did not necessarily have a soft spot for Prince Andrew but there was sympathy for what it must be like to be a royal younger sibling, knowing that your existence is merely ceremonial. Mocked by the press and jokingly referred to as the "spare to the heir," while at the same time you are free of power or clout, you remain left open to these attacks from the tabloids. Sometimes the best approach is to throw caution to the wind and embrace the black sheep concept, do your own thing and live your own way, run counter to the narrative, even try and grey rock method the press so they don't want to cover you. But this has never been Randy Andy's style. He always had a way of circling into the international spotlight every now and again, and this is something that not only drove his sister-in-law Diana bonkers but left her questioning Andrew's own sanity.

It was as if he couldn't avoid scandal or another embarrassing debacle. It was well known that he was easily wooed by women and wealth. There had been a decades-long focus on his love life. Perhaps it wasn't all his fault or making, rather a deep-running schadenfreude by the British public, a largely forlorn set of people. His own actions only fed the fire of the fodder, like when he married Sarah Ferguson in 1986 to then separate not long after. Then the spin off side dish tales of Fergie's own love life with other men. This semi-unattractive ginger woman with handsome Lotharios, of her photographed topless in the south of France, or leaked pictures of her toes being sucked by a wealthy American oil man. Andrew was framed by the tabloids as a playboy himself, but because of his homeliness, there was a suspension in belief required to make the jump to that particular narrative. So much of the intrigue was that here was a man who was on the "dating quotient" probably a 3, but as he was royal he became a 9. Andrew and Fergie remained friendly during their separation, as deep down, these were two people that, under any other commoner circumstance, would have been perfectly matched. Both unattractive, with penchants for kinky sex, and an alluring nod toward wealth. What many call ghetto fabulous would be their non-Royal label. A decade after their divorce there was fresh talk that they might remarry each other.

Then scandal struck. A tabloid reporter, undercover, filmed Fergie offering to sell access to the prince for $750,000 USD. When exposed she claimed that it was all simply because of her own dire financial needs. But this triggered further speculation that Andrew was in on the grift, because he needed money too. It was a well-known fact that Andrew served in an unpaid position as Britain's special representative for trade and investment, but his expenses were covered and his day-to-day life was funded by the British taxpayer. So why would he need any more money? He had an obsession with private jets, and flying to exotic locales to meet with any and all leaders who wanted, even briefly, direct contact with the British royal family. He liked to blend business with pleasure. He became friendly with Muhammar Qaddafi, and the president of Tunisia, even the leader of Azerbaijan. He sold an investment property he owned in Marbella, Spain, to the president of Kazakhstan for eight times the market value. Andrew was able to hide behind the front that he was brokering high level deals with these countries and the side investments were necessary to provide for his daughters.

Andrew first met Colonel Qaddafi at the Egyptian resort Sharm-el-Sheik during an official UK trade trip. Dining for hours they discussed the formation of a new bank in Luxembourg. It was implied by Qaddafi that if the Libyan government could park some of their oil wealth overseas that a small but significant broker fee could be paid to Andrew via the relief of over $1,000,000 USD in debts accrued by Fergie. There would be no paper trail. To entice the deal Qaddafi ordered his youngest Amazonian Guard--those exquisite all-female cadre of elite desert beauty bodyguards--to watch over him for the night. Protection included full body massages, but no sex, as anything involving penetration was reserved for the Colonel himself.

It was this type of hobnobbing that led to his friendship with Jeffrey Epstein. And it was around the time of their first meeting that Andrew stepped down from his official role as government liaison for trade. The Randy Andy playboy prince and his Army of Armcandy had finally met his perfect match in Epstein, an extremely wealthy, astonishingly connected pedophile. It was almost a mirror image of what Andrew had always aspired to become, and the tragicomedy of his life could now come full circle. Around this time is when he acquiesced out of the public eye. The public's love affair of William and Kate, as well the twisted obsession with Harry, had taken all eyeballs off of Andrew. The days of him bragging about his penchant for "flame-haired" women or that he might be into "the art of mistress-bedding" or that he isn't "opposed" to his romantic partner wearing a metal-spiked leather collar during intimate times, seemed to be over. As well these instances of moral indiscretion appeared to have been forgotten by the public and only regurgitated when needed. After all, this was mostly the Queen's problem, and #MeToo was becoming an ebbing and flowing feminist movement that tended to pick and choose their plights and targets with hit list narratives and politics in mind. Associates confided to me that Andrew felt he had finally, once and for all, stepped out of the "public's glare." But was he only moving into a new brighter spotlight?

As marginalized as Andrew was, there was the continued involvement of women who may have had less discretion than your typical lady, the gold digger types, or the occasional seeker of fame if even only on a B-level. His sole redeeming quality was his time spent as a helicopter pilot in the Falklands war. This is back before Fergie, in the early 1980s. And with nobody else in the Royal family pressing the hot talk meter, the tabloids labeled him as a "Warrior Prince" and his title of His Royal Highness was swapped with His Royal Heartthrob. It went to his head. He was not handsome, but compared to his older brother Charles he was indeed a looker. Years after their marriage, Fergie joked that Andrew had had 26 lovers during the time of their marriage. It was a big leap for the public to make. There was nothing sexually virulent about this man, and it seemed possible that these lurid infidelities were part of a bigger hype campaign, designed even to make Fergie herself appear more desirable, while simultaneously being casted as the sympathetic victim. Maybe it was best for his new global freedom that he was able to fly under the radar afforded by his homeliness, while attending sex parties, and Playboy-type pageants, traveling to places referred to as the "fast set," one notch above the boring "jet set."

When he met Epstein's lady pimp and playgirl girlfriend Ghislaine Maxwell, she was more than happy to groom him into an inner-circle confidant of Epstein, furthering the New Yorker's powerful network of titans of industry and wanna-bes. Andrew's own myopic view of the world, from his perch of privilege, allowed for a greater level of carelessness, something that began to wear on him, this life in the fast lane commingled with dustings of his own self-loathing. In his low-grade sociopathy there was always the quick out, that easy pre-established exit switch, because of the preloaded eye roll from the public should his own jolly recklessness come to light. It could be excused off because he really cannot be this dumb, now can he? Maybe it is a disability, like a secret diagnosis of Asperger's or Autism, something that if made public would only garner more sympathy from the commoners. And because of this, and everything else about the man, he was the perfect acquisition for Epstein and the Mossad.

Jeffrey Epstein Did Not Kill Himself

Anonymous ID; TB+ANS Sun 3 Sep 2:21:51 No. 141012 ViewReport
Super Bowl Trophy
Club of Rome
Prince Charles
Arab "child"

charm campaign
NYC Metro Correctional Center = MCC
6:29am
"cremated"
"Andrew drama" over?
Non-Disclosure Agreements (NDA)
Naomi Campbell
Victoria Secret stock value?
Ponzi scheme
~~Bernie Madoff~~
"underage sex scene"
Kryptonite?
Underwear = signal
Moldova or Colombia
Manhattan mansion
3 filmed rapes
Central Institute of Coordination TEL AVIV
Monica 2 Bill Clinton
Linda Tripp = trip wire?
"Generous pension" [handbag line]

Jeffrey Epstein did not kill himself. He is alive and well and, surprisingly, an advocate for kids, fighting human trafficking and those things that he was accused of while he was "alive." His best friend, Prince Andrew, in what the Mossad refer to as a "Super Bowl trophy" friendship, but what I call a dirty bromance, is very much a pedophile. Much of his geo-political moves that do not make sense, subtle chess moves, the stuff of the Rothschild conspiracies, or Club of Rome, even alluring mystical moments of magic, happen by the command of the Queen's hand. Andrew was always her special son, as Charles had his shit together and would be first in line for the throne. Andrew was always special in his needs, then the awful staged marriage with Fergie that nearly brought down the Monarchy. It was those years that Andrew really upped his pedo game, while raising two young daughters of his own. The British are known for their perversions but pedophilia is never acceptable. When British intel learned that Diana was pregnant with an Arab child it was then that Elizabeth made the difficult decision to have her taken out, killing the beloved mother of her two doting grandsons. So, years later, when the heat arrived on Jeffrey Epstein and the media wanted answers as to why he was not locked up they went directly to his bff and the attention, particularly from the FBI, zeroed in on Andrew. At first there was a media charm campaign, which played out awfully, resulting in his entire public relations firm being fired, and any subsequent interviews were canceled. Then when the FBI came knocking there was the air of cooperation, of course, anything for justice for these young women. Nothing to hide here.

Then before any trial could get underway, and before the release of Epstein's famed black book there would be Epstein's shocking early morning suicide in the NYC Metropolitan Correctional Center. What played out over roughly a thirty minute period was the discovery of Epstein's unresponsive body, wrapped in orange prison sheets, essentially thick grade paper, a severely deep cut along his neck, then the transport of his alive body by two paramedics to the New York Downtown Hospital, local time 6:29am. En route he suffered fatal cardiac arrest and was pronounced DOA. The alternative story is the alley transfer of him walking it off, and climbing into a black Range Rover, while the body of the recently deceased Tony Rodham, younger brother of Hillary Clinton, appeared on the jail gurney. Tony Rodham had died of natural causes weeks before and was "cremated." His funeral took place one week earlier. Planted paparazzi that were in fact Mossad agents were able to get several pics of Tony, playing the part of Jeffrey, being wheeled into the ER entrance. There was an uncanny resemblance between the two men. Designed as a message to Hillary to stop her own killing spree, and to Bill Clinton that Epstein is still alive somewhere, ready and willing to talk.

After the 45-minute drive to La Guardia Epstein was on a private jet to a safe haven in Africa. Believing the media reports that Epstein was dead, the Queen felt reassured that all the "Andrew drama" was surely over. But was it just beginning? Much was questioned and speculated but then downplayed and killed off by the media on how Epstein made his money, truly a vast and extravagant wealth that included mansions, compounds and private islands. Even two airplanes, both loosely referred to as Lolita Express. One that Bill had flown on 28 times, including a dozen flights without his Secret Service detail.

Epstein's safe haven in Namibia was not widely known, in fact its exact location still is unknown. Of course there have been many members of his staff, including young girls, that have travelled there but Non-Disclosure Agreements for the Epstein estate included a clause that nobody could speak for a minimum of thirty years after his death. To violate this would result in a judgement of $1,000,000 USD, ensuring even tabloid money couldn't surpass it. This Namibian oasis is said to have an exotic petting zoo, a resort-scale infinity pool overlooking a private jungle, and enough bedrooms to comfortably sleep over fifty guests. Word is that Naomi Campbell convalesced there after an emergency surgery in Switzerland to reconstruct her nose after years of cocaine abuse.

Back to Jeffrey's money. He was a master at numbers, in fact in his early adult life he was a Brooklyn math teacher that was tutoring a hedge fund manager's son who then recruited him to work some complex financial calculations. A friendship was born and stocks were gifted to him. Mostly Victoria Secret stock which would allow him at a later date more access to younger models. But like anything involving stocks and prestige in NYC there was an ominous grift, in his case large scale Ponzi schemes. Some so large they never were uncovered, even bigger than anything Bernie Madoff was able to consummate. One FBI agent has said, "There is about 75 percent about Epstein that we will never know." He did like to brag and boast. Much of this was lost on the American public as many have never actually heard him speak. He didn't get rolling with finance until his 30s, in the early 1990s, and this is when he met his long-term girlfriend Ghislaine Maxwell, a socialite that provided him access to the global elite, a link that ultimately led to Prince Andrew. They immediately got along great, maybe it was that deviant factor that only two pervs can connect, like some Bonnie and Clyde for the underage sex scene.

What Epstein learned from the beginning was that Andrew was weak and could be easily manipulated. He considered Andrew to be vulnerable. Underage girls were his kryptonite, while Epstein had access to the casting of Victoria Secret models, as well the lifestyle of jets and islands. It was perfect for the luring of unsuspecting girls. He had the toys that a very publicly broke Andrew did not have. Epstein maintained a cover as a pedo with his friends, but in reality behind closed doors he simply wanted massages, he even kept his underwear on to signal to the innocent girls that any funny business was not required. As a proxy Mossad agent he was equipped with the best surveillance equipment and everything that happened was filmed. Everything. Happy ending massages to low-grade orgies. Even the pathetic scenes of Andrew or Bill sitting with a teenage girl who didn't know who they were confessing to some ridiculous insecurity, crying and trolling for attention.

But sometimes the footage would produce a violent rape. It was then that Ghislaine would usually pay the girl $10,000 USD cash and send her away. There was so much more that could be done but during this era of intel and surveillance the best was to send them home, back to places like Moldova or Colombia. The disconnect with Andrew is that he is a royal so there is a cover for his own appearance to the public, an air of certainty that he was raised better than that, and was much too sophisticated for such nefarious behavior. Yet in reality, this was a man who never held a job, who never needed to make money to provide for his family, who failed at marriage and was not involved in the raising of his children. His relationship with the Queen could have been pulled from the playbook of mother-son relations in the trailer parks of the American south. A codependent man child and his controlling mother. Over a three week period in 1995 Epstein had lent his Manhattan mansion to Andrew and, during the course of the stay, there were three filmed rapes. Nothing extremely violent but definitely with an unwilling participant, girls who were repulsed by his body, and one screaming to not kiss her because his teeth were so awful. Watching the footage made Epstein sick and years later he would confide that it was a seminal turning point in his relationship with the prince and going forward he wanted nothing more than to bring him down.

Weekly reports, including the footage and personal notes by Epstein and Ghislaine, were transmitted to the Central Institute of Coordination in Tel Aviv. Much of his reporting took second place to the intel coming in

163

from Mossad agent Monica Lewinsky who was busy seducing President Clinton with her thong panties and penchant for sexualized cigar play. What was coming out of the White House was big and Israeli intel knew it could bring down the president. But we all know how that played out, with Linda Tripp's involvement the Mossad operation went dark and Monica was ghosted by her handlers. It would be years later that she was contacted and set up for life with a generous pension under the cover story of her handbag design business.

The Crimean Pyramid

The British once boastfully claimed that the sun never set on the British Empire, yet since the relinquishment of Hong Kong that is no longer the case. If Putin had his Russian version it would be that he could claim 11 time zones. But perhaps bigger news was coming his way with the greatest discovery of all time, something that would solidify his reputation as a savior of the motherland but also lift his status to that of a modern day Napoleon. Under a Gazprom resources exploration in Crimea oil workers discovered the ruins of the top of a pyramid. Much of the Crimean peninsula had a great history of battles between the Greeks and Romans, the Kumans and the Osman Turks, and coastal ruins were common. But this pyramid, after top secret carbon data testing, was confirmed to be older than dinosaurs.

The pyramid was well intact in a water cavern, and shaped more like an Egyptian pyramid than a more truncated top like that of a Mayan building. Within the foundation of the pyramid was a vault with a tomb for an unknown creature that measured over two meters in length with a crown where the head would be. More intriguingly there was a strong signal being emitted from this crown. Upon closer sonar investigation Moscow researchers were able to photograph a warehouse of metal boxes. When this was brought to Putin he began the planning of the annexing of Crimea. He wanted what was in those boxes as they seemed to pre-date history but were possibly from the future. His psyops team were ordered to instruct their operatives in programming at CNN to stick to the dying story of the missing MH370 flight as a distraction.

A dive team that entered the hollowed-out inside of the submerged pyramid emerged contaminated with highly dangerous levels of radiation. Samples from around the boxes were taken and tested for "non-earthly" matter. If this was parked goods from a previous alien race the potential value could surpass all wealth on the planet. It was Putin's hope that it was from the 140-mile long metal asteroid called 16 Psyche, also known as the Golden Asteroid. Rich with iron, nickel and plutonium its real value was in the unknown qualities of a new metal. Estimates of the valuation of the entire asteroid were in the quadrillions USD. It circulated Mars and was beat up with large pock marks, leading astronomers to believe it had been mined several times.

Putin was thought to be the richest man on earth with a worth just over one trillion USD. But he was heavily leveraged as was Russia, the country he wanted to leave debt free as his legacy. The acquisition of any significant amount of space gold would shatter the stability of earth gold, the gold standard, and subsequently crash the value markets of the US dollar. In that scenario Mother Russia would remain with the only economy and debt free, with neighboring countries pleading to join a new Russian federation.

The boxes would require a summer to be removed from their tombs, to then be transported by a motorcade convoy of flatbed trucks to the Hantsavichy Radar Station in Belarus, run by the Russian Aerospace Force. The two day journey coincided with the start of the Ferguson riots, and the watchful media eye was fixated again on racial tensions in America. This site was the only logical location to open the boxes, because of the required access to uranium in order to penetrate the space metal--uranium acquired from Hillary Clinton during the Uranium One transaction--and in the possible event that the contents inside begin to transmit a signal back into space, the space radar system could capture a reply.

A Coincidence Theorist

Anonymous ID; TB+ANS Tue 4 Apr 1:23:14 <u>No.</u>
<u>149025</u> ViewReport
Islamic terrorists
Narrator to the ~~public~~
Problem-Solution-Reaction
Patriot Act
Orwellian state?
NORAD
"Air sovereignty"
Cuba; ~~Castro~~
"Young dictator"
Pearl Harbor
Site R
"loose ends"
Alice/Wonderland

    Any of us of a certain age remember where we were on that September morning in 2001. Much of the details of that day I am not going to get into here, we have heard it all and frankly it is still painful to recall the terror imposed upon our nation. All of those everyday Americans going about their lives, just trying to put food on the table, then boom, everything changed. But I digress. Obviously it was the work of Islamic terrorists. But because of the bewilderment and shock it was easy to sell any story or narrative to the public.

The Problem-Solution-Reaction resulted in the Patriot Act and the loss of many rights, mostly invisible, but still significant. It had become a moment to seize the power, the world was in flux and before it could settle down it needed to be reordered. The new "problem" would be a constant state of fear and confusion, a flux of subtle horror that could lead to an Orwellian state. As anomalies and mysteries around 9/11 began to dissolve into confusion the official narrative was never questioned, to do so would be unpatriotic or sound conspiratorial. How could you ever be so callous?

Perhaps there was not an active plotting role by the government in the planning of the operation, rather an active role in permitting it to happen. We know that security precautions, like NORAD, had been told to stand down. Like most of the biggest assassinations, from JFK to MLK to Diana, there was an unusual evaporation of security at just the right moment, ensuring there would be no challenges.

From NORAD's mission statement:

...the monitoring of man-made objects in space, and the detection, validation, and warning of attack against North America whether by aircraft, missiles, or space craft, utilizing mutual support arrangements with other commands. Aerospace control includes ensuring air sovereignty and air defense of the airspace of Canada and the United States.

I know it always goes back to how and why would the US government do something like this to its own people? Yes, it seems implausible. But perhaps some of the higher ups don't consider the citizens their own, maybe they see them as nothing more than useful idiots for the manipulation. There is no question that the proof is there, you just have to look for it. Some evidence points to planning for the 9/11 attacks began way back in the 1960s. What would have been an attack by Cuba, orchestrated by Fidel Castro. Something to get the people to finally green light any means necessary to publicly take out the young dictator.

As we know now so many years on that what they were after was a new Pearl Harbor, something to spark a wildfire in the Middle East, to impose a Bush agenda, and to level his own score with Saddam Hussein. This was the cover. What went on in the private undisclosed meetings at Site R, deep inside Raven Rock Mountain, Pennsylvania, may touch upon what is unfolding now nearly three decades on. But more on these loose ends later.

*Nothing would be what it is, because everything would be what it isn't. And contrary wise, what it is, it wouldn't be. And what it wouldn't be, it would. You see?...*Alice in Wonderland

Tender is the Heart of Darkness

Anonymous ID; TB+ANS Thu 23 Oct 1:23:45 <u>No.</u>
<u>149035</u> ViewReport
Apocalypse ~~Now~~
A-Team
Lizard King
"Unmarked motorcade"
BBW booting up a desktop
Malaysian Airlines [logo]
Boogeyman
"1st world bodies"
Bering Straits
luscious native women?
poisoned arrow

Intel or, in my preferred parlance, the word on the street, was that the killer of JonBenet was on Flight MH370, and in some semblance to Apocalypse Now or nod to the A-Team, we would fight with our hearts for the end goal of finding those who do harm. We shall go to the end, we shall fight in the jungle, in the air and rivers, we shall fight with growing confidence and strength in mission, we shall defend our vision, whatever the cost may be. We shall fight in the streets and in the hills. We shall never surrender. Or some such uplifting banter. We shall travel upriver, upforest, upvalley, and upjungle. We can masquerade as a noble unit while knowing beneath the sheen we are a disorganized band of dead idols. Our humane institution will bring the light.

Our first stop will deliciously delight the crew, although they likely have never heard of the Lizard King, but word again is that Jim Morrison is uptheater. Every man has a breakpoint and we will find out ours. We will become accustomed to the horrors around us and the blank places of the map will fill with our desperation. My voice over to the shaky handheld camera documentation will roll out in your mind with the urgency of a loaded gun on your nightstand. The natives have nothing on the white man. All of the civilized world made us now, to this point, with the unhinged and nervous values, an unmarked motorcade of heroes and ghosts. And under the circumstances of our search party one could argue that amid all the insanity, the moments of tenderness and compassion are offset by a ruthless action, and the clarity to see what needs to be done to get there. To be unconcerned and untimid, to go beyond the morality and abide by newfound moral guidelines. When it's your own rescue in order to save the others, and any subsequent alternative thought is too sick to believe. Capable of new methods, and the idea that if we were still alive this is what we would have wanted, in the exhausting emptiness and platitudes of some other -ism. Life can be sustained on a life support of exhausting emptiness, but why?

We rely now on a lifetime of brutal instincts wielded like the machete in hand, our early lives sacrificed for the sake of an enlightened protagonist viewpoint now. This impenetrable darkness forlorn in the respective dark of narration, fore we cannot unsee the glimpses of the shared and hallowed terror.

Keyboard nutjobs had claimed to locate the tail, taller than the trees around it, perhaps several stories, and the shimmer of the windshield glint of a fully intact cockpit. These web sleuths did it for the dopamine hits, the chatter from their fandom, the accolades from their mothers, and the love from fellow trolls. A collective replacement, that with a heavy porn habit, and affinity for the BBWs, to downplay any actual involvement of a glimmering nod to a sex life as their virginity is played out on the down low through diversion tactics and a manic sense of hurried busyness to get back online, to continue the lead of the virtual search party. But all kidding aside we could not be here without them, hell, even I struggle with booting up a desktop.

They say they have the engine located but this runs contrary to our better intel that the plane is parked, fully intact and emptied of its passengers. Something 4.5 meters wide and 3.1 meters in length. A rival digital search party has a crash site several hundred miles away in the northwestern forests of the Cambodian capital Phnom Penh. Like the glimmer from fools gold in the sands of creek beds, this is the satellite equivalent, something shiny beheld from the heavens. Hope during another high speed fly by, talk of a large piece of aluminum with the Malaysia Airlines logo said to be the tail circulated in chat rooms but ran against my own instinctive intuition that it was just fodder for more attention seeking from a rival fringe search partier. These sleuths could be seeing something imaginary but like in the case of Fosset's crash, it could be other aircraft, smaller general aviation birds that never got the coverage when they went missing, or older shit from the Vietnam war era.

The natives are not Buddhists, rather they retain their local animist religions. They practice a slash-and-burn subsistence farming, or fire fallow cultivation. By cutting down and burning the plants they create a field called the swidden, where the layered ash creates a nutrient rich fertilizer. Their language group is the Mon-Kmer linking their migration from Siberia, settling now with over a thousand dialects within the jungle. The ghosts in the forest are mistaken for lost tribes, those clans that hid from the Khmer Rouge who still think the boogeyman is out to get them. Oh the sweet endearing thought to be detached from history like that.

Like the starry nights that had lit our pathway to now we had to rely on our own instincts and intuition. Because of a vacuum of knowledge many fantastical tales had arisen, some based on the modicums of fact, others purely from the imagination. With the absence of disproof and the repetition of storytelling there was the anticipation of a revealed truth. Fantastical tales of forgotten people in the jungle, and those who would be first contact. Wonderful and strange folk. Some that may die from exposure to our first world bodies. Those who may have descended from the Americas and arrived via the Bering Straits. Those luscious native women who would believe us to be gods, madly wanting to sire our offspring. But there was danger in small-scale orgies, and of being most vulnerable in those moments. The community vibe of us as devils in the human form. Anything can really set them off and a poisoned arrow into your bloodstream would seal your fate within minutes. But, first stop of order would be a visit with the Lizard King.

A Mystery with the Most Minimal of Clues

Anonymous ID; TB+ANS Mon 13 Jul 4:45:12 <u>No.</u> <u>149037</u> ViewReport
American West
227 "passengers"
"wiped"
Flight 93 = Pennsylvania
Compromised American press
[truthers]
"Good night Malaysia Three Seven Zero"
Russians?

Palau Langkawi landing strip?
Diego Garcia?
Kamikaze mission
Wormhole?
Fever pitch
Eyeballs ~~for sale~~
Andaman Sea
South Pole to Cambodia?
Maldives beach orb
Inmorsat?
"Rioters"
Sea junk
FAA inventory
Donald Trump
"vast empty oceans"
"greatest mystery in modern aviation"
Non-narrative
[Seeding] of madness
News vacuum
~~ISIL~~
Putin [annexing Crimea]
Ferguson uprising
~~Race~~ baiting

Flight MH370, oh that ever so mysterious missing
Malaysian bird, so intriguing in fact that CNN reported it
possibly had entered into the time space continuum
through the appearance, albeit briefly, of a black hole.
Something it flew right into and now those on board are
elsewhere in the past or in the future. The mental
imagery of the landed plane in an American West desert

surrounded by cowboys and indians, or parked on the deck of a spaceship being sanitized while the passengers are diligently quarantined. Like any good aviation mystery, the Beijing-bound 777 with its 227 passengers and 12 crew, we were left to untangle the mystery from the most minimal of clues.

We can go over the more plausible, less insane, more sane, possibilities of what came of the flight. You start with the wonderment of how a $300 million aircraft can go missing without some pinpoint of its position, that base technology that exists in all of our cell phones, what the government uses to track our movements. Early speculation by the American public, polling at 10%, was alien abduction. How else would all those signals be able to be "wiped." We had from the frightful experience of 9/11 the knowledge that cells kept working, and that even in the remains of the Pennsylvania field Flight 93 there were over 100 cell phone pings, in the burning ruins field, post-nosedive. Or, how when something like this happens in a politically-controlled country, without that *cough* fully free American press, the families of the victims become dissidents and desperate to weed through the mechanisms of blackouts and rose-tinted transparency traps, that sad image of family members running routes with their fingertips over aviation maps of the Indian Ocean, while shouting down the government to do something in conference rooms set up at the airport for the grieving relatives to cry it out, while constantly checking their phones, as if new information was coming out. The interviews where they shout down the politicians. Or, how early in the mystery, that traffic controller calls to the cockpit were calm exchanges between professionals, even laconic, and that there was nothing of significance to think that anything was amiss. When the first lost connection with traffic control took place it was noted to be nothing more than a radio malfunction. A more reasonable idea that lightning had struck the plane and it sat in the South China Sea floating while transmitting its signals to any satellite that so remotely could receive it, while running low on its battery charge. Later we would discover that the Believers, or the Truthers, would need only a small morsel to cook up their larger meals of theories that could last forever, or at least until the next big disaster.

The final handoff transcript, these six words that could be psychoanalyzed forever, "Good night Malaysia Three Seven Zero," and all that it could mean. What does it mean? Or, the rogue pilot theory that ranks the highest in polling, as the most plausible, but not without holes in the plotline, that co-pilot Fariq Abdul Hamid, with the most ominous name in the history of commercial pilots, somehow commandeered the plane after subduing the lead pilot, either through slicing his throat with a box cutter, in a nod to 9/11, or less dramatically with an ether rag, then suicided the entire plane into a nosedive. This theory is often squelched by the fact that investigators have never been able to find a motive on his behalf, just a most sinister name. Or, the theory, which had originally polled at 5%, that the

Russians had taken out the plane with missiles, but without any concrete evidence as to why, this theory has been voted down to zero. It did seem that Russia had a hand in most modern day air disasters, so why not this one? An alternative Russian narrative that was supported briefly by Rupert Murdoch was that it was a Russian special op to destabilize relations with China, and a well-trained agent that was on the flight was able to dismantle all of its electronics then fake the flight data to send the search parties wayward. Or, a cockpit fire caused the pilot to turn west, toward the nearest landing strip in Palau Langkawi, but then the pilots passed out, the crew took over the controls but didn't have enough time to radio in a distress call, while the crew passed out from the smoke inhalation and the plane flew ghost-mode for a couple of hours until it ran out of fuel and crashed. But there is no evidence to support this theory as there are no remains of the plane. Or, the furthest distance north with a full tank of gas would take the plane to Kazakhstan where there were plenty of runways and buildings large enough to conceal the plane. Simply, it could have been a large heist. Or, that the plane was headed to the atoll of Diego Garcia, specifically an American military base, on some sort of kamikaze mission, but before it could get there the plane was shot down, and the military was able to scoop up all debris, including the black box. Debunkers will say this operation is too large in scale and would require too many to stay quiet. Or, it was hijacked by Pakistanis, landed somewhere, refueled, then upon its arrival in Pakistan all aboard were killed and the plane was outfitted with a nuclear bomb. And the delivery of this most ominous of weapons will be at the choosing of the Pakistani military. Likely a suicide flight into Manhattan or London. Or a wormhole. Or a meteor strike that obliterated the plane into dust.

As the noise began to reach fever pitch--talking heads on television news and chat rooms on the web--there was a rhythm to the perpetual chatter, something I could pick up on, and as a chef with an inherent talent or noble ability to gauge a kitchen, what the servers were saying, what the sous chefs were grumbling about, the face the bussers were making, even the expressions from the dishwashers, I was able to surmise on my own that it was all fake news, the "officials say" addition on the front end of a sentence almost an automatic tag to discredit whatever was to come after it. There were no authorities or sources because there was no handle on what had happened. The mainstream media had become a trough of bullshit sourced from an "official" this or that then passed through a talking head who ran it past an "expert" then dropped as a droplet into a sea of misinformation called viewerdom. Your eyeballs were for sale, enumerated for advertising sales decks from one big corporation to another.

In the case of MH370 the bullshit meter was stuck at eleven. For example, the search started 400 miles off the flightpath in the Andaman Sea, then switched back to the South China Sea because military radar had recorded the flight managed a 180, which then got debunked by military officials. But was this a short-lived diversion to get officials away from the real crime scene? And like anything on the news, the more complex a story sounded the more legit it became to a casual viewer. Do you think some soccer mom in middle America gave a fuck about the minutia of geography, no, she wants the emotional carnage. She wants the Americans lost on the cover of People Magazine, pictures of them laughing and taking selfies in the days leading up to their demise. The memories of the fallen retold by family and lovers, how wonderful they were, that they didn't deserve this. That now someone has to pay. A plethora of mapping speculation took place with arcs of pings or through transmission handshakes between the bird and the satellites, plotting out where the last communication may have occurred was intriguing but not sexy. We needed human trauma. The arc stretched 6,000 miles, nearly double the footprint of continental America, reaching as far south as the South Pole, and as north as the aforementioned Kazakhstan, and encompassing the Cambodian jungle which piqued my interest. Or my instinct. What if the plane had ducked into the radar shadow of another plane to make its untraced path to Cambodia? Something about the jungle made sense to me.

One of the initial search parties found a mysterious metal orb on a Maldives beach, causing a whirlwind of speculation. It was downplayed by the mainstream media as nothing to see here, as the establishment's agreed upon narrative was to not find the plane. Yet the orb may have been a clue, even if otherworldly. A British satellite firm called Inmarsat had tracked the movements of this orb, or so they believed, and what was odd, through the triangulation of seven different satellites, was the slow movement of it. The pings and handshakes between the tracking devices in the sky recorded the speed to be at times a mere five miles per hour. Even the smallest of planes, like a Cessna 150, need at least 62 miles per hour to take flight. Was this orb extraterrestrial? Was it early drone technology? Was it being controlled by someone with a joystick on the other side of the world? To add to the mystery were the short moments of burst frequency offsets, when the signal's wavelength would dip below what the radars could receive. It was as if someone somewhere didn't want the movements tracked.

Ratings for the missing flight were phenomenal, the best in years, and finding the plane would end the intrigue. A month after the disappearance a next-of-kin protest took place by outraged loved ones at the Malaysian embassy in Beijing. The incompetence of the Malaysian government was being revealed. The "rioters" threw bottles of water at riot-geared paramilitary soldiers. The Malaysian president released a new and final theory, that according to his own calculations the plane flew directly south, and crashed somewhere in the vast ocean and that it was time to accept that there would be no survivors.

CNN loved this theory because it ensured months more of a missing plane. A frenzy of breaking news engulfed American media with the "discovery" of debris fields, mostly by the Australians, yet these debris would quickly be identified as "sea junk" or the remains of other maritime disasters. After a month the batteries to the black boxes would be dead so talk of their pings were discredited, or would lead to speculation of some other missing plane(s), regardless of the fact that planes don't just go missing. Yes, there are no Amber Alerts for commercial birds, but the FAA has an inventory of what goes up and comes back down.

The media were grasping at straws, and, a mere two years before the election of Donald Trump, were cracking at the seams, a reveal to their inauthenticity, and often large scale dramatization written by nothing more than fiction writers to drive a narrative that led to more intrigue, or outrage, whatever it took to get you to return to the screen. But like all good sagas, this story, like so many before it and after it to come, had to quietly die off, and come to a placeholder end in our collective memory. You've got to make room for the new, it was called news after all. And just like that everyone stopped talking about it. It was as if it never happened and somehow it was now okay for the mystery to go unsolved. All those screen time hours of expert testimony and raw speculation, the collective grief for the lost and loved ones, and the outrage at government officials. Poof!

But there was more to the story of the coverage than what appeared on the surface. From the moment CNN's Anderson Cooper went into full "breaking news" mode of the missing flight, coverage ratings spiked. Was it the mystery, the intrigue, or the droning calmness from aerial footage of vast empty oceans? Was it the crying family members? Was it the impending potential for thrill that at any moment the footage you were watching from the comfort of your sofa would reveal a floating fuselage in the white-capped sea? Coverage was 24 hours, the story never slept and was global in scale. Dozens of nationalities were aboard that plane. Prior to the disappearance of Flight MH370 CNN was in a nosedive of their own. An endless slide of ratings had the newly-appointed president/CEO Jeff Zucker in the hot seat. His orders for the correspondents and anchors was to now "go all in" on the MH370 story. It was finally the type of story that could sustain traction throughout the 24-hour news cycle. Defying the basic logic of what ingredients make a good news story, it was lacking in the in-your-face reporting, that live shot from the frontlines, instead the producers relied heavily upon the same loops of aerial footage, and the occasional official Malaysian news conference. Often with the only update being that new searches uncovered nothing. Lots of emotional foreplay without touching. And the more difficult the story was to explain--that intense throbbing mystery--the more compelling the entire non-narrative became.

It had fast become the greatest mystery in modern aviation. It was like a crime without a scene, a homicide without a body. The clues that trickled in would be followed up upon then debunked. Without evidence or facts, CNN found their formula, a barrage of endless talking and speculation. Hosts and guests were able-- instructed to, in fact--to run wild theories, essentially writing fiction of plausible yet impossible outcomes. They were just giving the people what they wanted. CNN was able to run any possibility they liked knowing there would be no consequence as there was no evidence of an actual factual event. Of course much could be questioned if the remains of the plane were found, but with each day that seemed less likely.

This new methodology of "reporting" would be deployed with the election of Donald Trump, planting seeds of stories that did not exist, so that any running mouths could never be called out. News had become speculation. It was the dawn of the post-truth media. CNN's new modus operandi was called "flooding the zone," go all in on the story and produce wall to wall coverage. Credible sources did not matter. There was a twilight zone element to the unquestionable reporting which culminated so deliciously with CNN host Don Lemon piquing his viewers with the idea that the plane may have been swallowed by a black hole. "A lot of people have been asking about that, about black holes and on and on and all of these conspiracy theories," he said. "Let's look at that." His guest that evening was a former inspector general for the Department of

Transportation, clearly an expert in black holes, and she countered with "A black hole, even a small one like that, would suck in our entire universe." This was a turning point in the coverage, it had reached peak absurdity, but what it also provided for was this seedling of madness, the black hole theory was now let out to the public and many ran with it. All they needed was that CNN had said it. This laid the groundwork for future reporting. It had appeared that the story had run out its natural life. But Zucker doubled down. "I get on planes all the time, I want to know what happened. There's a lot of layers to this story and as every day goes by and it isn't solved, it becomes an even greater mystery and that is what I think makes it a great story."

During the news vacuum that this story created, other news was neglected. In this case it was the formation of the Islamic State of Iraq and the Levant, or ISIL. As well, the disintegration from Syria's civil war produced a resulting diaspora to Europe with mass drownings in makeshift boats embarked for Mediterranean shores. It was the greatest refugee crisis of modern times, and equally "sexy" if you were a news junkie. Oh and also the power grab of Russian President Vladimir Putin by annexing Crimea, that beautiful and strategic coastal region of Ukraine. The next big all-in story would be the Ferguson uprising, and the birth of modern day hyper-mediated race baiting.

Adrenochrome So Hot Right Now

Anonymous ID; TB+ANS Sun 8 Nov 11:08:55 <u>No. 149039</u> ViewReport

Huma Abedin = HA

Eye bleach

"Aftershock"

Keep the flame ~~alive~~

Straight razor

Hunter S. Thompson

Ritual sacrifice

~~Debunked~~

Whack job

Campfire ghost story

Colonial subjects

Global labs

Well-paid shills

Hillary personal ER [Manhattan] "The Whitman"

*snopes

Small-scale trauma center

Chelsea

Rumors have circulated for years, first within the corridors of power in Washington DC, the private clubs of Manhattan and happy hours in the Hamptons, now blown out to the widespread reach of the interwebs and those who troll yet also conduct their own research, much of that which is based on nothing more than innuendo and crafty mystery, the existence of an extremely disturbing snuff film of Hillary Clinton and her down low lover Huma Abedin raping a prepubescent girl, then the mutilation of her body. Somewhere this is parked on the edge of the parking lot of the dark web. Of course many have not seen this video and considering its dark subject matter and theme why would you want to? Yet everyone seems to know someone who has seen it, and they claim it falls into the category of that which cannot be unseen, with mentions of eye bleach being a welcome treatment to the haunting aftershock of such disturbing material. It's one of those things that you question with your inherent intellect, or whatever remaining brain cells you may possess, that you muster for the sake of personal clarification, do you personally know someone who has accessed it? If it's only someone who knew someone or a cousin of a friend at work your own numbers game comes up dry through voodoo logic. But for the sake of the possibility that it may well exist you keep the flame alive.

This girl, like many others like her, need not be forgotten. Does someone know her? A certain description of the video is so disturbing that you can only believe that it is real. The details of how they fillet her face with a straight razor. Then, wait for it. These are sick people. They take turns wearing the girl's face like a mask. Why such extreme evilness? Well, it is a process to harvest adrenochrome, a fountain of youth serum, produced by the oxygenation of the adrenal gland when the subject is undergoing an adrenal rush. Like a satanic ritual sacrifice you drink their blood. It's all about getting high while chasing immortality. In the 1950s it was theorized that adrenochrome is essentially LSD made by the human brain. American journalist Hunter S. Thompson brought the semi-secret to the mainstream and out into the light with his description: "There's only one source for this stuff...the adrenaline glands from a living human body. It's no good if you get it out of a corpse."

The elites love it and it comes from children. That is all you need for the ingredients of a hot conspiracy, anything to get attention away from the possible truth, those delicious morsels of spice and intrigue, a nefarious element combined with disbelief, and abject horror. It is then that you have built a protective layer, a paranoid segment that can quickly be disregarded and weaponized should anyone dare believe the hype.

There is the immediate reaction that something so wicked cannot be true but this is the default byproduct of anything of non-mainstream interest that can quickly be debunked through a dismissive offhand remark or labeling of a believer as a conspiracy theorist whack job. It's almost as if the narrative is written for that visceral thrill, tailor made for the reaction. The imagery is barbaric and medieval, drinking from a chalice made of the child's skin. It's like imagining a composite sketch of the worst horror villains, then crank that up to eleven. Sick cannibalism which nobody can get behind. Is there a suspension of disbelief to arrive there? Yes, I suppose, much like any conspiracy racket out there. But like anything worth its weight in silver there is work involved to get there, versus the lazy consumption of simply taking in and consuming that which is told to you. The easy route versus the sometimes more difficult truth. This is the conundrum of any conspiracy theorist. It's the campfire ghost story come to life. The immediacy for the conscious skeptics. Pedophiles aided by some supernatural drug and the fears of child abduction. The best of horror film tropes recycled for the fear effect, while any ancillary themes are glorified legends taken from the town square of yore to retroactively engage your most vulnerable sensibilities.

A visceral disgust is followed by the dehumanizing of the subjects, much like how colonial subjects were once dehumanized in the early days of the New World. And the blood of children will always set a frenzied tone with its gory rhetoric yet another component to the personal genocide within. In Aldous Huxley's essay "The Doors of Perception"--published in 1954 and the inspiration for the name of the band The Doors, by Jim Morrison himself--it was about the author's experience with mescaline, and how the effects of adrenochrome are strikingly similar to those of the psychedelic cactus. The fact that it was only "spontaneously produced by the human body" made it even more alluring. The next big pop culture reference was in 1962, in the novel A Clockwork Orange. Adrenochrome was offered as an additive to libations, in this case a glass of milk, resulting in a cocktail referred to as the Moloko Plus. The cover story for the usage of it, in a professional hospital setting, is to slow blood loss by promoting clotting in open wounds. Its synthetic versions are available for purchase from certain global labs. "A sexy and cool name but not a very exciting compound," one researcher has said. But is this just part of the downplay, and anti-hype brigade, from well-paid shills?

Back to Hillary. It was no doubt that adrenochrome had become necessary medicine for her at this point. In what was becoming increasingly frequent, she would often faint at public events. Her private medical team, consisting of a half dozen paramedics dressed as Secret Service agents, were quick to catch her when she was about to fall. Her daughter, Chelsea, had a personal emergency room built for her in the ground floor of her New York City apartment building, The Whitman. This was required so that no actual emergency room visit occurred, possibly revealing publicly any of Hillary's numerous health concerns, and when out and about within Manhattan her team could quickly get her there. Debunker sites like Snopes were quick to discredit this story as completely false even though detailed construction plans of an elaborate small-scale trauma center were available on the internet. Years on, when Chelsea listed the apartment for sale, in the listing was mention of a private medical facility among its many amenities.

The Murder of Hunter S. Thompson

Anonymous ID; TB+ANS Mon 4 Nov 21:34:11 <u>No. 149031</u> ViewReport
"counselor"
Woody Creek
[Dick Cheney] code name: Angler
~~Johnny Depp~~
WTC
Explosive charges
Bush 2 Nazis
[bushy-haired strangers]
mujahideens
Super Drug
HRC

    Staged suicides share some commonalities, but in the case of the death of famed American writer Hunter S. Thompson there were various undeniable clues. He had a broken leg at the time but he was free of any terminal ills. His lengthy suicide note ended with the word "counselor" lending to the idea that he was mid-sentence when he was killed. He was in the middle of a project exposing an alternative theory of what happened on September 11, 2001. He was crazy about his young wife and didn't even say goodbye to her. He mentioned to a friend one week prior to his death that he feared he would be "suicided." And finally there were no witnesses. It took place at his fortified compound in Woody Creek, Colorado, while his wife was in town running errands. His nearest neighbor was former vice president Dick Cheney who lived .8 miles away.

I was able to reach by phone a friend of his who, understandably, needs to remain anonymous, even here. But let's say he is a big Hollywood star with his own eccentricities, a pirate's gait, and Native American blood. Oh, and he has a fetish for scarves.

"He phoned me the night before his death. He mumbled that there was something he really wanted to understand. He'd been working on a story about the World Trade Center attacks and had stumbled across what he felt was hard evidence showing the towers had been brought down not by the airplanes that flew into them but by explosive charges set off in their foundations. Now he thought someone was out to stop him from publishing it. 'They're gonna make it look like suicide, I know how these bastards think.' These were his last words to me."

To add to the intrigue his wife Anita claimed that his suicide note was written four days prior to his death. And if this was the case why would nobody in his family try and save him from his misery? It was a series of quotes from two years prior that encapsulated the intrigue. During a local radio interview Hunter said: "Bush is really the evil one here and it is more than just him. We are the Nazis in this game and I don't like it. I am embarrassed and I am pissed off. I meant to say something. I think a lot of people in this country agree with me...we'll see what happens to me if I get my head cut off next week. It's always unknown or bushy-haired strangers who commit suicide right afterwards with no witnesses."

The deputy who arrived at the scene of his suicide noted that the pistol used had spent a shell casing, but there was no cartridge in the firing chamber. A bullet from the magazine should have cycled into the chamber. The only explanation to this was that Hunter had been coerced into self-inflicting the gunshot wound. Perhaps a threat against his wife.

It would be months before his editor was able to thoroughly pursue his various writing projects. In true Hunter fashion he had several stories going. An investigation into professional sports, a fluff piece about fly fishing, and a Rolling Stone deep dive into the mujahideens of Afghanistan in 1980. But the biggest story, well over 20,000 words, was one he had, oddly, never mentioned to the editor. It was the story of adrenochrome, that super drug harvested from children, the product of the decomposition of adrenaline. Titled ADRENOCHROME: The Elite's Super Drug. The story opened with a first hand account of a satanic ritual sacrifice attended by none other than Hillary Rodham Clinton.

NXIVM & Other Unpronounceables

Anonymous ID; TB+ANS Sun 9 Jan 14:00:11 <u>No. 149161</u> ViewReport
Self-Help = MLM
"sex slaves"
Vincente Fox
[throuple]
Dominus Obsequious Sororium
Knife of ~~Aristotle~~
"straw donors"
keylogger virus

     Let's clear this up before we can proceed any further. NXIVM is pronounced NEKS-ee-em. You may want to say it out loud. If you go to their website you will see they are a self-help multi-level marketing company. Yes, apparently you can fuse together two rackets. Oh but there is more. They had a secret society platform for recruiting sex slaves. It was called The Vow and young girls were branded into the trade. Like any cult there was a semi-charismatic leader, and the doting followers to build up the hype that surrounded him. The "self-help" component of the message was that of "experiencing more joy in life." Simple, right? In order to get there required a range of self-development, including gimmicky programs like the "Executive Success Program" and classes that were named from characters in video games. Their most well-known follower was the ex-president of Mexico, Vincente Fox. But they reached their peak--and notoriety--with the acquisition of B-list Hollywood actress Allison Mack.

Mack went all in on the multi-level marketing aspect of NXIVM, likely to seek a consistent source of income. Bringing new followers in ensured a downline that would ultimately pay dividends when those under her were able to acquire new followers of their own. Only in America can such fringe business behavior be tolerated. Then Mack fell in love with the leader's girlfriend, and they became lesbian lovers within the existing relationship. A sort of proxy version of a throuple. In the early days there was no sex between Mack and the leader. It was only girl-girl that he enjoyed watching. In court filings at a later date it was reported that all three were eventually to become equal lovers. Regardless, Mack's role was quickly solidified as the "procurer" of new young girls. In the hyped-up fantasy realm of any cult you needed someone with connections to the outside world, a charismatic connected player who could bring new blood to the group. In many ways Mack was perfect for the job and she was able to bring over two dozen girls within a year. These girls were groomed with lesbian affection, the promise of guaranteed income streams, and the potential of ultimately belonging within something much bigger than themselves.

The Dominus Obsequious Sororium (DOS) was that sisterhood that any girl with daddy issues could find comfort within. Structured loosely as a sorority, there was corporal punishment for those who misbehaved. This typically involved the leader men paddling the bare asses of the girls while the others were made to watch. Photographs were taken of the girls to document these compromising positions, and they were told that the pictures would be released to the public if they ever tried to flee. Surprisingly, many of the girls found comfort in the conformity required of them.

NXIVM had its own media outlet, named The Knife of Aristotle, which pumped up the ideology of the cult with testimonials and stories of success from "graduates" of the program. Beyond the fabricated hype stories, the cult's own journalists were tasked with paying off outside reporters to write favorable stories. But this all blew up after a two year run. The FBI raided their corporate offices, arrested the entire upline, including Mack, and indicted the operation and its officers with racketeering and sex trafficking charges.

Later revealed in court were the contributions to Hillary Clinton's presidential campaign. There was a laundering aspect of straw donors over-donating with the surplus amount being refunded to other entities. Court filings exposed that NXIVM "agents"--many of whom were the same ex-Mossad agents who worked for Harvey Weinstein--were able to "gain access" to the

Chappaqua, New York, home computer of Hillary Clinton and install a keylogger virus to act as a trojan horse to transmit the computer's data and activities to "Mr. REDACTED, a New York City individual of social prominence and influential wealth." Speculation was that Weinstein was spying on HRC, but that theory could be disregarded as a decoy to the real espionage operation of Jeffrey Epstein. The biggest catch of the intel world, the object of the FBI, of Interpol, of China, of Israel, and of Putin himself, was the video of Hillary with Huma Abedin and that child. It would be well worth the investment spent in acquiring it as global bidders would line up.

The Lizard & His Kingdom

Anonymous ID; TB+ANS Tue 7 Dec 5:28:54 <u>No. 149041</u> ViewReport
The Man
Bounds of "reality"
Poet Laureate Americana
Hippies [Costco food courts]
Public indecency [Florida]
art = stoned = immaculate
Lizard Kingdom
Colossal synchronicity
Operative locales
~~Beginnings~~ of the world

"bender after bender"
Ambiguities of modernism
Rhyme the abstraction

The American 1960s were a clashing of the utopian ideal of a well-cultivated and perfected existence versus the boundaries and confines imposed by capitalism and The Man. Nobody embodied the position of figurehead, with the ethos of the counter cultural times, as much as James Morrison, aka the Lizard King, the lead singer of The Doors, and poet laureate Americana.

"Let's just say I tested the bounds of reality because I was curious to see what would happen. That's all it was, Tony. Can I call you Tony? Just a boundless curiosity really."

Sixties art--the music, film, visuals, writings--all somewhat were heavy in these feelings of countercultural movements, surged forth by the infamous hippies--many of whom are now the boomers who crowd Costco food courts--once fed heavily with their experimental advancements into marijuana and LSD. Within that explosion of color and a tethered sensation for heightened sensitivity and free love, was the birth of this mythical rock god. He blew the doors wide open on psychedelics while acquiring a bad alcohol problem, especially a love for whiskey. Alcohol was his muse, fueled by an underlying desire for the rush that came from drinking his sorrows away, something that he knew he could not sustain for a lifetime. His weight gain was directly in correlation with his diseased liver, and this is why for much of his mid-twenties he looked much older, like a man in his forties, if not early fifties. An added elusiveness to his wisdom factor was that old soul reincarnation, multiplied by his Adonis looks, he was someone all the girls wanted to fuck and all the men wanted to embody. This led to a well-devised manic sex appeal on stage, including a sequence toward the end of shows where he would pull down his crusty leather pants and moon the crowd. A stage move that landed him in jail for a few days after a Florida show, on public indecency charges. His sense of self was immortalized in words. This poem he wrote in 1965:

I can make the earth stop in
Its tracks. I made the
Blue cars go away.
I can make myself invisible or small.
I can become gigantic and reach the
Farthest things. I can change
The course of nature.
I can place myself anywhere in
Space or time.
I can summon the dead.
I can perceive events on other worlds,
In my deepest inner mind,
And in the minds of others.
I can.
I am.

Looking back from this perch of modern-day hyper narcissism, what was Jim trying to say? That he was some omnipotent figure in the universe and could manifest destiny at his own beckoning or was this a more humbled approach at inner peace, that he had complete control over his mind and was calm and accepting of his impending fame?

"No, Tony, it wasn't like that. I didn't understand what was coming for me in those days. I was fucked up most of the time. The stuff I was writing, this poetry, I would write it at night and wake up the next day and none of it made sense. It only got hot after I got the fame. Look at it, it really is just some jumbled word salad that doesn't mean shit. But the kids liked it so I kept it going. I knew I had to sell the performer in order to sell the words. Then I had my legit bandmates who made timely music, the final piece was my debauched performance. I look back on it now like performance art, much like how porn is made, it's staged. It involves a heavy mood, nobody is getting fucked without lube, you know. In many ways I was a fraud, I even lied about my family to build up the mystery. I knew it would all catch up to me at some point and I just couldn't handle it. I went into exile in Paris and with some reflection I devised a plan to fake my death. I didn't foresee it being such a big deal. Once I pulled it off, during the first days, I knew that I had done the right thing. It was a rebirth of sorts, but it was also a return to the real Jim. My art didn't matter so much because much of it I considered a fraud on the fans. Sure we had some hit songs, The End certainly was my favorite and will live on forever."

From a 1966 journal entry:

I'll tell you this…
No eternal reward will forgive us now.
For wasting the dawn.
Back in those days everything was simpler and more confused.
One summer night, going to the pier.
I ran into two young girls.
The blonde one was called Freedom.
The dark one, Enterprise.
We talked and they told me this story.
Now listen to this…
I'll tell you about Texas radio and the big beat.
Soft driven, slow and mad.
Like some new language.
Reaching your head with the cold, sudden fury of a divine messenger.
Let me tell you about heartache and the loss of god.
Wandering, wandering in hopeless night.
Out here in the perimeter there are no stars.
Out here we is stoned.
Immaculate.

"So much was made of your emotional volatility and apparent cruelty to those around you, namely your band," I mention.

"Those were relationships that were supposed to last a lifetime, that loyalty and camaraderie that you get being on stage, making love to the crowd, an orgy of sorts, those wasted days on the road, the build up to show time, those dudes with their instruments, sound checks before the fireworks, that foreplay. There was that emotional connection between our hearts and souls. But nothing is forever my friend. I became unrecognizable to myself, and that scared me. Call it arrested development or whatever psychoanalysis you got for me, I will listen, but I felt like a child thrown into a candy store. The drugs, and the women. I could have it all but I would take on too much and not be able to enjoy any of it. Do you know how many orgies I attended where I sat in the corner with my whisky dick and took in all the sucking and fucking through a hazy fog of beer goggles. When I wanted to join in I harbored the secret that I couldn't get it up, even when the hottest young girls tried to coax the lizard kingdom it got nowhere. It was years of sobriety before I got full boners, my man."

How often in your life is what you think you should do at odds with what you feel you should do? When your heart stops beating to sing at the prospect that your meta-thinking has been kicked in the balls and is now doubled over, unable to thwart your intuition, with you now pinned inside the reality zone. It's as if the programming has glitched just long enough that your standard logic no longer applies, and even though you have lived it for so long you can't suppress the clairvoyance. This is when your body-computer is strung out for the pre-eminence, and any robotic programming,

202

the 'you can't do this' type of unrelenting pressure, folds inward and infinite awareness becomes reality. This is what takes place in the jungle. The flow becomes the guide, and a colossal synchronicity becomes your potential. I know this is daydream believer psycho babble but next time you find yourself staring out a window, losing concentration, a sudden touch of fatigue, an overall fuzziness with your droopy eyes swelling and tearing up, know you are under the spell. You go to yawn but your mouth doesn't open. This is the ultradian response, and within the jungle it ceases to exist through ever present danger and the lack of wavelength signaling.

Cambodia, a hopeful land for the disappeared, and an opportune locale for cynical rock stars of yore, away from the neon-lit marquees, freed from the spiritual graveyard of their former lives, now long dead, with their subsidized rebirth amid the anonymity of uncaring natives. To feed the spiritual pangs there was still a low-grade fandom directed at the tall whiteman, and Jim was well over six feet, with a large belly that Asians loved, exemplifying his wealth, appetite and, most importantly, access to food.

"I wanted to travel back to the beginnings of the world. Even if it's up to the front door, where I can knock and wait for some local to answer. In some ways I wanted to become a prehistoric man. My kinship is with the savages, and for me going native was simply to invite the wilderness within me. You see, it wasn't about what was happening around me, but inside of me. There was eloquence in the clarity, away from the drugs, because I had become the drugs. I was tripping, on bender after bender. I am coming off of one right now, man. My problem was with the ambiguities of modernism, and therefore modern man. I'm all good with it now, and as a poet I rhyme the abstraction, that's right, to spin the chaos into order. Tony, did you get that down?"

Neurotic Dividends

Anonymous ID; TB+ANS Thu 12 Dec 18:14:24 <u>No. 149043</u> ViewReport
False applause
Memory weaponized
Negation
"labels the pigeonhole"
DOC = drug of choice
China ~~White~~
27 Club
Magic number
To Boddah?
peace, love, empathy
Closing years of the [Aughts]
7/11 misadventure
Marcus Aurelius
The longest posthumous ~~fame~~

Funeral [manic banter]

It has been said that only ghosts wallow in the past, and that the meta-descriptors base a life on what they choose for today. Who are you? How would you best describe yourself? To answer any kind of question like this you must relive or re-visit your own past, perhaps a history that you so desperately have tried to escape. All those little labels you have amassed over a lifetime of self-definitions, those tags that were thrown your way that stuck and perhaps led to your own inefficiencies or false applause. It's not that your recollections are inappropriate, it's that your memories can be weaponized and used against yourself, those labels as deterrents to growth, with the only remaining factor the further subjectification of your negation. When you own those trademarks you may be slowing your very potential for growth. Now is the best time to look back at it all as nothing more than a bucket of ashes. Take a look at your self-canceling behavior, the fruitless sentences you have been trained to repeat that play on some kind of mental looping keeping you from real growth, and more importantly real talk. Labels that pigeonhole you into categories that may have begun when you were a child. These are your neurotic dividends.

And you do it because you lack self-worth, unable to believe in yourself you are unable to achieve your goals. This includes self-confidence which equates to self-worth but when you are constantly telling yourself you are not qualified enough you act accordingly. Without confidence there can be no attainment of full potential. And these fears equate success to stressors, causing for worry that you may be exposed as a fraud. But you don't stop there, you need to place blame elsewhere that way you can justify the procrastination. Accepting that since you already committed yourself to the failure that it's just a matter of time. And you may put up a front that you control you, because this makes you feel better on the surface, as you have already accepted the negative outcome. You now control the negative outcome through patterns of self-sabotage. To have a goal is not enough, it's easier to come up with reasons, and place cards for the sympathy, you try and garner from those around you, regardless of the fact that nobody is paying attention.

Enter substance abuse, be it food, psychoactive drugs, sex, porn, you name it we got it. My own drug of choice, or DOC, back in my twenties was heroin. You look in the rearview mirror and think it should have killed you, but so goes the saying that what doesn't kill you makes you stronger. In some twisted way heroin made me the man I am today. I didn't need a gateway drug to get there either. One night, after a long shift, a bus boy invited me to his apartment to inject some "China white." The chemicals change the brain, the rush of euphoria wipes away any co-morbids like depression or anxiety. And when the thrill is done it comes down to the rebound effect, how hard it affects you coming off of it. Thankfully now I look back and that wasn't my case, I was able to kick it over a weekend, alone, without help. I was 27 years old.

Alas, the 27 Club, that hapless motley crew of deceased celebrities, be it mostly musicians, succumbed to their vices and addictions at the ripe age of twenty seven. Jim Morrison would be one of the founding members but we know his real fate. Icons like Kurt Cobain and Jimi Hendrix really did die, as far as I know. It can't all be faked, right? Janis Joplin was a big name and so was Amy Winehouse. You have to wonder if there is some coincidence, or is 27 a magic number, like a peeking out curve in life when you are burning out, spinning out of control and you either get clean or take the plunge into the unknown. Statistically it could be argued that it's all coincidence, that with the sheer number of dead celebrities any certain amount will have died at any given age. But this class is special.

Included is Brian Jones of Rolling Stones fame, this poor bloke founded the group then after a falling out, mostly blamed on his alcohol problem, the rest of the band, led by Mick Jagger, fired him. From his own band. Two weeks later he was found drowned in the pool of his country estate. The circumstances were suspicious, and at the time certain circles believed that Mick had actually killed him. The official autopsy announced that he "drowned by immersion in freshwater, severe liver dysfunction, and ingestion of alcohol and drugs."

Kurt Cobain, as the founder of the grunge band Nirvana, was the early MTV face of a generation that was to become known as Gen X. But he didn't live long enough. Fame and the music business drove him mad and his penchant for heroin was a recipe for disaster. On an April day in 1994 in a quiet Seattle neighborhood he blew his brains out with a shotgun, suicide note and all. It would be three days before anyone found him. The red flags were there. A month prior he had ingested over 50 pills while in Rome on tour and was hospitalized. The cover story was that he was suffering exhaustion and influenza. He flew home and entered a rehab center to quickly check himself out. His dealer later recounted that he gave him enough heroin to "fuck him up into oblivion."

His suicide note:

To Boddah
Speaking from the tongue of an experienced simpleton who obviously would rather be an emasculated, infantile complain-ee. This note should be pretty easy to understand. All the warnings from the punk rock 101 courses over the years, since my first introduction to the, shall we say, ethics involved with independence and the embracement of your community has proven to be very true. I haven't felt the excitement of listening to as well as creating music along with reading and writing for too many years now. I feel guilty beyond words about these things. For example, when we're back stage and the lights go out and the manic roar of the crowds begins, it doesn't affect me the way in which it did for Freddie Mercury, who seemed to love, relish in the love and

adoration from the crowd which is something I totally admire and envy. The fact is, I can't fool you, any one of you. It simply isn't fair to you or me. The worst crime I can think of would be to rip people off by faking it and pretending as if I'm having 100% fun. Sometimes I feel as if I should have a punch-in time clock before I walk out on stage. I've tried everything within my power to appreciate it (and I do, God, believe me, I do, but it's not enough). I appreciate the fact that we have affected and entertained a lot of people. I must be one of those narcissists who only appreciate things when they're gone. I'm too sensitive. I need to be slightly numb in order to regain the enthusiasm I once had as a child. On our last 3 tours, I've had a much better appreciation for all the people I've known personally, and as fans of our music, but I still can't get over the frustration, the guilt and empathy I have for everyone. There's good in all of us and I think I simply love people too much, so much that it makes me feel too fucking sad. The sad little, sensitive, unappreciative, Pisces, Jesus man. Why don't you just enjoy it? I don't know! I have a goddess of a wife who sweats ambition and empathy and a daughter who reminds me too much of what I used to be, full of love and joy, kissing every person she meets because everyone is good and will do her no harm. And that terrifies me to the point where I can barely function. I can't stand the thought of Frances becoming the miserable, self-destructive, death rocker that I've become. I have it good, very good, and I'm grateful, but since the age of seven, I've become hateful towards all humans in general. Only because it seems so easy for people to get along that have empathy. Only because I love and feel sorry for people too much I guess. Thank you all from the pit of my burning, nauseous stomach for your letters and concern during the past years. I'm too much of an erratic, moody baby! I don't have the passion anymore, and so remember, it's better to burn out than to fade away. Peace, love, empathy. Kurt Cobain

It was easy to write him off as a sufferer of depression, you could see it in the note and mostly in his music that sounded on the surface like angst but was really primal in the child wanting to scream out through the man. For years there were conspiracy after conspiracy floated about his death, but most of it was played down because of the characters involved, seedy trailer park relatives, private detectives, and everyone Cobain ever pissed off. There was a pot of money as a focus, but none of the theories garnered any plausibility and these many years later his death has been solidified as a suicide.

Amy Winehouse brought to the closing years of the Aughts the British version of the hot mess, a disheveled drunkard woman with homemade tattoos and a plunging bust line. Oh and that drooping beehive. It was fast becoming a played out look, but when she would sing all was forgiven and she was hoisted back onto some pedestal of exquisite regard. She ran fast and loose, and you had to wonder how much was for the cameras, running out of her flat with her bra falling off with a burning cigarette butt dangling from her pouty lips, or collapsed on a sidewalk with her endless list of junky boyfriends. Was it merely a test run for a certain downfall? When she did die of alcohol poisoning in July of 2011 it was no surprise to her fans. She is said to have told her doctor hours before her death that she did not want to die. Her body was discovered next to two empty vodka bottles. The official inquest listed her death as a "misadventure."

The point to these side digression stories is to counter the fake death stories, to show that there are indeed very real deaths. Ones with backstories and plenty of proof in the lead up to the demise. It isn't all conspiracy and smoke. Death is never a fun subject, and certainly it is disturbing when the dead are young. We all harbor a certain anxiety of what we will leave in our own death's wake, how our loved ones will feel when we are no longer here. Few emotions on this earth garner the uncertainty we feel when we ponder death. But we cannot go about our days with this wasted energy, as anxiety surrounding the end of our lives only distracts us from enjoying the time we do have.

There is an assurance in death, that comfort in the finality and the slip into oblivion, and the waning of memories of you, to a point that they cease to exist. Peace comes about in knowing that mistakes you make in life will soon be forgotten, and that alone should permit you to live with a stronger level of authenticity, and a newfound ability to embrace life's risks. The stoic philosopher Marcus Aurelius once wrote:

Brief is man's life and small the nook on the Earth where he lives; brief, too, is the longest posthumous fame, buoyed only by a succession of poor human beings who will very soon die and who know little of themselves, much less of someone who died long ago.

Stop living like you are being watched, or that somehow you will be remembered for this or that, like some romcom scene of your funeral with the manic banter of storytelling about how epic you were, because it's not going to be like that. All that will remain is how you made people feel, those endearing sentiments that when felt again will remind someone of you. May that be your legacy.

Lost Empires & Other Aspects of Collapse

Anonymous ID; TB+ANS Fri 11 Jan 15:58:14 No. 149051 ViewReport
[red man]
Vietnam ~~War~~
"cloud of light"
Evacuation
LSD
WWII or WWIII research?
Chinese technology = UFO?
Delirium triggered by fever
Fourth Kind = alien abduction
Alien hotspot
"millennia of dynasties"
Angkor Wat what?

Capuchin friar
~~NASA~~
1,000 x
"willing nymphs"
3-fingered hands
[official] narrative
"Golden Age"
"only one way to find out"

I am in your chants and laughters. I am in the tears that flow from sorrow. I am in the bright joyous eyes of the children. I am in the substance that gives unity, completeness, and oneness. I am in you when you walk the simple path of the red man. I must leave you now to appear in another age, but I leave you with the red man's path... Sioux medicine priestess, White Buffalo Woman

In May 1970, well into the Vietnam War, Private First Class Gary Conover and his regiment found themselves assigned to a top secret mission deep in the Cambodian jungle. During their preparations of a temporary campsite they witnessed on a nearby hill, an "attacking light." A pulsing thrust could be felt through their bodies. The light began a rolling movement down the hill and toward their position, while invisibly causing all of their munitions to discharge. Pistols in holsters began firing, while a grenade launcher launched at the same time as a bazooka fired into a nearby tree trunk. This "cloud of light" was an amber orange but as it passed by it changed its color to green. They shot at the light and there was a force field effect that caused the bullets to ricochet off of an invisible wall. It began targeting the soldiers individually, emitting pulses and waves like a sweeping searchlight that would cause a burning and tingling sensation. They scrambled for cover as the ball of light finally hovered off the ground then abruptly took to the heavens. Desperate requests for evacuation were called into command and the men were evacuated two days later.

During medical treatment it was discovered that they had dangerously high white-blood cell counts, almost as if they had been under months of radiation treatment. The stories of their experience were brushed off by the brass but what the brass did know that they did not know was that similar stories were coming in from other remote parts of the battlefield. Mostly tales of unidentified flying objects, crafts that resembled flying saucers. In fact, the command had 53 corroborated witnesses in 35 reports in just under a month. Much of this was kept from reports back to Washington DC as nobody wanted to be mocked or told to hold off the LSD. The easiest explanation was that it was Russians experimenting with anti-gravity technology based on German WWII research. Could it have simply been that the witnesses were highly stressed and exhausted men? Maybe it was Chinese technology that Americans were not aware of, as the Vietnam War was a testing ground for future wars. The force field technology is what piqued everyone's interest. Bullets fired at the light ricocheted off. The thing with UFO sightings or abnormal things of this nature are later to be found as ordinary phenomena, often gas clouds. Statistically they are easily debunked 80 percent of the time. But this story from the Cambodian jungle lingered for fifty years on and was in that 20 percent of the unexplained. Chatter among different regiments of similar experiences went unreported as filing a report would just make you look crazy and your own account would be discredited as some form of PTSD. It very well could have been some kind of hallucination brought on by the terror of war, or a delirium triggered by a fever while the spike in white blood cells could be explained off as a jungle bacterial infection.

The US Navy's top secret UFO division classified the encounter as a "close encounter of the first/second kind." First Kind observations were classified as no interaction, while second kind observations included the "visitation" of a vehicle, device, or UFO. Third Kind observations involved seeing actual beings. Fourth Kind was alien abduction. Fifth Kind was defined by "response from UFO to human desire for contact." Close encounters of the Sixth Kind involved injury or death caused by the UFO. Seventh involved hybrid offspring between humans and aliens. Eighth involved the aliens mentally controlling the humans, while the final close encounter, the Ninth Kind, something strictly for the annals of Science Fiction involved humans partially or completely transforming into aliens. Some futurists and alien hunters have wanted to complete the list with a Tenth Kind, one that has humans fighting back, successfully. This has not been implemented because most of these theorists know full well that humans have no chance against a hostile alien force.

The point of this UFO back story is that much of the jungle ghost talk may be rooted in an actual alien hotspot, somewhere that on planet earth they choose to land. Within remote tropical forests that are off the satellite radar grid, with bountiful forest canopy cover. This is why parking flight MH370 deep in the Cambodian jungle made sense. The stories of these rich wildernesses harbor ancient tales through civilizations that have come and gone. Detailed expressions of people who had figured it all out to then disappear, cease to be, or end in quiet demise. Millennia of dynasties. All those warriors and chieftains, all that bloody sacrifice and orgiastic lovemaking. Natives doing what natives do best. And the increasing possibility of extraterrestrial visitors over, say, any century really. But I digress.

Oh the mystery and charm of Angkor Wat, the gloriously moated 12th century Buddhist-Hindu temple deep in the heart of northern Cambodia. Discovered in the late 1500s by a Catholic Portuguese Capuchin friar, who was unable to describe "its glory with a pen since there is no other building like it in the world." Elaborate and decorated with every conceivable refinement reserved for man, the building is the physical manifestation of human genius. Built by the Khmer Empire and dedicated to Vishnu, its ultimate legacy would be that of a fallen city. Europeans encouraged a deep archeological effort in order to solve the riddle of this potentially lost civilization that possessed their own Asian Michelangelo capable of such elaborate architecture. A barbaric people able to outdo the best of Greece or Rome, it was inconceivable that it could be built by them. Unless of course they had help. The 500-plus acre compound was completed at the zenith of their empire in the year 802, and sustained for another 600 years until being conquered by the Thais. Palaces, terraces, pools, reservoirs, much of the auxiliary buildings, and foundation footprints have since been mapped by NASA and its forensic aerial topography and ground-sensing radar methods to discover what was the largest empire at its time.

But something else was discovered. A mirroring city to the north, buried in the jungle, yet just as elaborate. It was older, by many millennia in fact. This lost city was deemed "Top Secret." After the Vietnam war was wrapped up a team of NASA archeologists made a trip to the jungle to laser scan from helicopters the ground below. The technology allowed for topographical mapping through the jungle flora, with an ability to see 1,000X that of the human eye. What was described as "mind-bending," those on the team were able to recreate lotus-bud towers, the friezes of demons, kings, warriors, willing nymphs, battle scenes, and small people with cartoonishly large heads and eyes, complete with 3-fingered hands. The official government ruse for the downfall of the city-state was overpopulation which triggered unsustainable deforestation, leading to the failure of the topsoil and an overwhelmed irrigation system. This is the official narrative to this day, repeated over and over again to the millions of tourists that visit each year.

As civilizations are born and completed over and again they also become forgotten. What is has been. As we learn that our inventions are merely reinventions and our discoveries are rediscoveries, it's hard to not think we are on a time loop of sorts, always taken aback by a "golden age" which once existed that now we strive to return to. When men lived with gods, commingling their passions and vices with divine beings, there was more joy and tranquility. It was about mutual confidence, and the bounty of earth and the boundless variety of life. People spoke through telepathy, and on average lived to one hundred. But then again is this mythology for something to attain or is it a true account, and we are here now in modern times jaded and wide awake from such a gentle slumber? Could we return to this paradise without the purging of evil, the toxicity of ignorance and ways of the bad guys? There is only one way to find out.

Imagine All the People

Anonymous ID; TB+ANS Tue 19 Feb 21:08:54 No. 149055 ViewReport
50 "years" of misery
If you survive infanticide

"dragons"
Orphan girls
Patriarchy [playbook]
Brokers = lepers
Purveyors = flow
Needle in the HAYstack
Still ~~fucking~~ peasants
"folks on the hill"

John Lennon figured if he remained in the spotlight for the remainder of his life that it would be 50 more years of misery. He knew from his early travels to India that there was a saddening cultural phenomenon at work, that of unwanted girls, abandoned children, victims of a male-biased culture. India's girl orphans needed help, and John was obliged to do what he could. Girls at birth were killed at a striking rate, something like half a million a year. And this is how India has the most imbalanced gender ratios. And as a result, the highest rates of teenage rape. There isn't much to look forward to if you do survive infanticide.

Known for some of the most famous lyrics of the 20th century, he had a way with words, but this gem was a quote he told an interviewer in the mid 1970s. It's something that has always stuck with me, there is a vulnerability in such words of honesty:

"I believe in everything until it's disproved. So I believe in fairies, the myths, dragons. It all exists, even if it's in your mind. Who's to say that dreams and nightmares aren't as real as the here and now."

Low key, and settled at the end of a suburban street of well-tended gardens is the orphanage that John Lennon calls home. His days are spent, along with a dozen helpers, tending to the needs of the rotating guest list of girls. Cots comprise most of the larger rooms, and babies are sorted from the toddlers and teens. The baby rooms are oddly quiet, as they are diligently fed on schedule. Other rooms are not so quiet, those that consist of the more insane kids and those with other physical ailments. When you see the array of disabilities you cannot but think of some cruelty from above, how could God create in his likeness such broken humans. The more damaged children have a harder time getting adopted, mostly from Western countries. Some of the orphan girls stay in touch with their birth parents, mothers who did not want to abandon them but were forced under the patriarchy playbook. When the wealthy white Westerners arrive to pick up their babies it is quite the sight. The genuine love that the couples, often heartbroken for years, have for a child they already love so much before a physical touch. For John this is what it is all about.

"That peace and love, man, it never gets old."

But like anything in India there is a quick bounce back to something strikingly polar opposite, that of the government-encouraged and funded programs to find child brides in the orphanages.

"It's total bullocks, but you know it's part of their traditions so we just have to go with it."

There are grooming tours of young men, mostly in their early twenties, who visit the orphanage with their families, parents and siblings, looking for that ideal child bride. The decision isn't based entirely on attractiveness but on how the girl may look within the caste system, the levels of darkness in her skin, is she void of deformities, does she have a hopeful glint of elegance, all those aspects that cannot be learned. For the girls of destitution there is only one way, and that is up. Many are excited by the prospect. The wedding costs--jewelry, dresses, receptions--are paid for by the state. In some ways the program works for India, of course out of the context of this sweaty and overpopulated place, frankly, this shithole, the concept is quite absurd and seemingly illegal. But when you can get a kid off the streets while taking out another incel or potential bus rapist, so be it. Those that remained behind still had John's focus, including that of much needed education.

"You see, the problem is ignorance. These girls know absolutely nothing, so they go with the flow. What they need is education, in order to obtain a larger life view. Think of all the culture they miss by not having a family, so we have dance classes, music classes, even talent shows."

This is where I need to jump ahead to the more ominous reason for The Beatle in the slum, that of ongoing attempts from global child predators to mine the fields of Indian orphanages for sex slaves. Of course the purveyors and "brokers" have no interest in the lepers or severely disabled but there is interest in the needle in the haystack, that beautiful child that can move up the ranks and within a life of luxury and opulence gifted by pimps and johns, emerge as a beauty queen. John's focus is to keep the children from that darkness, to ensure a most merciful life is bestowed upon each child he comes into contact with, knowing there is only so much that he can do and that there are sometimes forces beyond his control. And this is why I came to meet with him. He had information that was almost too unreal even for my jaded mind.

From John's song "Working Class Hero," the first single off his 1970 album "John Lennon/Plastic Ono Band," his first music after the breakup of the Beatles:

As soon as you are born they make you feel small
By giving you no time instead of it all
Til the pain is so big you feel nothing at all
They hurt you at home and they hit you at school
They hate you if you're clever and they despise a fool
Til you're so fucking crazy you can't follow their rules
When they've tortured and scared you for twenty-odd years
Then they expect you to pick a career
When you can't really function you're so full of fear

Keep you doped with religion and sex and TV
And you think you're so clever and classless and free
But you're still fucking peasants as far as I can see
There's room at the top they are telling you still
But first you must learn how to smile as you kill
If you want to be like the folks on the hill...

Zorro Ranch & the Honey Pot Trap

Anonymous ID; TB+ANS Wed 9 Feb 8:11:12 <u>No. 149059</u> ViewReport
Big Sky ~~America~~
"Super strain"
Armand Hammer United World College of the American West
Charles/Andrew
Trementine Base
"Sex chambers"
Trinity project
~~White~~ Sands
Bikini Atoll
Blast radius
B. Gita
"Demon core"
33rd latitude
Roswell - Bermuda - Hiroshima

Zorro Ranch
Supermodels = Cool Americana
Heyday = angels
Local "arts"
Bill Richardson "energy scty"
Bill Clinton "ex potus"
Sex enclaves
Kingmaker
cover [story]
Club of Rome
Eugenics
Bill Gates = underage boys
cloud vault
empire

Oh New Mexico, the Land of Enchantment, that big sky America, a state of secrets, from the White Sands nuclear bomb test sites to the Manhattan Project, so why no better place for Jeffrey Epstien's isolated Zorro Ranch, a sprawling 1,159 acre desert compound, a place guaranteed to ensure his most sacred secret, that of his desire to clone himself, while engineering his DNA into a super strain of human. Yes, you read that correctly. An experiment that involved rogue international doctors, and his own sexual prowess that required sex with forty different girls/women over a thirty day period. When Epsetin bought the property in the early 1990s it wasn't about the beauty of the barren land, or some peaceful respite far from New York City, no, it was more about the protection afforded criminals. After all, this was the state the Catholic Church sent their accused pedophile priests to hide out in parishes. This is home to the Armand Hammer United World College of the American West, made famous for being the boarding school of Prince Charles and Andrew. This is where Pueblo Nation can be bought off with truckloads of booze and tobacco. And of course, this is the home to the most elite order of Scientology, the Trementine Base, a vast network of underground vaults and bunkers, which "officially" hold and preserve the original writings of L. Ron Hubbard, while unofficially are consisting of panic rooms and sex chambers. Oh, and when Mr. Hubbard returns to earthly human form it is here that he will appear. It's all about preparation for that divine event.

Folklore carries the stories of the desert forth. This is the theory when there are few witnesses. The truth becomes second hand stories and riffs on what took place with only the wind and wild animals as witness. It's within this same spirit that the conspiracies surrounded the very public Trinity Project, that first atomic bomb test two hundred miles south of Santa Fe on the White Sands Proving Ground. The year was 1945, a full year before the second test that occurred in the Bikini Atoll of the South Pacific. As legend goes there was a blind teenage girl named Georgia Green who claims she was able to see the flash of the test from over a hundred miles away. Her doctor quickly dismissed her claims, but she continued a regimen of staring at the sun, eyes wide open, and within a year had cured her blindness. She was able to see for the first time. When medical journals began discussing this miracle in the desert it was to discredit her as someone who had lost her mind by being within the blast radius, that the radiation was eating her brains.

The chief scientist of the nuclear project, J. Robert Oppenheimer, after witnessing the mushroom cloud of the first atomic bomb, quoted from the sacred Hindu text, the Bhagavad Gita: "I am become Death, destroyer of worlds." The choice of the codename Trinity became mysterious on its own. Did Oppenheimer choose it? Did it refer to a three-personed god? Did it have anything to do with the "demon core," the name of the fourteen pounds of plutonium in the bomb? Theorists would extoll the prevalence of the number 33. The site of the test was on the thirty-third line of latitude north, as was Roswell, New Mexico. The thirty third latitude north ran through the Bermuda Triangle as well as the Japanese cities of Nagasaki and Hiroshima. The president at the time, Harry Truman, was the thirty third president of the United States. He was also a thirty three degree Freemason, the highest ranking possible. But the hook to the conspiracy is that an extraterrestrial spacecraft was on its way to the White Sands Proving Ground when it crashed. These technologically superior aliens were coming to warn the US military of the inherent dangers of nuclear weapons. That the splitting of atomic nuclei is never a good idea, that you might as well release a demon on humanity.

To say New Mexico is a pedophile's wet dream is to understate the most obvious, this vast land has been established as a go-to for the uber wealthy and power elite. And that is why Zorro Ranch fast became a known secret. When Epsetin applied for a permit for a grass landing strip, the county commissioner said they would need to send an inspector, which Epstein did not allow. He went ahead and built the strip anyway. It was his interest in theoretical physics, cryogenics and eugenics that brought him here.

The mid 1990s were the heyday of the supermodel, the likes of Cindy Crawford, Claudia Schiffer, Linda Evangelista, and Naomi Campbell. Those most-photographed women of the era, the high gloss advertisements and cat walk swagger raising the bar for Cool Americana, while paving the way for decades more to come. Whatever these tall skinny women touched turned to gold. And it was with this in mind that Epstein devised a plan for the turnaround of his fledgling brand Victoria's Secret. What consisted of affordable mall lingerie for soccer moms, the brand needed a facelift. Epstein was quietly the majority shareholder of VS, and it was his idea, as a self-described connoisseur of fine women to raise the "consciousness" of the brand, to embed it into the American subconscious. Thus he began the nationally televised fashion show. And he paid the high fees for the best models. He had stores begin selling plus size, and the ever-growing in demand push-up bras. The brand blew up. And this was all the cache he needed for his own procurement farms of hot young girls with the dream of being an "Angel," allowing them to let down their guards and travel to Zorro Ranch. The ranch's all-night parties became legendary. The lights were so bright that they would drown out the starry nights and could be seen from neighbor ranches miles away. Nobody complained because of the insanely large amount of property tax that Epstein paid which funded so much of the community, as well his generous donations to the local arts. He was a city slicker that knew how to buy a wink and a nod.

And this is why even after his Florida conviction for prostituting a minor, local officials never required him to register as a sex offender. These power plays are what added to the hive of secrets. Patterns of deception that involved government bureaucrats, an invisible force field to shield himself from accountability. And all of this remained a secret to the girls who visited the ranch. It was later revealed that his most frequent guest was Bill Richardson, the governor of New Mexico, and former Energy Secretary and UN Ambassador for Bill Clinton. It all led back to who benefited by knowing Epstein, and the potential downside when it would all be exposed.

The compartmental world that we all know and live by allows for us to look away from things that are too exotic or foreign for our ways, like futuristic cults, or hideout sex enclaves, high tech laboratories and black government ops. As humans, it's as if we need to see it, or to go through it with our own emotions, before we can register as something viable and with the potential to exist. For most of us we perceive the world through the prism of the media, with so much left out, like those mad scientists and the high-end orgies with billionaires and young beauties. This is how things went down in the high desert of New Mexico. This is why the elites traveled in the same circles, this is why they kept things under wraps. Not just for their own pleasure but for self-preservation. Someone always had dirt on another.

As the kingmaker of blackmail, Epstein never used anything he had, just the threat was enough. And this is where Bill Gates, of Microsoft fame, enters stage right. The affable Seattle nerd was not so much the nice and decent man portrayed of him over the many decades of his celebrity. No, this was a man on a hell-bent mission to prove his haters that he was more powerful than God. With the cover story of his philanthropy he was able to go about with his plan, backed by the Club of Rome, of population control. And he was interested in Epstein's eugenics works. He even funded him with a cool billion to bring in the best doctors, many of them Germans who had quietly carried on the studies of the Nazis. But also Bill had a fetish. He liked his toes sucked. Yes, sick and twisted I know. But add that he wanted it done by underage boys and now you had a story. Epstein arranged for a series of sessions at Zorro Ranch, which was secretly documented by Mossad cameras and uploaded to a cloud vault. This alone may not be enough to bring down such a man and his empire, but what he did at the end of the session, beating himself off and yelling, "Not today Satan," was enough to get anyone else admitted to an insane asylum. And as he had fallen into Epstein's honey pot trap he now would be under his command.

Weiner's Hard Drive

Anonymous ID; TB+ANS Thu 6 Apr 20:12:34 <u>No. 149059</u> ViewReport
Schumer "protégé"
full length mirror
abruptly resigned
HA
Obama "distraction"
Carlos Danger
Target ~~audience~~
"Let a lot of people down"
Sydney Leathers
NYPD acquires Weiner laptop
Pay-to-play schemes
Clinton Foundation
Life insurance
"A mystery for now"
Saudi Ministry of National Guard
Jailhouse suicide?
Heart attack?
Potassium chloride
Bicarbonate
Harvey Weinstein

"Final" demise?

New York Senator Chuck Schumer was Anthony Weiner's mentor going back to 1985 when the newly graduated high school boy interned for the then-Congressman. When Schumer ascended to become a US Senator his protégé began a career in politics of his own, assuming Schumer's Congressional seat for NY. It was a short-lived career for Carlos Danger, his online handle, when he was swiftly brought down by a scandalous sexting maze of deceit and deviance culminating in his resignation from public office. To this day Schumer will not mention Weiner's name. Weiner claimed to have had his social media account hacked, but everyone knew what he posted was from him, that of a picture of himself in bulging underwear. That is the one the public saw, it looked like a banana stuffed into a pair of tighty whities. It was fairly innocuous for what adults tend to share with each other, but in his case the recipients were underage girls. Also, they received two more photos--ones never made public--located on his infamous laptop, of him totally nude, fully erect, and posing into a full length mirror. When it became apparent that he sent these to young girls his actions were abruptly condemned by those on both sides of the aisle and he resigned.

His wife, Huma Abadin, moved out of their apartment and into Hillary Clinton's NYC residence. Hillary was her boss and alleged lover with the cover story that she was like her mother, and Bill was like a father, after all he officiated the wedding between Huma and Anthony. Even then-President Obama chimed in, "This is a distraction and as a Congressman, Weiner has said it himself, that his behavior was inappropriate; dishonesty was inappropriate. He should resign." A series of online chats were released to the media between his virtual ego Carlos and several minors. Most of the content was harmless, with nothing indecent or explicit. It appeared to be nothing more than a lonely man with dustings of megalomania seeking out an online dopamine rush. But he was married, with a small child of his own, and his target audience were underage girls.

A few years passed of Weiner in self-imposed isolation, only to emerge announcing that he would run for mayor of NYC. "Look I have made some big mistakes and I have let a lot of people down, but I also have learned some tough lessons. I am running because I've been fighting for the middle class to make it for my entire life and I hope I get a second chance to work for you." Everything seemed fine and the public was behind his comeback story. He was back with Huma. Their toddler son was an adorable mix of Jew and Arab. Then a new sexting scandal surfaced. This one involved 22-year-old Sydney Leathers, and a picture of himself in boxers, fully erect, with his sleeping 4-year-old son curled up next to him in bed. This led to an investigation that revealed Weiner was having an unrelated sexual affair with a 15-year-old. It was reported that the girl was "troubled" and that the relationship was consensual as she was obsessed with him.

This is when the NYPD first came into contact with Weiner's laptop. The hard drive was a treasure trove of undisclosed emails from Hillary to Huma. And within this was Huma's own "Life Insurance" folder to protect her from assassination by Hillary. It included evidence of their sex crimes, other child exploitation, money laundering, pay-to-play schemes, perjury and various felony crimes. It was enough to put Hillary away for life, and for that matter Bill as well. It contained information on the Clinton Foundation and an elaborate money laundering scheme of billions siphoned off from Haiti relief funds. It contained payout ledgers of Bill's rape victims. And it included a video of Hillary in the act of adrenochrome extraction. The laptop had been examined by two retiring NYC detectives and one digital forensic expert. It was parked overnight with the Property Clerk in Evidence Room #4, at Precinct 1 of NYPD where it was lost in the early morning hours. This laptop may or may not be in my possession. That piece of information will need to remain a mystery for now.

Huma was considered safe, even if she was the target of Hillary's rage she was deeply rooted in Saudi intelligence circles and had the Kingdom's Ministry of National Guard surveilling her. That wasn't the case for Weiner. He was shaken to the core with fear of a jailhouse suicide or sudden heart attack. The playbook for heart attacks worked best with the healthier and in shape guys as it was scary to think if it could happen to them then why not you?

And in that narcissistic exchange there was a suspension of belief over one's own self concern. What could appear as a heart attack was nothing more than a stopping of the heart through potassium chloride. The same ingredients used in capital punishments. Any excessive dosing can be detected in an autopsy so the administered amount is important. An alternative is bicarbonate which increases blood pH causing an adrenaline rush making the heart pump harder against blood vessels that cannot handle the pressure. This results in what appears to be a most conventional heart attack. Grayanotoxin combined with ricin is a direct toxic shock to the heart which induces an actual heart attack. Someone on the physically stronger side may survive, someone like Weiner. Someone like Harvey Weinstein would die. An air embolism occurs and fills up the heart's chambers with oxygen, blocking the entry of blood. In order for this to work the embolus must be massive. With the blood vessels open, normal amounts of blood get to the heart, ensuring there is no heart damage yet. Then a constant pain sets in--those classic heart attack characteristics--from the partial blockage leading to the final demise after several minutes and the lights out moment of death.

Afternoon Tea with the Walrus

Anonymous ID; TB+ANS Sun 9 Apr 2:32:44 <u>No. 149061</u> ViewReport
Legend on Arab Street
"Big floor puzzle"
Mexican cartels
rejected disabled class
Destination ~~unknown~~
Jewish mathematician
Panama Papers
"Self-contained"
Electronic record
Border enforcement [not]
~~Black~~ communities
Democratic party "highest levels"

John's favorite part of the day, like most Englishmen, is when he takes his afternoon cup of tea. In India he has migrated his taste from Earl Grey to Mint, a taste he acquired in Marrakech, Morocco, where he briefly stayed with Jim Morrison shortly after his own faked death, early 1981. There is something about mint tea that is exquisitely delicious when piping hot and you are there sipping it in 100% relative humidity. Legend on the Arab street is that it's the only way to cool your body down, from the inside.

"When you ask me what I know, I don't want to go on some kind of rote memory riff of all the rather strange things I have seen, but I can tell you this, Mother Teresa was not involved. At least her involvement was not conscious on her part. She was a pawn, a useful idiot if you will," he said.

We were seated in the backyard of the orphanage. Stucco walls draped with bougainvillea, it was a tropical respite from the overwhelming heartbreak inside.

"Lady Di visited in the mid-80s I think it was, along with Mother Theresa, and frankly I was nervous they would realize who I was and out me to the paparazzi. Diana assured me with that wry smile that I had nothing to worry about. I still don't know if she knew who I was or that's just how she works the room, you know. A very attractive bird, my mum would have been so proud that I had come so close to royalty."

"Is there anything present day that could help us out?," I finally ask to steer him to the point of our meet up.

"It's like a big floor puzzle Tony. Lots of pieces, some missing and some not making sense. It's only when you can assemble enough that the picture comes through. Then the benefit of distance, to be able to stand back and take in the entire image. Only then can you connect the dots."

One of the older orphan girls interrupts us with a fresh decanter of tea.

"I can tell you that the Mexican cartels have been here."

"All the way to India?"

"Yes, they are procuring the girls."

"Have they been successful?"

"From some orphanages, yes. Not with mine. I play it off when they come because I don't want a fight. It's almost like those American Western movies when the bad guys come to town. I get them to leave me alone by telling them my kids are of a rejected disabled caste."

"Jesus Christ."

"However, the word from other orphanages is they will take several girls back to a nearby abandoned airstrip and fly them off. Destination unknown. But into a world of trafficking and blackmail."

"Tell me what you know about the blackmail."

"C'mon you must know this already."

"Maybe but I gotta know what you are seeing."

"There is this New Yorker named Epstein, small Jewish mathematician. He is filthy rich, but that is his cover story. He is an agent for someone, or a country, and he has his hands in all of the trafficking. And he is a high level blackmailer."

"I have heard this too."

"He uses the cartels to get the girls, then he is tasked with entrapping a high level mark. Have you ever heard of the Panama Papers?"

"Yes, of course."

"Did you notice how that story self-contained so quickly, even though every wealthy person on earth had money in those companies. It was killed off fast by the media because of those involved, but mainly by the bankers. Even low level bank employees wouldn't talk because they had all been compromised."

"Caught in Epstein's web?"

"Yes, there was some form of electronic record of them being with kids."

"Why are the cartels involved, shouldn't they be dealing drugs?"

"It loops back to drugs. Stay with me here. Their biggest market is the US, like America alone consumes half of the drugs in the world. So they want access to the cities, to highway routes, to housing projects. Enter the Democratic Party. High level players are paid off for favorable treatment, either through lax border enforcement, or the defunding of police departments, even the ruin of American cities. They can do this without anyone raising an eyebrow. Americans don't expect much of their black communities so this all goes unquestioned."

"Yes, it's called the soft bigotry of low expectations."

"Any counter talk of border enforcement or economic zones in these inner cities is shot down as xenophobia or racism and nothing changes. But invisibly the drug flow remains."

"So the cartels have compromised the Democratic party?"

"Yes, to the highest levels."

<u>Choke On This</u>

Anonymous ID; TB+ANS Thu 10 May 4:42:14 <u>No.</u>
<u>149063</u> ViewReport
"Accidental suffocation"
American private detectives
"appetite for deviant sex"
Bangkok renegade
"spiraling opiate addiction"
[satellite] phone
Thai jungle = JBR
Large database of blackmail intel
ATMs [filmed sex]
"gradation of perversions"
Refund gaps
Asian "flat ass"
Neo-vagina = holy grail
Pamplona
John Mark Karr
Peel the onion

Death scenes do not get much seedier than that of
David Carradine's early demise in the cramped closet of
a Bangkok motel room. In what was ruled by local
authorities as an "accidental suffocation during lone sex
play" his ex-wife countered with he "never flew solo" so
he must have been murdered. In fact, all four ex-wives
revealed his penchant for autoerotic asphyxiation but
with the caveat that he liked others around. Mainly for
the thrill of scaring them, but as well as protection if
things went too far. This narrative could also be
countered for insurance purposes, that his policy would
pay out if there was indeed foul play but not a suicide.

For David it was enough to confuse all those following the story and ensure his own escape into the Asian jungle life. Being choked out to the point of orgasm was a major piece of contention in his third marriage, so why could it not be the reason for his premature demise. American private detectives hired by his widow, the fourth wife, knew that he liked to carry cash and wear expensive jewelry. This could have attracted the wrong crowd.

In Bangkok working on the film "Stretch," his body was found in the Swissotel Nai Lert Park Hotel by an unsolicited young woman, one who authorities let go after a brief interview, someone the family believes was involved in a hit of sorts. The Carradine family attorney even went so far as to blame the death on a secret sect of kung fu assassins. This allowed for Carradine's plan to fall into accordance while he settled into the final chapter of his life, that of a non-famous, and non-bothered, wallflower. Away from the exes and the attorneys that he loathed so. Lawsuits were filed against the production company of the film he was making, alleging breach of contract and wrongful death. At least one of his ex-wives tried to clear his further tarnished legacy by claiming he never wanted to hurt anyone intentionally, that his appetite for deviant sex need not be aired to the public. His "life as a renegade was mystified through a constant infusion of alcohol and drugs, and his early demise need not leave people with certain thoughts of him."

The body used for the scene of death was that of a German sex trafficker, your standard low-grade local pimp, but tall and thin, bald. After the brief autopsy there was the required cremation as morgues were not an option as space was limited. Wife #1, "We must understand him now as a human being, not a celluloid fantasy, with faults and his own demons, and for people to understand why he was like this." But wife #3 would have nothing of this polished gem of a memory of the man. "Our marriage was derailed by incest, yes, you read that right. It was a relationship he had with a younger relative, I will refer to only as X, which spanned at least two of his marriages." She had caught him in a compromising situation with X and pleaded for him to get counseling, to no avail. More accusations of a spiraling opiate addiction fueled the flames of the suicide narrative.

It would be a decade later that I made contact with David, deep in the Thai jungles, at an undisclosed location, somewhere even I was not privy to, as we chatted by satellite phone after a brief email exchange. He had information on JonBenet Ramsey. This time it was a lead not about her potential killer, but the shattering notion that her death was faked.

"Tony, I know all the pedophiles down this way. I also know about the stuff that doesn't take place. It's kinda what I gotta do, get to know them, let them think we're friends, take pictures with them, stuff they send back to England and Germany, allow them that access to a Hollywood star. You have to remember, I was way more famous in Europe than I ever was in the States. So with access comes a certain level of comfort, where they may ask me for particular favors, or for specific needs. Of course it is always perverted stuff. Like if I know any kids for sale or where to buy poppers. Much of it is sick, and I am beyond the point of being disgusted, because it really is just what is here in Asia. Am I on their level? No, but do I like the girls young, yes, but I do the 18 over thing. And the rumors of me liking choke play are true, can't really hide that when you have a bunch of ex-wives all telling the same story over and again. I just like it here. The humidity is good for my arthritis. The steamy air does wonders on my face, it's like I haven't aged since I moved here. My diet consists of rice and fruit, and tight pussy if you catch my drift. Sometimes the pimps send me girls to try out, to introduce to the business. I go easy, hell I am an old man. I like the sex to be as vanilla as possible. And I am not here on vacation. This is my home. You remember that saying, don't shit where you eat? Well that's my mantra for life."

Carradine had his unique style of charm and it worked in a place like this. Stateside living at this point wouldn't be an option. Woke culture and political correctness were not something he could process. This was a man that lived on the fringes of 60s and 70s Hollywood, at best a B-list star really, who operated with a scummy patina, within a glossed-over biker culture rebellion, mixed in with the mystery of the East and his affinity for martial arts. He was a chameleon, someone who was comfortable playing the part, especially that of his own production, American-made shaman, viral and ready to pop. He had built a large database of blackmail intel, most of the perps were unknown wealthy businessmen from London, Munich or Berlin. Executives with big global brands like Mercedes and Bayer. The varying levels of acquired intel consisted of pictures and receipts. Even far off photos of men withdrawing money from ATMs with young girls by their side, or the real jackpot stuff of filmed sex, sometimes on the perp's own phone, for his private collection, which was then stolen by the girl while she quickly escaped the room. This move was risky but if it was done when he was asleep and naked there would not be any chance of him taking chase. Without his cell he was screwed. Local cell phone stores were another racket. Often selling burner phones for $1,000 USD. Rolexes were big too, either as targets for being stolen, or used as trade for a cell phone. For an additional $500 USD the "techs" were able to clone your original cell number. Sure your contacts were lost but when you called your wife at least it was from your number. Any evidence acquired was bagged and secured outside of town. These pimps and girls never knew who was who. They graded levels of wealth by how fat a man was. However some of the more fit guys were actually the titans of industry, the whales that you wanted to target, not some low-level mid-manager from middle America. Often under the cover of scouting for new factory and production operations, these businessmen were personally scoping out the poon scene, and for some the boy, or boi, set.

In a gradation of perversion you had at the top of the food chain the guys who liked children, I am talking infant to toddler, next level from that are young boys, next would be those who were into older boys, next up those who liked the young girls, then those who liked the trannies, of any age. "There are no chicks with dicks, just dudes with boobs," was an expression we reminded ourselves when we came across some of the more attractive ones. Plastic surgery, though fairly barbaric compared to Western practices, was more common than one would think. The most standard was run-of-the-mill breast augmentations, either on the aforementioned he-shes or on actual females who, as was common with Asian women of all descents, were small-chested. Most went from A-cups to C-cups. The most dangerous silicone was used, often re-used from upgraded operations Stateside, with a certain guarantee for them to leak within a couple of years. These girls ran the risk because the bigger their tits the more they could charge for their time. Of course there were johns who liked the flat chest aesthetic. What they were after, for obvious reasons, was a semblance to a child, or even a boy. It kinda reminds me of the heroin chic that Gianni Versace ushered into the fashion world early 90s. That whole Kate Moss look, small buds for tits with the only real definition being the nubs of her areolas.

These plastic surgery operations were often botched, sometimes resulting in unmatched implants, or large scarring from the base of the breast all the way vertical to the nipple, then the full 360 scar around the nipple footprint. The consequences of full numbness of feeling was nothing for these girls as many, without really knowing it, were dead inside, so why not expand that lack of feeling to the tips of their tits. "Refund gaps," that resulting procedure where the breasts are separated by several inches was normalized and even desired by some girls, making you ponder how desire can be manipulated by the environment or newly offered goods. Ass lifts, the infamous Brazilian Butt Lift Miami ideal, were catching on but the Asian flat ass remained in demand. It was a lingering look that ran contrary to the fake big booty ideation that had so rapidly empowered the Western aesthetic. For many it was refreshing to see smaller ass, besides, for the johns they said the smaller the ass the bigger their dicks looked. Vaginoplasties, those dreadful labia reconstruction operations, involving the slicing off of extra skin from the pussy lips, in what looks like garbled deep-fried calamari rings, was hot, and reserved for those in their early thirties, or anyone with more than three kids. Usually a stateside surgery reserved for the American milf, even gilf, those who in later stages of life want to tidy up the garage, those cougars who are dating again and feel shame for the flaps. I could go on but you get the picture. Neo-vagina and neo-penis surgeries were the holy grail. These could easily run over $10,000 USD, and were mostly performed on visiting foreigners, known as surgery tourists. American and Euro transgenders who were eager to chop it all off, or build it up. Bring that phantom penis to life. Or slice it off and invert it. Make that prostate into a G-spot. In many ways the local surgeons were at the forefront of transitional surgery, much like the doctors of Pamplona are the most adept, globally, for treating bull gorging. But I digress.

Carradine claims to know who may have been responsible for JonBenet Ramsey's untimely demise. And it isn't who you think it is. Not her mom, not her dad, not her brother, not Santa man, not the maid, not the electrician. Not even John Mark Karr, the creepy as fuck school teacher arrested in Bangkok. In order to unravel this mystery within an enigma I must unpack for the sake of storytelling a small tale of the Panama Papers, and in the peeling of that onion and subsequent tears the forces behind one of the biggest financial frauds to date, and cover story for the money side of the worst global child prostitution rings.

Panama Papers

Anonymous ID; TB+ANS Sat 10 Apr 13:12:14 <u>No. 149062</u> ViewReport
Mossack Fonseca [11mil docs]
80 countries
Vladimir = CCP

~~Organized~~ crime
Lack of transparency
"undermines global economy"
"jaw dropping"
Origins = Antwerp
[onshore]
Delaware, Joe Biden
Lithuanian Shopping Centre ☐ ~~U2~~
Maltese national
Published dispatch
Initial stratagem
Bush ~~Dynasty~~
Deep State
Fellow citizens
psychological weapon
avoid the ~~spotlight~~
Deflection
Talmud
Warfare
Fog the public's eye?
Pandemic?
weather vane
New Testament

In early 2016 eleven million financial documents detailing offshore banking activities from thousands of individuals, some ultra-famous others unknown, broke down what financial forensic experts claimed were "jaw-dropping" and "terrifying" money moves in what would soon become known as the Panama Papers. These documents originated from the Panamanian law firm

Mossack Fonseca, detailing over 200,000 incorporated entities in offshore accounts with owners that were impossible to trace. Over 80 countries were involved. The dizzying complexity of how these businesses were structured were beyond the skill sets of the investigative journalists who were first involved. It was beyond even tax collectors and law enforcement. What was known was that it all led back to money laundering for the purpose of covering up varying levels of nefarious activities.

When the story had picked up some steam, and the mainstream media were no longer able to keep the genie in the bottle big names began to be leaked. The prime minister of Iceland was the first casualty. The father of then-British Prime Minister David Cameron was named several times and the PM had to publicly explain why. Putin's name was everywhere but journalists were careful to name him as they knew his assassins had global reach in the event Vladimir wanted them permanently silenced. All the heads of the Chinese Communist Party were in there, but China spun the narrative that it was a smear campaign instigated by the West to defame the country, and was nothing more than "racism." The papers were peak corruption in the form of economical organized crime. And much of it was circling back to child prostitution rings. The World Bank came out with their own statement of diversion, alluding to the fact that "tax evasion was bleeding these developing countries dry" when all they needed was "more development." One American senator, the first

US politician to speak of the papers, spoke of the "lack of transparency" that undermines the "functions of the global economy."

As the onion was peeled it kept getting worse, the web was more complex than anyone could imagine. Strange occurrences began to happen around the globe. A Russian oligarch drowned during his morning swim. A top EU financial official was struck down and killed during a hit and run while on his evening walk with his family in Antwerp. A banker in Finland hung himself. People began to act nervous. At last there was that alarming calm that comes before a storm. The vice president of Panama called for a special commission to be set up. The intrigue was right out of an espionage thriller but was playing out on the world's stage, with bit players in all corners of the globe reacting, evading, covering up. What the public did know about is what angered them the most, and that was how the havens were tolerated as a means for the ultra-rich to benefit further. All this money that was escaping taxation while third and fourth world countries were enslaved by debt service. How the elite were protected from the prying eyes. It brought heat to the "onshore" operations being run out of secrecy centers in Delaware and London, where any enforcement or legislation was shielded by corrupt politicians. For reasons unknown these havens were exempt from the "multilateral automatic exchange" of information among tax authorities. Much of this was written into law from legislation pitched in the 1980s by then-Senator for Delaware, Joe Biden.

On the surface this was a political thriller like no other. Battles ensued between government agencies over who had jurisdiction over who and what, or the origins of certain offshore accounts and where they had begun and ended. A globally-spun network of cleverly hidden digital traces like no other, designed to further confuse and lay the groundwork for the impossibility of indictments. But heads rolled, top dogs were forced to resign. Celebrities caught in the web had to devise elaborate excuses for their involvement, with blame casted toward wayward money managers. Rock star Bono, of U2 fame, outed as a buyer of a Lithuanian shopping center through a Maltese account, was forced to release a statement to try and save his good name as a crusader for the poor and disenfranchised. "I would be extremely distressed if even as a passive minority investor anything less than exemplary was done with my name anywhere near it. I take this stuff very seriously. I have campaigned for the beneficial ownership of offshore companies to be made transparent."

The hypocrisy was rich. Peak do as I say not as I do. In what was turning out to be the largest data leak of all time, the lead journalist following the story explored the deep involvement of the global mafia. Daphne Galizia, a Maltese national, with her last published dispatch connecting a payment from the government of Azerbaijan to the prime minister of Malta, was abruptly taken out by a car bomb in her driveway. No group came forward to claim responsibility. Malta's president called for calm, "In these moments, when the country is shocked by such a vicious attack, I call on everyone to measure their words, to not pass judgement and to show solidarity." However, Europe's underworld was now on notice that perhaps her death would lead to more data drops, as often the insurance that is set up by these journalists is a file release in the event of their untimely demise. At this point 11.5 million documents have been released.

The entire initial stratagem of the Panama Papers, or the web of global financial deceit before it had a name, was for the sole purpose of an undercover financial pipeline to arrange for child trafficking. Of course there were do-good wealthy people who were innocently pulled into this nefarious labyrinth of laundering and deception, and those folks should have their names cleared. But for the real actors, those players that went all in with their investments and direct deposits to then be delivered on the other end a child of their pleasing, they will pay, and dearly. Many names may be familiar while even those that are unfamiliar are involved with others, or companies, that somehow directly affect you. The political class is anyone who has been around politics for over forty years, your Clintons, your Joe Bidens, even the Bush dynasty. Collectively they have pulled the puppet strings of dare I say "the deep state" to ensure there is enough division within government, and between its fellow citizens, that nobody gets around to looking into the papers, as any deep dive would unravel the mystery.

A common psychological weapon used by politicians on the public is to draw attention away from one's self. It's a defense to deflect blame to others. Like blaming your kid brother for breaking a lamp. Anything to avoid dealing with negative consequences. This is what they do to avoid having the spotlight shine upon themselves, they go all in on false narratives that take your eyes off the real crimes. Or they create some manufactured crisis, but more on that later. The deflection then can morph into shame dumping, or the more technically termed "psychological projection." Oh that glorious act of denying the existence of their own negative ways while attributing bad to others. The Babylonian Talmud from 500 AD even warns of this: "Do not taunt your neighbor with the blemish you yourself have." In this technique politicians can hide behind anything, spinning personal crisis away from themselves, redirecting the heat of outrage elsewhere. You see, this is how much of the world works. It's a finely tuned machination at this point. When the deflection doesn't work the backup plan is any psychological warfare that can throw a fog up into the eyes of the public. A manufactured crisis like wag the dog bomb dropping, nuclear threats, even pandemics. And you, if awake to the contrivance, will act like a weather vane, as the storm winds blow they can point you to what it is that is being covered up. Remember this the next time there is a manic panic event that doesn't really make sense. And this from Jesus, his New Testament warning, "Why do you look at the speck of sawdust in your brother's eye and pay no attention to the plank in your own eye?"

<u>Long Live JonBenet?</u>

Anonymous ID; TB+ANS Wed 11 Jun 7:52:32 <u>No. 149067</u> ViewReport
JonBenet Ramsy = JBR
Pageant child = Momager
Boulder Police
NAMBA
~~Black~~ market
"Heaven on earth"
"big money"
MH370 [CCP?]
"Disappear"
Kamikaze ~~mission~~
Bill Gates [vaccine code]
abandoned airstrip
Australia?
CNN "busy" w/ Ferguson riots
...wait for it...

There has been talk--much of it in the child sex dark web--of JonBenet's death actually being faked and that she is an alive adult woman somewhere in hiding now. This of course kills off the fantasy for these guys, the thought of a grown woman disgusts them, so they fight the narrative. For them, JonBenet was forever locked in that sheen of beauty pageant child, gilded into foreverdom on some hotel conference room stage under glaring track lights while momagers bickered over whose kid had the best hair and makeup. The feather in the cap for the members of this dark underworld has yet to be anointed, as the killer of JonBenet has still not been confirmed. That last hero to hear her talk, to see her last breath, and the final one to assault her sexually.

This led to confessions around the world, and Boulder police, over the last twenty years, could not keep up. For a while there was an outpost set up in Asia for all the leads to be sorted through, prioritized by relevance, even plausibility. Most of the operation was paid for by JonBenet's father and caring donors. It resulted in the occasional extradition to the States, but each time the confessor was somehow eliminated, either through statements that ran contrary to the facts or through DNA.

As the internet grew so did the ability for these guys to stay in touch. Hell, many of them were computer nerds. Message boards in the early days of the internet were invented solely for the purpose of sharing each other's fantasies, and vast private collections of pictures. Sadly, without these creepers, the internet wouldn't be what it is today. Then when they realized they were not alone in their kink, and that the wider world consisted of others just like them they became more brazen. They ventured out. They traveled to conventions. The North American Man/Boy Love Association was formed. Better known as NAMBA. They saved up and got passports and traveled to Asia. Thailand was big, known as a British hotspot for young boys that looked like girls. A crossover type of sexual bent that allowed for repressed homosexuals to at least feign interest in a girl, yet someone who indeed was a boy with boy parts. The Thai government knew that sex tourism was good for the economy--as the black market funded their bribes--so they pushed it, running ads in European and American magazines with pictures of beaches and smiling locals. It was heaven on earth while simultaneously the devil's playground. Neighboring countries caught on, and they didn't want to miss out on the tourism so they pushed child trafficking even harder. Jungles and villages were procured as recruitment sites. Those chosen young kids moved to the cities, to make "big money," to send home to their parents and extended family. It was a win win for everyone. City slicker pimps cherry picked those without deformities or disabilities. They made sure that a small portion of the loot went back to the village, often a few dollars a month, just enough to seem like a windfall to these peasants who had no gauge on wealth.

In the transaction of the child there were a multitude of players. After the initial contact with the john, there was the point man/woman who offered up the child for 30 minutes, then the hotel room attendant, then the child, who was often on a salary of sorts, then the shakedown actor who confronted the john after the sex act and demanded some form of blackmail, usually $60 USD from an ATM. The johns knew that the shakedown was all part of the rues and were willing participants in it. These scam artists were also the players who arranged for Johnny Walker, or for drugs like coke, heroin, Viagra. But I digress, you get the gist of it, and how it came about.

Flight MH370, I may know why it went missing. There were some people on board who had hard drives, zip drives. Stuff they had sold to the Chinese Communist Party. They were on the final leg of their trip to Beijing. Word is, it was all the evidence needed to take down half of the world leaders, and after that initial wave, the secondary tidal assault would take down the other half. The chain reaction from the fallout would cause the world to spin out. All of the spiritual leaders would be implicated, the Pope, the Ayatollahs of Iran, American Evangelists. CEOs, corporate board members, half of Hollywood and the music and sports world. So what happened is the dark forces that wanted this evidence to "disappear" ordered up the pilot, that Ahmad Shah character, to be paid $1,000,000 USD into an offshore account, arranged by the same Panama Paper players, and this fund, once the plane was successfully crashed in his own kamikaze mission, would be distributed to his children, $800,000 USD to them, and $200,000 USD to Islam. He had gone through a bitter divorce and was suicidal anyway. A covenant in the payout to his kids was that if they gave any to their mother it would all be taken back.

Oh and the Anthony Weiner hard drive, stolen one month prior from an NYPD evidence room. A priceless item, that if offered for public bidding would fetch billions. And finally within the terabytes of hard drives was a vaccine code owned by Bill Gates, for an unknown virus. The only possible value of such a vaccine would require the release of said virus on the population. And all of this was headed to China, what could go wrong?

The disappearance of the plane was the perfect cover for what really happened. The forces for good in the world, I will get to them later, heard about this transaction and knew that any counter offer to this was worth billions. Yes, that much. Everything was on the line. Those in the know had short sold the US dollar. US senators sold their entire stock portfolios. There was the anticipation that it was all going down soon. The good guys swept in and arranged for the safe landing of the plane in an abandoned airstrip in Australia. The precious cargo would be extracted and the passengers would be let go, with other commercial airliners flying in for their rescue. But, as we all know now, this is not what happened. The plane did go missing. The searches for it were very real. There was an obsession from CNN, and now you know why. Then after wall to wall coverage for two months, the story got dropped and the Ferguson riots became the new focus of media coverage. But that's irrelevant to what I am about to tell you. I know where that plane is. And it's safe, intact, and everyone that was on it is fine. And those hard drives are stowed away safely in the cargo hold. It's in Cambodia and I will get us there.

JonBenet is Dead, Long Live JonBenet

Anonymous ID; TB+ANS Thu 14 Jul 9:21:35 <u>No. 149070</u> ViewReport
$118k ransom
"sexually assaulted"
break in
Santa Claus
Family housekeeper
"Quiet the demons"
Cape Cod
$2k ~~loan~~
Patsy
grieving father
"Hurt a little girl"
Phone cord
John Mark Karr = US Air Force jet
~~Love game~~
Pacific Northwest
JBR is Jonie
"High level cabals"
Malaysian Royal Family

Janet Reno
Closeted lesbian or [something] else?

Some undisputed facts included that just before 6am on December 26th Patsy Ramsey called Boulder Police from her home's landline. Her daughter JonBenet was missing from their sprawling McMansion. Found was a 2-page ransom note with the demand of $118,000 USD for the child's safe return. Local authorities arrived at the house and began a casual search of the premises. There was a promised time that the kidnappers would call yet they never did. A more thorough search of the basement, by JonBenet's father John, resulted in him discovering the gagged and bound body of the deceased child. Strangled and with head trauma, she was possibly sexually assaulted. Without signs of a break-in, the perpetrator must have been familiar with the family, and the large house. This is what we know.

From there, it has been three decades of media speculation. Theories abound that her brother Burke had killed her. Suggestions linger that the family housekeeper Linda Hoffman Pugh killed the child out of some jealous rage. Or Santa Claus suspect, Bill McReynolds, completed his fixation on the child by snuffing her out, to "quiet the demons" in his mind. An interview with McReynolds included this quote, "All children are special to Santa, and she was extra special." A colorful local character, with his long white beard, as Santa he would visit the homes of wealthy families in the suburbs of Boulder. He had been at the Ramsey home for a holiday party just days before JonBenet's death. He told authorities, "She just happened to be extra special to me. She was very thoughtful, a very caring little girl and she actually gave Santa a present. You can imagine how rare that is." Detectives found a note from him to JonBenet in her toy bin. It said she would "receive a special gift after Christmas." An added ingredient to the mystery of Santa's involvement was the abduction of his own daughter in the early 1970s. That intriguing aspect to the story was compounded with a stage play his wife wrote about a true crime murder of a 16-year-old girl who was tortured, molested and left to die in her family's basement. Santa doubled down on his friendship with JonBenet, telling the authorities that "When I die, I'm going to be cremated. I've asked my wife to mix the star dust JonBenet gave me with my ashes. We're going to go up behind the cabin here and have it blow away in the wind." Hair samples given by Santa and his wife came up empty on DNA traces in the Ramsey home. After intense pressure from the community the couple quietly moved to Cape Cod.

This left new speculation on the family's housekeeper. Her testimony revealed that JonBenet's brother Burke had smeared his own feces over the walls of JonBenet's room, even leaving a large shit in her bed. Shortly before Christmas the housekeeper had asked Patsy for a $2,000 loan. When the authorities were alone with her, their questions moved onto questions about Patsy. What kind of underwear she wore, what she liked for breakfast. The cops knew that the housekeeper's intel was important. She unloaded on her boss, claiming she was a violent woman with multiple personalities, that she was verbally abusive to JonBenet, going from a good mood to cranky in an instant, arguing with her children constantly. The housekeeper even said that if she had to guess, that Patsy did kill JonBenet, but by accident.

There were more suspects, adding to the suspense but also to the mystery that would further grip the nation. The possibility that it was her father who ended her life was inflamed with the initial police report detailing how he found her body in the basement and that his first move was to remove duct tape from over her mouth and cover her body with a throw blanket. This made detectives think he knew something. He was destroying evidence and contaminating the crime scene under the guise of a disheveled and grieving father. There was sexual abuse innuendo, like in any situation of this magnitude. There was the brother's possible involvement which theorized that he had hit her over the head with a flashlight. The eight-inch gash on her skull mirrored the possible blunt force of the flashlight found at the scene.

Further speculation of persons involved included a town drifter. There was a drop of blood in her underwear and this particular drifter was a known convicted pedophile. An interview with police revealed that he had a cut out picture of JonBenet from a magazine in his backpack. He was cleared but the family were resolute in saying that Boulder police needed to pursue him more. Years later a high school friend of his alerted the media that he confessed to killing the child, "that he hurt a little girl." He added that he choked her out with a phone cord. This drifter was convicted as a teen for assault and battery on his own mother when he choked her out with a telephone cord. A follow up interview with him by Boulder PD produced a cache of kiddie porn and he was subsequently convicted of that crime and put away.

There was the electrician. Michael Helgoth worked in an auto salvage yard near the Ramsey home. There was a property dispute with the Ramseys. This led to motivation for the possible kidnapping and ransom demands. Years later when the police announced they would be having a press conference to disclose new information on the case, he committed suicide. He posthumously has been cleared through DNA.

The schoolteacher. John Mark Karr, the personification of creepiness and epitome of evil, was arrested in Thailand where he had been on the lamb from child porn charges. During his interrogation he haphazardly confessed to killing JonBenet. He was flown on a US Air Force jet to Boulder for questioning but was cleared after his DNA did not match any of the samples on JonBenet's clothing. His confession included diary entries detailing the scene of the crime, even noting that he strangled the child when a "love game" had gone wrong. His diary entry closed with "Close your pretty eyes, sweetheart. I love you so much. Oh God, I love you, JonBenet. And my lover's eyes are slowly closing…" Detectives were not able to trace him ever being in the state of Colorado. Since the very high profile false confession he has now transitioned to a female and is living in the Pacific Northwest.

Turning thirty was a big one for Jonie, it didn't carry the thrill of twenty but it did carry the weight of having two kids and the fortune of a happy marriage. The void of her past nuclear family now was filled with her own, with her role at the matriarch realm. Much of the past she didn't remember, not out of any specific reason but surely for her own emotional survival. Besides she was just a kid. Who remembers childhood past the taste of food, the shows you watched, certain pivotal days like picture day at school or attacks from the school bully? Her memories of that time involved caked-on makeup and bright lights on a stage looking out at overweight moms with judgmental stares. The doting qualities of her father offset the harshness of the stage life. Her brother was nice and she would look forward to seeing him when she was home from beauty pageants. But like anything that seemed too good it was.

The dangers of the pedos are what led to that eventful escape on Christmas eve, so long ago. "The name JonBenet is dead to me. I took on Jonie because if someone yelled it out in a waiting room it was close enough that I would know that was me. Witness protection was an adolescence with my adoptive family,

Bill and Susan. Wonderful people who were not blessed with the ability to have children of their own, but abundantly charmed with warm hearts and a love for our savior Jesus Christ." High school consisted of cheerleader practice and short-lived relationships with boys until she met her soulmate in David, one year her senior. "We married the summer I graduated high school, in a small ceremony in my backyard. He worked a combine harvester on the corn fields. Life in Iowa certainly can have its moments. When I get bored I remember that I once was JonBenet Ramsey and this gives me a small private thrill knowing I was the source for so much international news coverage. Really jarring if you think about it. Does it bother me that people still believe I am dead? No, not really, I mean wouldn't this alternative scenario be better, that I am still alive, even if it is under a new identity?"

The switch from that life to ultimately this, saved her from an undeniable demise. "My mother was compromised with certain high level cabals and I was headed for slaughter. She essentially had pimped me out, but without knowing the severity. At least I need to believe this in order to somehow retain space in my heart for her, rest her soul. These were bad people. She really didn't know. But she liked the bling, and those secret direct deposits that my father didn't know about, that allowed her untraced walking around money, and lots of it."

What was learned at a much later date was that JonBenet had been ordered by a far-off Malaysian royal family member. He was seeding the funding as a way to further entice her mother for a private jet visit to his compound. "I would hope she didn't fully understand what was being arranged but that is between her and her maker. My father and her weren't that close during the time of my disappearance. They didn't talk much except for the minimal dialogues about the kids, or who was coming to the house to clean. Most of it was notes they wrote to each other and left in the kitchen. So my dad, who is still alive mind you, got a tip from a high school friend who was an FBI agent."

There was intel about an international pedophile ring that had infiltrated the child beauty circuit. Of course, why not go directly to the source. Many of these overweight single moms were known to be living out some vicarious existence through their children, either reliving their own failed pageant past or trying to make some point for their envious relatives that their own daughter would be the next Anna Nicole Smith type and pay off everyone's mortgages.

"It was a weak crowd of lambs ready for slaughter, really. I think that my mother fell into the hype machine, and the competition between the moms is what led her to make the reckless mistakes she did. My father, along with the help of his FBI agent friend, traced an elaborate payment scheme that was going on in the pageant community. Something was close to happening and it was going to be big. He knew that if he brought this to my mother it could be the final straw with her moving out and taking the kids." She was in too deep herself. She got her rocks off from the dopamine spikes of recognition. She was Patsy Fucking Ramsey after all.

"Long story short my dad and his friend found a digital trace to a high-level ringleader of the racket. That was none other than Attorney General Janet Reno, a closeted lesbian that had a predilection for dollish children. After the connection was made to her, through some back channeling communications she learned she was compromised and with this as blackmail a private jet was arranged to be on call for a Boulder pick-up. Destination unknown. So on that eventful night, when my father found my body and he brought me upstairs, wrapped in that blanket, then to the ambulance, and finally to the jet way, it was his own sacrifice for my survival. I was then placed in witness protection in a small Iowa town. I still think, much like other adopted people, about the alternative reality. How my life did end up playing out, and I can say I am happy with it and would not have wanted anything else."

<u>Chinese Deception</u>

Anonymous ID; TB+ANS Fri 18 Aug 7:31:55 <u>No. 149072</u> ViewReport

[Houston] CCP Consulate
11 Front St BROOKLYN
"closed circuit camera"
Web of payoffs
GAMBINO
Item #67439 (personal laptop)
La Guardia
Authentic or decoy?
false flag?
Sinaloa Cartel
BBVA Bancomer Bank
Nancy Pelosi HoR
Hillary Clinton [HRC]
Indictment "½ of Washington w/ me"
"honey pot"
dreams of the ~~middle class~~
~~revolution~~ of sorts

    The Communist Party of China, a ragtag group of overweight career politicians, failed businessmen and shady dealmakers, arranged through a trade ambassador in the Houston Chinese consulate to purchase the Weiner hard drive for $10,000,000 USD through a wire transfer via an unmarked Cayman offshore account redirected to a bank in Andorra. At least this was the story. Now, the task of stealing the hard drive from the evidence room located at 11 Front Street, Brooklyn, was perhaps more daunting of an exercise than planned. Through an intricate web of payoffs, mostly arranged by the Gambino family, yes that iconic mafia family, $10,000 USD cash ended up at the Staten Island doorstep of the property clerk who was scheduled for the graveyard shift to guard the front door of the evidence room. He had two commands, and if executed correctly another $10,000 USD cash would be delivered the following day. One, accidentally kick the wires behind the computer running the closed circuit cameras, enough to disable the surveillance. Two, act like you fell asleep for at least ten minutes between 2:15AM and 2:25AM. The visitor that would arrive to pull evidence would be another paid off cop, paid a more significant amount, and he would not bother his sleeping coworker. He would retrieve Evidence Item #67439 ("personal laptop"), while replacing said evidence with a decoy laptop. Once the Weiner laptop was out of the building a driver would take possession and deliver it to an awaiting unmarked Gulfstream 500 in the general aviation field of La Guardia Airport. With the decoy hard drive securely in place in the evidence room nobody was the wiser resulting in a successful heist, or was it?

The Gambino family had skin in the game because they wanted to expose the Sinaloa Cartel for their involvement in the drug invasion of the Northeast, and the corruption of politicians who were now under higher payrolls by the Mexican giant. The Gambinos were old school in that they still operated with honor, they didn't kill women or children, and they weren't interested in doping up half the population. Facilitating the Weiner hard drive into the hands of anyone not named Clinton would surely guarantee the release of its contents. But the big question remained, was the heisted computer in the evidence room authentic or a decoy?

False flag operations are acts committed with the intent of disguising the source of responsibility, pinning the blame elsewhere. The term goes back to the 16th century, and was initially used in naval warfare with vessels flying the flag of a neutral or enemy country to hide its own identity. The tactic would deceive other ships to come near, then be ambushed. In more modern times it can include when a country stages an attack on itself, like domestic terrorism, in order to drum up a response. If you are paying attention at all these days, you know it's hard to keep track. It is in this spirit how much of the Gambino crime syndicate worked. Every action they took had some cover that was used as a distraction. Smokescreens in deception over here while the real crime was committed over there. The media and public were none the wiser when they took out the competition, or put up their own underworld resistance to the Sinaloa Cartel. It was called the underworld for a reason, right? And with that you have to wonder if the decoy of the decoy of the hard drive is a decoy itself?

In the hard drive were payout schedules from BBVA Bancomer Bank, Mexico City, Distrito Federal, Mexico, in various amounts over a twelve year period totaling approximately $500,000,000 USD to American Democratic politicians. The list doesn't matter, but it includes Nancy Pelosi, the speaker of the House of Representatives. This fact, if aired to the public, would connect the dots back to the fervent battle against border fencing and stronger enforcement. And the neglectful concession of the homeless population explosion, as these were the people consuming the most drugs. This revelation would make sense to the public, and surely trigger the downfall of the majority of the Democratic Party. So, you see, a lot was on the line.

In these moments of revelation I always ponder how it is that people can be so brazen when heading down the road of corruption, without a concern for the paper trail, or the people involved who may turn state witness. As a man I compare it to standing there with a raging boner with a less than homely woman and in that split second moment of horny rage all you can think is "Let's go." But then you spend your remaining days nervous, paranoid that someone is onto you. Your behavior may even become erratic and not make sense to those in your midst. Your mission in life becomes one of self-preservation. And avoiding going to jail. You may even begin threatening those in the know, or laying down veiled coded messaging that if anything comes out on you then it's going to come out on all. Very much like how Hillary Clinton operates. That evil bitch approach. "If I'm indicted I will take half of Washington with me" kind of verve. Under this prism so much of Washington began to make sense. An elite political class so corrupted by money that they no longer cared about the working family, just more taxation to fatten the honey pot while choking out the dreams of the middle class. In many ways we are on a one way street to a revolution of sorts, and I am ready for battle.

Unearthed Revelations

Anonymous ID; TB+ANS Sat 19 Aug 10:34:51 <u>No. 149074</u> ViewReport
Jungle Girl (JG)
N12.0159, E104.1520
"electronic world"
ANS = midlife crisis
Softest nipples [divine stroke]
Switzerland of Cambodia
PARIS "moveable feast"
Disneyland ride
Virachey NP
nocturnal wildlife
Khmer ruins
~~Kooky theory~~
AW laptop secured
Bell 206
Email NYC
500 Pearl St ☐ final destination

Jungle Girl was mute and played deaf but she had other ways to effectively communicate. A wild variety of facial expressions and a basic sign language that even the abled hearing could somehow understand. She was happy with the task of leading our crew to N 12.0159, E 104.1520, or more simply the Kampong Speu province, specifically the base of Phnom Aural, Cambodia's highest peak. You know how when a child starts losing focus and abounds with a shotgun blast of energy, but you task them something fun and you see the clarity in their mission, this was Jungle Girl. On a side note, not much was discovered about her after she appeared in the modern world, no legitimate family member came forth, those that tried failed out on the DNA tests, and she remained more mysterious than ever. Kind of like a human Bigfoot or jungle Abominable Yeti. The big global tabloids ran occasional stories, even if completely fabricated, because there was so much public interest. Maybe it was that we all wanted to be her. To have that primal experience away from the electronic world, checked out from the mayhem and the media, and returned to a spiritual sense of calm. I can counter that fantasy by telling you it's not that glamorous, she is a charming banshee and her dislocation from modernity has given her a manly disposition. Likely a virgin, she is lean, buffed, aggressive, almost roid rage-ish but without the roids. In other words, I would never want to bed her. But I digress.

Anna Nicole Smith, my midlife crisis crush if you will, has rekindled a lost connection to herself while in the jungle, meaning she, more than anyone I know, benefits mostly from being untethered to the distortions of modernity. Some of us just do better in nature. What would have become of this woman if she had stayed in

Houston and never ventured to Hollywood, or had more children with her first baby daddy. I can tell you with most certainty, she would be a hundred pounds overweight, covered in tattoos, likely diabetic and riding in one of those scooters when she shopped at Wal-Mart. Sad but true, sometimes the truth hurts. In some ways being in the spotlight forced her to constantly check herself, at least in the looks department. These last few years out of the spotlight have been good to her, she has found a private spirituality that she can visit when the demons arrive. I know I have already mentioned her billowing breasts but I would be remiss if I didn't offer praise again with this mention. The sanguine outer hang and suspension of such godly orbs, detailed out with the ski slope profile projection of the softest nipples, are at minimum a divine stroke.

Our version of trekking within the jungle could be best labeled as glamping. Di and John wanted their own space, understandably, as did I when the lights went off I wanted Anna far enough away from the others that her muffled passion screams weren't mistaken for nighttime monkeys descending on our campsite. Jungle Girl never slept, she was our all-night security, and she did make us feel safe.

Our journey took all of seven days. Imagine the wettest of hipster dreams in the glorified offline experience of travel and leisure, that polished sheen of better than thou digital sharing of your best analog life. This is how it was. The hiking felt good while looking forward to nightly sex was even better. Day one we left the capital city Phnom Penh, a charming town that some have dubbed the Switzerland of Cambodia for its rolling green hills and picturesque lakes. I always found it funny how places would compare themselves to others versus trying to be unique on their own merit. How about for once being the Phnom Penh of Phnom Penh. I think the only city that has never compared herself to others is Paris. You just never hear it, instead she is likened to a moveable feast. She is there for you always, in your thoughts and dreams, but whenever you return, like a good mistress, she will not have changed. You get what you expect. There is comfort in that. Our first hours involved a jeep ride through dozens of miles of plantations, with the heartfelt endless waves and blessings from children and elders. I got the group going with roadside home-brewed rice wine. Nothing more authentic than that. Imagine sweet prison wine, but this pruno was smooth and without the carbs. I didn't bother to inform anyone that it was supposed to be drunk via shots, not continuously sipped. Oh but that head-spinning humidity buzz is unrivaled. To be honest I throttled my intake to avoid any whiskey dick in the night. Yes, I thought about these things. Oh, the responsibilities of middle life!

Day two and three consisted of actual hiking, no longer transported by jeep, we followed Jungle Girl on a trail that only she claimed to know. Like something out of a Disneyland ride we walked under waterfalls, and stood in the doorways of caves for that refreshing cold

air blast. John and I swam in our underwear, I even tried
to get him to go au naturel but he said he wouldn't do
that to Di, exposing himself in front of Anna. What a
gentleman. We lunched on bamboo soup. And in the
night ate barbeque that Jungle Girl provided. We didn't
ask what the meat was but it tasted like chicken.

Day four and five were increasingly difficult with
the density of the jungle becoming an uncomfortable
factor for all involved. The girls were spent, and we had
to slow our pace. Anna became that annoying child in
the back of the car asking on repeat are we almost there
yet. Not yet sweetie, but we are close. The reprieve was
our arrival at the riverside town of Kratie. From there
we would travel day six by fishing boat up the Mekong
river. These waters were known for freshwater dolphins,
and local legend had that if your boat was escorted by
the dolphins your journey was blessed by the local gods.

Day seven consisted of hiking through rice paddies
to the base of the Virachey National Park, then the
ascension to the highlands. Evening spent around the
campfire sampling exotic vegetables and fruits, even
medicinal plants. This is when shit could go sideways,
any hint of a dosing of psychoactives could trigger a
relapse in Anna or myself, or bring about an episode for
Diana. And the nocturnal wildlife. Everything was on
the line but at this point Jungle Girl knew us well, she
understood our frailties, and her indigenous instincts
kept us safe.

Day eight would be our final day. As we got closer to the plane the jungle animals joined us. Small primates, and jungle cats. Almost as if they were domesticated. We came upon Khmer ruins, something that I knew was likely 9th century, but what Jungle Girl claimed was from the sky people. She tells me through sign that when she was here last a glowing orb appeared to protect her. The glowing orb is another jungle story that goes back to the Vietnam war era, and like the freshwater dolphins the logic was that it was here to help. Local folklore says it was a leftover technology from the previous civilizations to protect the jungle. It was a benevolent god of sorts. It defied logic in how it moved through the trees and foliage. The last time it got testy was with the soldiers so many decades earlier who fought over the jungle, sometimes the soldiers would light it up with napalm. Ever since, it has had a calming effect.

And it was awaiting us when we arrived at the airstrip. A once fully militarized landing area had now been overgrown by encroaching jungle to the point that only the fuselage of the plane was exposed to the sky. There were no buildings and apparently no people. Certainly a forgotten city atmosphere. This would remain the mystery, what happened to the passengers? The energy became more and more eerie as we approached, finding that the door of the plane had been removed and a makeshift ladder hung from the doorway. I let John have the honors and board the plane. He went alone as we anticipated his quick murder by screaming monkeys. It would be a few minutes before he gave the all clear. I boarded the plane to find it surprisingly barren, void of belongings, almost as if it had been professionally sanitized. Meanwhile John retrieved the metal box from the cargo hold, and we verified the contents. One Anthony Weiner laptop. Now you might say, is this another decoy laptop? Well, the fact that it was here, lost in the jungles, lent it all of the authenticity we needed.

Jungle Girl hiked us out another mile or so to a football field-sized clearing demarcated with four small steeples. It looked like a well-maintained soccer field replete with terraria wiki grass, like the ruins of a sepak takraw field, the ancient kick-volleyball sport popularized by the Khmer Empire. Upon closer examination of the corner spires' friezes and entablature were bas-reliefs of faces of aliens. Yes, large eyes and big heads, void of anything indigenous in their appearances. Jungle Girl was quick to point out the three finger salutes. John used his satellite phone to call in for our helicopter extract. It bothered me that we couldn't find any trace of the passengers, and for the sake of not leaving a hook in the story unresolved I must conclude it was alien abduction. And there we stood in their spaceport for over an hour until our ride arrived. Kooky theory yes, but as a plausible theory it made the most sense.

Our Bell 206 chopper arrived like a welcome fantasy from the southern sky. The pilot greeted us but remained anonymous as John said he is black ops and that is all we need to know. Jungle Girl stayed behind, as we informed her there would be plenty of people descending on the plane in the coming days. She wanted to remain in order to help protect the spirits and the animals.

Six hours into our eighteen hour direct flight to New York City I emailed my old producer at CNN. I used a burner email account but did sign it Tony, knowing he would know it was me. I sent the jungle coordinates of missing Malaysian Airlines Flight 370. It would be another 24 hours before I walked the hard drive, securely locked in a silver briefcase, into the 500 Pearl Street courthouse offices of the Southern District of New York. You may think to yourself, why return it to the authorities that sat on it for all these years? That is a good question, and thanks for asking. The difference this time is we will force them to show their hand, and to finally bring justice forward.

A Great Awakening

Anonymous ID; TB+ANS Sun 17 Sep 10:11:05 <u>No.</u> <u>149079</u> ViewReport
"Conspiracy Theorists"
Gearing up [for battle]
shield yourself
American patriots

Dismissals, willful blindness
"Reflection in the castle"
follow the $$
Tripcode = Nostradamus
greater hole
JFK Jr, access to highest ranks of Navy intel
"You are the news now"
...enjoy the show...

The thing with conspiracy theorists is it's hard to discern if one is an adherent on looks alone. We tend to look like any other American. You could be that hopeless individual on the bus bench, or the mom in the minivan on her way to pick up the kids. You could be your favorite dentist, that highly successful immigrant you so much admire. Or your tax guy, your grocery clerk, your mysterious online friend. You cannot be identified by appearance or demographics alone. And this works in your favor if they ever do come for you. You are beyond caring if you sound crazy because you believe in the dark forces and the manipulators in the shadows pulling the strings, those evil doers who harm and damage children without the fear of retribution or consequences. You see the world as a ravaged place where evil exists and a plague of badness is gearing up for a battle against goodness. How the other denizens cannot see this is beyond you, so you remain on guard at all times, and shield yourself from the ignorant as you prepare to fight.

Headlines about the movement are laid out to establish a sense of insanity for anyone who would believe such malarkey. How possible really is it that a cabal of powerful elites is abusing children and continuing to get away with it? Have we collectively lost our minds to the increased chatter of that connectivity of the internet, something that pre-world wide web would have gone unnoticed, or is it indeed right there for our consumption? If you are paying attention you see the recycled premises of the debunking playing out over and again, it doesn't matter what the topic is, as long as it's about bad intentions and maligned actions there is an invisible shield to protect the perps from the preying eyes of American patriots. That was a mouthful. Essentially the moral degeneracy is protected. And the questions from deep within your own gut are needed to sustain a movement of inconvenient facts and contradictory details, as there is no argument that can prevail over these nefarious actors. They will use their strongest weapon against you, that of the useful idiots, those limited thinkers who believe the party line hook line and sinker, dropping reverse psychology back onto you forcing you to question your own sanity. Regular everyday people who have been weaponized for the sanctity of keeping the narrative going. These could be family members, coworkers or online friends. Tasked with the dirty work of enforcing what you should believe, and anything outside that may leave you exposed to ridicule.

In the offhanded dismissals that leave you reeling and asking if you have indeed accepted willful blindness, you then know this is not what civil society is about, that democratic governance is too important and your warped reality need not be derailed. Your enthusiasm comes into question as the narrative is that Americans are susceptible to conspiracy theories, that you are nothing more than a part of a loose collection of rag tag internet trolls. It gets dissected in claiming you have abandoned reason, rejected objectivity and whatever else can be used to label you as a fringe actor. They break you down by slandering you as paranoid and missing something in your personal life so you go hard in the fervent hope of belonging to something, anything.

But what's inside you is a primal verve and preoccupation, along the lines of a reptilian brain just looking for answers. It may seem radical but it's nothing new, and it doesn't mean you are all about the end times either. Others may consider it a new religion for you, they may throw out goofy terms with "-gate" added to them, or the more ominous sounding New World Order. Confusing enough that you question which side you are still on, that perhaps you have gone full circle and are now a puppet for the enemy. When chat rooms use commands like "Find the reflection in the castle" there is surely a nutty afterglow. And this is by design, to throw off any real investigation or reporting. Closing communiques with "Follow the $$" or "I have said too much" all but ensures continued reading.

For the online profiles that I have used as avatars they simply existed to build up a more important account I ran. Using a tripcode--a series of numbers and letters to signal continuity--to further verify my unverifiable identity, I moved from one image board to another. Places like 4chan, 8chan, 8kun and reddit, all once and still considered the anus sites of the internet but now more importantly a message passthrough billboard. Safe harbor places for the believers to believe. Discrediters can move along. Were the predictions all played out as described? No, never, that would be impossible. I am not Nostradamus. Was there a morsel of truth in each of them? Yes, and often they overlapped. If you have one big rabbit hole in the entire internet you will inherently have a number of recursive rabbit holes within the greater hole, and then it becomes a game of choices for where to travel next.

Early on I knew I needed an airtight persona or character, someone nobody could question nor easily identify. I was friends with JFK Jr. on the down low. He had his access to the highest ranks of the Navy. Officials who worked under his father while they were young men. Information gleaned had to be clean, it couldn't come from world leaders or anyone in the deep state. Otherwise it wasn't intelligence but propaganda or misleading detractors. In the broader context by character needed a catchy name and in order to battle the apostates and the mainstream press a rallying cry. I came up with "You are the news now." And for the impending apocalypse "Enjoy the show." And for my codename I kept is simple, "Q." The highest US government clearance for accessing top secret documents.

Much of this had its conception while I was still very much alive and working at CNN. I needed something to counter the narrative of fake news coming at the public with such dogmatic force. Call me deviant but I kinda got off on my intel drops. I got most of it from John, and my creative side would seed in something juicy here and there. Clues that led toward a bigger mystery or the next hot conspiracy. I was getting off on the followers, I could see them, they were truckers and housewives, businessmen and other professionals. The people were thirsty. We were all spectators to the impending doom and we had our popcorn. Well that moment has arrived today.

A Calm Before the Storm

The most common touchstone among the followers is the "calm before the storm" phrase as that dangling carrot of sustained excitement and build up. I used it in my first post, now three years ago. It coincided with a picture of POTUS with his military commanders. High dramatic effect indeed. The ambiguity worked well in the recesses of a hungry mind, even if the meeting was about a covert military attack in the Middle East why could it have not been planning for the takedown of Epstein's Pedo Island, or a raid on some adrenochrome lab in Hollywood. The ambiguity is rich and popular. After that initial post my followers grew exponentially. Redneck dudes morphed into soccer moms which led to small town mayors and congressional candidates. Every single one of them helped lift Q from obscurity. Eventually it hit the mainstream and that is when the smear campaigns began.

I resorted to out-cunning the press. I threw smoke bombs their way and patiently waited to see if they took the bait. If the President wore a yellow tie I would post that he was telling us that war with Iran is imminent. Crazy stuff like that. There was no logic to it but the followers were then able to run with these morsels and construct elaborate scenarios of their own. Some of the better ones I would modify and reshare. When small predictions happened it lent to the credence and validity of the Q posts and emboldened my own political instincts. Leaving me to wonder if I went into the wrong line of work by reporting on food?

I could never go wrong with invoking God or the Bible or the Lord or capitalizing He and His. Our savior's pronouns remained male, sorry folks. This followed with any mention of the wickedness of the elites. Pizzagate was huge but that burned out of interest after the mainstream media went so hard on it. Mentions of the coordinated propaganda from the powerful brought its own sense of hysteria, as Q followers were intelligent and never wanted to be outsmarted. Even newcomers were humble in asking questions as this growing army wanted to get it right. And finally we didn't like bad news and as you know that's kind of all that's out there, so I would close my communiques with something uplifting, and the acronym WWG1WGA. Where we go one we go all. How beautiful of a hook is that? A delicious delectable of connectivity in these disconnected times. Community over disunity. A battle cry from your living room and solidarity in your allegiance.

The goal was to predict events that in all likelihood would occur in order to strengthen the brand and believability. But of course there were majorly bad predictions that flamed out upon take off. Most significantly the arrest of Hillary Rodham Clinton. Of course this still could happen. Some followers of Q believe that the fact she hasn't yet been arrested is all part of the plan and nothing more than a deception play. Who knows at this point?

We do know that it all leads back to Hillary wanting JFK Jr. dead. And the potential for her success in killing him if he had not faked his own death. She will not be tried for that crime as it never materialized, but it will not matter when the video is played for all to see. The Storm is at the shore and the high winds are beating at the doorway. And on the other side of the storm is a great spiritual and intellectual revival, where we become aware of our own depravity, and reclaim a self-awareness of sin. Having been exposed to the unimaginable perversion of the elites we will no longer be enslaved to the corruption.

Postscript Diana

Di had gone under the knife several times since the age of nineteen. First a small shaving of the bump off her nose, then a small breast augmentation after her son Harry was born. It was a present to herself and the public never knew, only those who were most intimate with her would notice a firmness to her C-cup breasts, and they would not see the scarring in her armpits. That operation was done sometime early 1995 in Switzerland under the cover of a family ski trip.

The last photos of her were from August 1997, and these images were burned into the memory of the global public, of her on a yacht in the Mediterranean and the final photo of her, in the security footage of the elevator in the Ritz. Like all fallen heroes there is that magical quality of never seeing them as old people. A lifelong aversion to being in direct sunlight has resulted in Di embodying 60 as the new 40. Wrinkle-free except for a dusting of laugh lines, she looks the same and would be recognizable except for the fact of her well-published untimely demise. In order for her emergence she would need the best plastic surgery, even vocal cord work. Much of her British accent had subsided to more of an American monotone. But like ears and tongues, something that never changes is the tonality of voice. Slicing alternating vocal cords allow for this change.

With the distance of the faded memories of a 36-year-old Diana combined with a minor facelift and dark hair coloring there would always be that resemblance, that stopping glare from a stranger, the comments that you may remind someone of a celebrity, but in the mental confusion and absolution afforded from a very public death there would be nothing more than a piqued mental curiosity. With the news of Prince Harry leaving the Royal Family to move Stateside, specifically to the glint of Malibu, with his child, Di's third grandchild, along with his American wife Megan, it was Di's ambition to make contact with him. She knew through intel that her children had always partially believed that her death could have been faked. They certainly believed as well that their grandmother, the Queen, very possibly was behind the assassination. Their young minds couldn't fully sort it out, but did leave a level of wonderment for an alternative ending.

In this thinking was Harry's own concern over the paparazzi treatment of his wife and child. He knew deep down that if the Queen could have killed Diana she certainly would have no problem killing Meghan who she so despised. Many royal watchers had a hard time understanding his devotion to what some royal critics had referred to as the "mulata." With an unconventional white father, the stereotypical obese American man, easily casted as the villain in any narrative involving the diluting of the royal bloodline, paired with her simple black mother, who very notably sat alone at their wedding, was fodder for the press. The vilification of Meghan was obviously a planned hit campaign by the Queen. It began with the ideation that the fallout would be a divorce, something the royal family was comfortable with, yet it culminated with Harry standing by his woman.

What many could not understand was that she was his sexual kryptonite. He had only been with one other woman before her, and there is no denying that she is an exquisite beauty. The kid was pussy-whipped pure and simple. Much was made in the press about their child not being biologically theirs, that Megan was actually never pregnant. Conspiracies of faked royal births go back to the year 1456, when Queen Margaret's son, a two-year old Edward of Westminster, was alleged to be a nonroyal. A stand in, an impostor, a changeling. It had to have been true because the Queen began executions of anyone who spread this gossip. Hanged in town squares. The wombs of royal women have always been fodder for speculation, and understandably so, this pending offspring will be born with such a burden over their head, and directly into the limelight. A life that nobody can imagine, yet, like a fish is unaware of water, this will be the only form of life they will know.

With the advent of the internet those that had succumbed to the vilification offensive of Meghan took the story to the next level with a bombardment campaign that while Meghan was supposedly pregnant she indeed was not and wore a prosthetic called a "moonbump." Why would this be? Maybe because she was such a narcissist that she didn't want to do any unnecessary damage to her body, maybe she couldn't get pregnant and rather than be raked through the burning embers of the British tabloids, being blamed for her own misfortune, she chose to fake it. Her sister-in-law the Duchess of Cambridge, Kate Middleton, had been dogged by similar accusations because she looked too good right after giving birth. Some floated the idea that Meghan suffered from pseudocyesis, the phenomenon of a false pregnancy induced by desiring to be pregnant. Mary Tudor, Queens of Scots, was also known as Bloody Mary for her high profile bout with this aforementioned affliction. Way back to the mid-1500s, months after Mary had stopped menstruating and had gained a significant amount of weight one morning she felt nauseous. Her doctors were called and Parliament was notified of an impending royal birth. As a precaution in those days, the government anointed her husband Philip the king in the event of her death during childbirth. It was only April but out of concern that things could end badly Londoners celebrated Christmas services. Then another month passed without word from the Royal family. Much speculation was that the baby was born prematurely and everything was fine. Then it was announced that due to her extreme desire to have a child

Mary had conducted a "false pregnancy" and that her infertility was enough of "God's punishment." Immediately after the official announcement Prince Philip ordered attacks against France while Bloody Mary fell into a deep depression.

This tale further exemplifies the disappointment that comes along with infertility, and the hatred from certain women toward expectant mothers. With that, Archie Harrison Mountbatten-Windsor was born to the Duke and Duchess of Sussex in a London Hospital, specifically the Lindo Wing of St Mary's Hospital, contrary to reports of a home birth. He is seventh in line to the throne.

But I digress. Diana has been busy working the back channels to get herself placed as the family nanny, in Malibu. It will require a lengthy discussion with Harry, about what happened, but also why she wasn't there for him in his adolescence. It will be painful but healing for both. This new chapter of their lives is yet to be told.

Eyes on the Castle

That juicy and delicious talk, reverberated online chatter of imminent mass arrests that never seem to take place. Or with the covert campaign to root out an elite child sex trafficking ring by POTUS and the Attorney General. Word settled within the Anon-world that everyone is now waiting on JFK Jr. to re-appear, to join forces with the President, and to run along with him as his Vice President, ensuring his own eventual 8-year stint as President of the United States. This kind of talk tends to get discredited as conspiracy theory from those on the fringe of American life. But something that cannot be downplayed or disregarded is the temptation to believe. That lofty hopefulness that so easily spreads and is increasingly difficult to combat and thwart. Granted there are low barriers of entry into such inclusive and hopeful thinking, when the stark reality of life and its limitations are juxtaposed with the Great Awakening, and the cryptic missives of an open-ended and absorbing messenger. When you take in the breadcrumbs you are left with, your own theater of mind will concoct the rest of the story, and write your own ideal ending.

You know what they say about conservatives, they may be nuts but they have more sex and the women are hotter. It's a game on many levels, often requiring fantastical and magical thinking, with a tendency to stretch one's own personal experience beyond bequeathed levels of logic. It can escalate to violent encounters like at Comet Pizza or a hijacked armored truck blocking traffic onto the Hoover Dam. Or it can bring about a personal demise that involves a quiet suicide and ghosting of one's online presence. What some call a "bloodless revolution" will bring to its knees an incredible historical movement, that of the revelation of JFK Jr. very much alive, and the promise of those years of deciphering posts now to promote the truth and no longer vigorously to deny the truth, when the live-action went from the digital to the analog. And your role-playing avatar now ascends to the physical realm, when the government will see you now and the media finally pays attention. And we will no longer need to bend our realities to theirs.

From a hangar in Philadelphia, JFK Jr. emerged from the shadows of his own death to the shock of the world. What at first was disbelief as another conspiracy hype event, all was quickly discredited when he took to the podium. He had aged well, that jawline still intact, and with a full head of hair he looked young. And unlike your average overweight American, he was able to wear his father's WWII bomber jacket. A large screen was positioned to his right, while to his left was an American flag. The screen was blank for now. It was connected to a laptop with the files from the Weiner hard drive. A loosely edited 15-minute long sizzle reel of its juiciest highlights.

He began by apologizing: "I know that my presence today is shocking, and I can live with that if you can accept me back into your hearts. I must first apologize for what I did. First to my sister and her family. As if they had not gone through enough, Caroline did not deserve to lose me. But what I did was necessary for my own self-preservation. I had learned I was in the cross hairs of Hillary Clinton and my murder was scheduled. A bicycle accident in Central Park or a mugging that went bad, maybe even my own suicide. So I decided to fake my death as a way to survive. It was as simple as that. You may now ask what have I been doing for all these years, well I have been busy. Along with some friends I have gone after child sex predators, and with amazing success. Why I have assembled the press here today is to announce my candidacy for Vice President of the United States of America, if the President is so inclined to choose me. After this short video presentation I will take your questions..."

Afterthoughts During An American Sunset

Imagination is the biggest part of us, and lends to our potential to fly, to seek out immortality and to travel in time. It goes beyond what our eyes allow us to see, showing everything else, beyond the situation, and most gloriously our free will. We go as far as pinpointing global hotspots of crop circle formations with a whimsical conviction of their authenticity, or the idea that Hitler is still alive, that Saddam Hussein escaped a falling Iraq with his own stargate machine, even that the world is flat, because there is a society for that.

You feel that urge to tell them what you know. That within the short window from Cro-Magnon man to the current Neolithic not much has changed. Maybe the cave drawings or how the kitchens moved inside, that simple advancement which made us become sedentary, leading partially to our impending demise. Setting up shop meant we were done settling, so we built towns and cities, and called off our nomadic hunts. This misstep played out for all the great civilizations and look how they ended. Egypt and its Pharaohs, ancient Greece and Rome. We waged on into a series of jarring events that took scar tissue, like the Declaration of Independence, fighting communism, and coming to grips with the death of our beloved Elvis. In some ways the flowcharts were nothing more than false predictors of where we were headed, not where we came from. Everything finally did mean *everything.*

Now it was about the latitudinal line. It started with the agricultural spread of Eurasia. A starting point in Ethiopia on the mystery line of 45 degrees East, that is where the fossil record first evolved. Following six degrees north you arrive at Mecca, the site of the Black Stone meteorite and the mystery of what possibly lies beneath it. Westward takes you to Jerusalem, then onto the Tigris and Euphrates Rivers, those mythical places that played crucial roles in our humanities studies, on such a pedestal for the advancement of life it's almost as if they don't really exist. Then to Mount Aratat the final resting place of Noah's Ark. From there the topographical mystery has you turn due north, tracing the migration routes of the first humanoids. The prehistoric importance of this line is that it traverses an alignment of gravitic and electromagnetic forces where it is rumored that both in the Arctic and Antarctic are underwater UFO bases. But here is the hook, there is a constellation map of this, yes a galactic explanation of where to go. Finally, human evolution played out over a mere ten thousand years--a blink of an eye in the time space of Earth--a timeframe that counters the Darwinian narrative with its lengthy and unproven explanations so successfully sold upon the public that any counter thought is disregarded as junk science or holy roller platitudes. With that said, we had to have had help in advancing the species.

Why go there now in this tale? Because any awakening requires cracking in the concrete. As your life changes the spiritual world around you tends to fall apart. It becomes about what your computers decide to read or to ignore. Anything that can heighten human perception above the depression and fear. As you are being asked to change you are turning yourself inside out, arriving in an exalted state over the collapse of an old matrix.

As for myself I choose life in hiding. As much as I miss the fame and that dopamine spike every time someone on the streets recognizes me and yells out "Tony!" I prefer this more muddled existence. Besides, I am not safe, never will be. Mine is a life of wanderer and that means away from the threats and toward that shiny sparkle of a new discovery. What is the heart of the matter? When did you last see a truly happy chef? Maybe it's because we know everything and in the case of life too much information is not your friend. We started out as dishwashers then worked upward, self-educating, from station to station while navigating the intricacies of a kitchen, that metaphorical mirror to life, and the struggle was overcome again and again until it was burned into our cell structure, and this is how you want it, not some easily triggerable "artist" who may be having a hard time because of the pressure, no, you want the culinary warrior, with an expectation of excellence, of an accumulated guarantee of character, with that most delicious characteristic, the ability to endure. Take the chef out of the ludicrous and feigned hostility of a kitchen and put him into real life, that truly raw-dogged existence of corrupt politicians, despotic regimes, bad cops, and dirty extortionists, and from the get-go the chef will be ready for it all.

This all-encompassing patina of a well-tenured professional will embrace the meeting of very much-alive dead celebrities as if there is nothing to see here. Those thoughts of, is it just me or is my head about to explode. My role as some kind of crazed wanna-be of my own life's making, an impostor syndrome of the down, with blazing trumpets announcing my departure from a collective yearning for the truth with the pull of a simultaneous rush for the rigors of a reflected glory. When the internal monologue leads to re-runs of the Death Row Game, choosing those dishes that you would want to eat if you only had a few hours to live. Or what ingredients you could not end your life without. And what albums or books or movies. Then the fantastical spank bank sizzle reel production of those fantasy women, some famous and others anonymous, that you would love to bed for the last time, even the first time, and the comfort that arrives with this altered worldview. As I cherry-pick the next morsel or delectable nipple, or side view of an elevated hip on my latest crush. Like Paris for Hemingway it is truly a moveable feast. And any predisposed inclination toward one certain meal or individual woman is nothing more than a soft lie to myself, as like the hungry wife on a long drive I am no better suited to decide what to eat, and in the fantasy of a new willing partner why end with her when there could still be more in line.

When life is treated like a casual eatery with you there cherry-picking the more mouthwatering from each plate and your personal flavor spectrum gratifyingly devoid of extravagance, even along the lifestyle racket you remain in an invisible semi-straightjacket with the ability to see the future. The less full of yourself the more prone you are to encourage a convivial revival of self, and ultimately for those around you. The talk of uplift is jazz to me. And the cheerful implication that right before you go on a killing spree you implicate the children. The American children. And the sneaky thievery of downtime and an unreliable conspirator lot. A relentless adherence to the doddering schizophrenic in our midst. The creatures of a certain newfound netherworld, embattled in the jihad of their lives. What else is left to be done to become a made guy. The inevitability that your hijacked life is made into a romcom a year after your confirmed demise. Who will play the bad guys of the future? A bemoaning apocalypse full of government informants when daddy finally disappears.

While we move through life we get banged up, small paper cuts to daggers into the heart and this changes us ever so slightly, making more room for that beloved scar tissue. In return the experience of life leaves profound marks on you. Even though it hurts there is beauty in the trauma. And in the strangeness comes the good, served on white table cloths void of a sense of time, hopping with enthusiasm along with predictable names. A newfound curiosity when it all gets sorted through, or figured out for the umpteenth time, getting to know if you are indeed alright. Or are the scoundrels and misfits newly tormented pawns in your industry of bitches and hoes. When the fear porn is finely tuned just right, that idea that what you see grabs at your reptilian brain and heart, with the appeal for Generation X, Y, or Z indiscriminate in the rock and roller holler back when you re-learn English as your second or third language, because your foretold misfortune never involved basic communications, simply a rabid enthusiasm like gunslingers of the Wild West, those venerable early fur traders, with the manic after-hours verve of a hunter-gatherer on their afternoon big box shopping trip. Genuine benchmarks for spirit-lifting activities guaranteed with inspirational exclamation marks!!!

The emphasis is the envy of all of your friends, like the tribal markings on the lowrider of a painted rendition of the OG's old lady, that Latina queen chola forever captured at the age of nineteen on the driver side of the 1964 Chevy Impala. When we talk of legacy there could be worse, there could be none, so if your visage is immortalized know that you are special, it could be void. So go on with your bad self. I for one find comfort in knowing my legacy lives on in my books and my daughter. But also in the memories that my friends have of me, those fantastical nighttime beats in their hearts when they are acquiesced into something warming, like wetting one's pants, and the lingering pleasantry that comes about when my name is mentioned. It's not so much how you leave someone but how they feel when you are gone.

As for all of my sardonic bad behavior I would hope that I could outweigh that with moments of one-time wondrous hits from the jukebox of my life, for we are not merely the collective of every single beat from the beatbox, but selective ingredients that work, in unison, in harmony, like the salty with the sweet. My savory life an assiduous and hard-core original concept menu of every comfort food pilfered, with signature dishes and those main plates that got me through the harsh times. Life doesn't need the garnishes when the meals are served uncompromised and non-composed.

It's more about what's playing in the background, the ambience of vital tunes from the swanky to the dive bar favorites. And that roadhouse element that keeps you alert enough to never fully rest or take your eye off the exit. It's really about what in your life actually saved you. Family, friends, lovers, idols, icons, the memory of ghosts, and whatever invisible companions that were with you along for the ride. When you look back there wasn't so much to complain about, really. Just unhinged madmen and mere mortals in the despotic futility of a crushing emotional turismo, and the remains of a troubled mind and damaged heart. A heartbreak beat indeed. Playing all night long. And how we handled the troubling times, those flashes of catastrophic difficulty, dead giveaways to your status as an American or an American't. And the diligence in knowing you built that.

While you career from a nightmare into a happier happenstance, with all that low-hanging fruit, by design, you as citizen of the world, with a particularly invested lifestyle, having endured and risen multiple times, and flushed out the desire to drive your vehicle into a group of pedestrians or to climb a tower and unload a clip onto the crowd below. We, as inherent emissaries of evil, tasked with returning to good, making a joyride out of life and enthused by the transformation. Staying humble friends, it's not so much about the profit but the margin, if you catch my drift. And when life comes at you with near-gale-force winds how you weather the rat-tat-tat of your slow demise.

What you do with your life is what you are. Esoteric I know. Nebulous, I don't think so. What it means is that your actions are extensions of your own personal history, political leanings, your ancestors and the tribe. You are inseparable from that, and excuses need not be made. You learn from people when you spend quiet time with them, away from the noise of electronics and those distractions that the cave dwellers before us never had to suffer from, and when you deep dive on others it is only then that you find out if they have pride in their ways or love in their hearts, how indifferent they may be or if they are people pleasers. It becomes about how you discern the aftereffects of your life. When you let your confidence shine as a way to better those around you or in small acts of kindness the effect it may have on someone who feels invisible.

It's also about the small rituals of life, doing dishes or filling up the gas tank, bringing groceries home for your family, significant reminders of your purpose and how collectively it is something so much more, the fabric of our lives, layered upon layer, that eventually envelopes you in a weighted blanket, a comforting shield from the darkness of the outside world, but also your comfort zone, a buoy where you dock when the sea gets rough. These are the things we don't talk about and why would we? We don't brag about the sex we had, or the epic nap we took after hot yoga. If you do go that route not only do you sound like a douche bag but your tale now becomes questionable. The perfected balance is when you allow life to remain as much a mystery to you as to those around you, to somehow teeter on the edges of the unknown while having one foot solidly planted in reality. Just enough to leave a mark, a wound, and the subsequent scar tissue to build you up. Those marks left on you, you can now leave on others. A tribal handing down while ascending the totem of your own id.

Embracing life entails going against the narrative and flipping a bird at the outdated nonsense of how and what to do, or what has been deemed attractive or appropriate. You might find your own inherent likings and inklings to be somewhat deviant or kinky perhaps, but by what standards? This wisdom in knowing how small you are but also that if you are feeling something that there are others feeling the same way. A reverse narcissism if you will. Breaking free from the confines of memory and context by allowing for the grand reveal even if it breaks your heart, the change that comes as you sync your consciousness with your body to fully absorb the experiences. And the voids in your life that become stale points to avoid, you must let the happy accidents happen, that magic in the bad experiences, all that's not on the itinerary. When risk is now a factor in the equation, like mob life or low-level street crime. Having to watch over your shoulder, for a healthy tinge of paranoia never hurt anyone. Be that mercenary warrior who takes pride in what they do, donning the noble cap of honor and satisfaction. And with every ending there is the beginning of a new story, a regeneration in the passway through to an exiled life, something of a rebirth from the ending of this story.

Acknowledgements:

For her enormous heart and compassion, my wife. She provides for a wonderful life that affords me a great gift, that of time to write.

About the Author:

American writer Tennison Long is the author of Glorious Verve, When We Ran The Master Plan, Of Tribe & Empire, On Becoming Yesterday's Actors, tex•tu•al, How to Fake Your Death (& Other Illusions of Exile), and The Devolution. He likes to take his readers on a psychological thrill ride, blending the macabre with the sublime while sewing seams of mental confusion with emotional clarity. He offers a uniquely imagined prose that sustains moments of sputtering haunted brilliance. He lives in Northern California and would love to hear from you.

Visit his website at www.tennisonlong.com